Love On The Red Rocks

Visit us at www.boldstrokesbooks.com

LOVE ON THE RED ROCKS

by

Lisa Moreau

2016

LOVE ON THE RED ROCKS

ISBN 13: 978-1-62639-660-9

This Trade Paperback Original Is Published By
Bold Strokes Books, Inc.
P.O. Box 249
Valley Falls, NY 12185

First Edition: February 2016

Credits
Editor: Shelley Thrasher
Production Design: Susan Ramundo
Cover Design By Sheri (graphicartist2020@hotmail.com)

Acknowledgments

What you hold in your hands is a dream realized. I'd always wanted to write a novel, but stuck to shorter pieces. Writing a book seemed like such an overwhelming task, so I kept putting it off. When my father passed away unexpectedly June 2013, it was a not so gentle reminder of how short life can be. One month after his death, I began writing this book. I'm not sure how he'd feel about having a lesbian novel dedicated to him. Regardless, he was not only the catalyst, but also the inspiration for my first novel.

It's been a whirlwind, eye-opening, exciting year since signing a contract with Bold Strokes Books. I'll never read another novel the same way again. So much work, from so many individuals, goes into a published piece. I owe a tremendous thanks to Radclyffe, Sandy Lowe, and everyone at Bold Strokes Books. Thank you for your guidance, professionalism, and taking a chance on me. Bold Strokes Books was my number one choice in the hopes of getting published. I've been a fan for many years since the writers and editors are top-notch.

Speaking of editors, they are the unsung heroes, and I had the best. Shelley Thrasher, you improved my manuscript greatly. Thank you so much for your suggestions, encouragement, and keen eye. I look forward to working with you again.

Thanks to my family and friends for their ongoing support. A special thanks to my sister, Carla Cotton; and niece, Sasha Kelton. I always think of us as the Three Musketeers. You are my best friends and greatest supporters. Even though we're separated by many miles, I feel your presence in my life every day. I love you guys.

And for anyone who has a dream: don't delay, don't fear, don't make excuses. Go for it with all your heart and soul. Dreams do come true.

Dedication

For my Dad
See you later, alligator.

Prologue

The Kachina Woman

Fifteen Years Ago

I'm not sure what I expected to find. Maybe an hourglass-shaped, voluptuous figure with lots of cleavage. Something with peaks and valleys in all the right places. We were, after all, looking for a woman. And considering I was fifteen years old with raging hormones, it wasn't crazy to want to find a buxom beauty, even if she was a rock formation.

Sweat stung the corners of my eyes and rolled down my back. My dad and I had been hiking in Sedona, desperately looking for a woman. But not just any woman. The guy at the Red Rock Visitor Center called her the Kachina Woman. She sat on top of a ridge, towering over Boynton Canyon. How could we possibly pass up an opportunity to see that?

The hike started out well enough. We were excited, anticipating a new adventure. But it didn't take long for us to tire in the ninety-degree heat, trudging uphill through rough terrain. My legs burned, my shirt became drenched in sweat, and my heart pounded. If it wasn't for the woman, I think we would have turned back. We stopped often to stand in the shade and chug down water.

I liked the pause between activities with my dad best. That was when we had some of our best chats. I could tell him anything. In fact, I came out to him during the Super Bowl half-time show. He didn't even bat an eye. He hugged me and said he'd always love me no matter what. He was cool that way.

"She's got to be around here somewhere," Dad said. We'd been walking for miles, climbing over rocks, dodging lizards, and with no woman in sight.

"Howdy," Dad said to a hiker passing us on the trail. "Does this lead to the Kachina Woman?"

"Yes. It's just around the bend and over that hill. You can't miss it."

"Do you hear that?" I asked no one in particular, picking up a faint strain of music in the distance. "It sounds like a flute."

"Oh, you'll hear and see lots of strange things in Sedona," the hiker said.

"You mean like blue lizards, 'cause I almost stepped on one back there."

"That and more." His blue eyes twinkled in the sunlight.

My dad thanked the hiker as we continued on our trek. The longer we walked, the louder the music sounded, like the melody was being carried along the warm breeze, swirling around our bodies.

The hiker was right. After we turned a curve and fought our way up to the summit, the woman practically smacked us in the face. She was tall, sturdy, with an air of confidence. Honestly, at first I didn't see a woman. All I saw was a big glob of red rock. But then I remembered what the man in the visitors' center said, so I relaxed my gaze and squinted my eyes. And there she was. Cleavage and all.

My hand brushed the ankles of the Kachina Woman as we walked around the base, looking for the cause of the stirring music. As we rounded the corner I spotted an Indian with a flute sitting cross-legged under a twisted juniper tree. He looked about a hundred and five, with deep crevices in his face and hands.

When I gazed in his eyes a jolt of electricity coursed through me. I know this sounds weird, but they were an exact replica of my grandmother's eyes. The color of brown sugar, they brimmed with joy and anticipation. Even on her deathbed, as Grandma was taking her last breath, her eyes never dimmed.

Perhaps feeling our presence, the Indian stopped playing and rested the flute in his lap. He allowed a few moments to pass before he spoke, staring straight ahead.

"You know this place?" he asked.

"This is our first time here," Dad said. "It's beautiful."

The Indian motioned for us to sit beside him. My dad and I sat cross-legged under the tree, one of us on each side of the Indian.

"This sacred land is home to Kachina Woman," he said. "She guards and watches over all who enter the canyon."

Chills cascaded throughout my body when the Indian stared directly at me with Grandma's eyes. In one graceful move, he held out his fist as though he was handing me something. Not knowing the protocol in this particular situation, I sat there like a lump.

"Take," he said. Peering past the Indian, my dad nodded his approval. The man placed a red sandstone rock in the palm of my hand. A heart-shaped rock. Within seconds it warmed my palm.

"Fear is of the mind," he said. "Love is of the heart. Kachina Woman say always listen to the heart." The Indian tapped my chest with his fingertips three times as his eyes twinkled with what resembled delight.

I looked past the Indian to the Kachina Woman. The rock was the exact color as she was, a fiery red that came alive in my open palm. Shards of limestone imbedded in the rock sparkled like diamonds in the rays of the sun. I ran my thumb over the smooth surface, tracing the perfect outline of a heart. Then I slipped the rock into my pocket to keep as a souvenir. How many people have heart rocks handed to them by an ancient Indian on top of a sacred site? It was too cool not to keep.

The Indian raised his flute and began playing as my dad and I closed our eyes. The haunting melody reached deep inside me, swirling up all sorts of emotions in the pit of my stomach. It made me want to laugh and cry all at the same time. When the music stopped, my dad and I opened our eyes and the Indian was gone. We glanced around the juniper tree, even got up and looked down the trail and around the Kachina Woman, but he was nowhere in sight.

My dad scratched his head and looked as confused as I did. The Indian couldn't possibly have gotten up that fast and down the trail without us hearing or seeing him. For a minute, I wondered if we hadn't imagined the whole thing. I slipped my hand into my pocket, feeling the warmth of the rock against my fingertips. I wasn't so sure about the Indian, but the heart rock was definitely real.

Chapter One

A Funny Thing Happened on the Way to Sedona

Present Day

One minute I was in heaven and the next screaming my lungs out. Lizzie and I were cruising down Arizona Highway 179 on our way to the Rainbow Lodge in Sedona. Just the two of us, for three solid weeks, all alone. Well, mostly alone. Eighteen other lesbians would be there, but who counts them? It's not like I was planning to make friends. I was on a mission.

So we were traveling down the highway when all of a sudden tires were screeching, the nauseating scent of burnt rubber filled the air, and my heart thumped so loudly that the pulse in my ears practically made me deaf to my own screams. Then I saw it. Panic in the eyes of a deer. It was one of those fight-or-flight moments, except I couldn't run or punch the deer 'cause I was stuck in the passenger seat of a Lexus. So I did the irrational thing, of course, and grabbed the wheel, causing the car to skid across the deserted, thankfully, two-lane highway and right into a ditch.

After all that drama, coming to a jolting halt made everything seem eerily still. Shaking my head a few times like the coyote does in that cartoon after falling off a cliff, I saw Lizzie rubbing her forehead. I hate to admit it, but I felt a pang of joy. Maybe I'd have an excuse to hold her hand, caress her face, and even kiss the boo-boo.

Don't get me wrong. I wasn't a pervert who took advantage of injured women. I was in love with Lizzie. It didn't matter that we'd never dated, or kissed, or even touched for that matter. I didn't have to do any of that to know she was everything I ever wished upon a star for in a soul mate. Sounds perfect, huh? Well, it was, except for one small problem: her girlfriend, Heather. Actually, it was her ex-girlfriend. For the moment anyway.

"Malley, why did you grab the wheel?"

Because I'm a control freak? I thought it better to leave that conversation for my therapist, so I chose a more mature response. "I'm sorry. I panicked. Oh my gosh, Lizzie, are you okay?" With trembling hands I carefully pushed her bangs aside. God, her hair was soft.

"You have a bump. Did you hit your head on the steering wheel?" I regretted bringing up the wheel the moment it was out of my mouth. We probably wouldn't have been sitting in a ditch in the middle of nowhere except for my quick thinking.

At that point I was about as close to Lizzie as I'd ever been. Our noses almost touched, and I could feel her warm breath tickle my lips. As I gazed into her eyes, looking for signs of a concussion, of course, I thought for a moment we might actually kiss. Even the remote possibility of our lips touching made me breathless.

"Malley, what are you doing?"

Oh my God. I was staring at her lips while unconsciously running my fingers through her hair. I may have even rubbed her shoulders. God, I hope I didn't try to kiss her. Maybe I was a pervert.

"I'm checking to see if your eyes are dilated," I said, which made no sense whatsoever since I was staring at her full, sensual lips at the time.

"I'm okay. Just shaken up. Thank God we didn't hit that poor deer." She was so considerate. "But we do seem to be stuck in a ditch. A very deep ditch." I wanted to wipe the worried expression from Lizzie's beautiful face.

"You sit here for a minute, and I'll go out and survey the damage," I said, and stepped into the ninety-eight-degree sweltering heat. Was I insane—attending a retreat in the desert in the middle of June? Jessie was probably sitting in her West Hollywood apartment with the air conditioner on full blast, snickering at the thought of me dying of heat stroke while buzzards flew overhead. But then I remembered why I was going to Sedona and smiled broadly. Lizzie had finally done it. She and Heather were history. Granted, they'd broken up and gotten back together a million times over the past year, but Lizzie had actually made Heather move out this time.

So when Jessie had told me about her friend Clarissa's three-week lesbian retreat in Sedona, it didn't take much effort to convince Lizzie that she needed a relaxing vacation away from the drama of the breakup. Little did she know, I had an ulterior motive. Now that Lizzie was single and free, I could show her we were perfect for each other. In fact, I even had a three-week plan mapped out in Excel to convince her of just that.

Tab one of the spreadsheet included various retreat activities perfect for us to spend time together, like leisurely walks, hiking, and biking, with romantic spots highlighted in each category. Hiking trails included location, mileage, and elevation so we didn't do anything too strenuous and make Lizzie realize I was horribly out of shape. Tab two of the spreadsheet included romantic restaurants around Sedona, which I Googled beforehand and included Weight Watcher's points so I'd know what to order.

During a romantic dinner at the end of the three weeks, I planned to tell Lizzie how I felt about her. Just the thought of that confession made me queasy. It's not easy putting yourself out there. What if she laughed or, God forbid, never wanted to see me again?

I popped my head back into the car. "Start 'er up and see if you can go forward or backward."

Lizzie cranked her Lexus, which was a good sign, but the wheels did nothing but spin in place as she accelerated. After a few unsuccessful attempts, she opened her door to let a hot breeze in.

"We're not going anywhere, Malley."

"Don't worry. All I have to do is call AAA." Just as I grabbed my cell phone we heard a thunderous roar, coming from a quickly approaching motorcycle. A yellow motorcycle. A yellow motorcycle with a figure that looked curiously like Jessie. Oh my God, it *was* Jessie!

"Thank goodness for dykes on bikes," Lizzie said as she got out of the car. Jessie pulled up behind us and cut off her deafening motor.

"What in the world is she doing here?"

"You know her?"

"That's Jessie."

"*The* Jessie? To quote you, the exasperating, frustrating, irritating Jessie? The next-door-neighbor Jessie? Wow, you never told me she was a babe." I gave Lizzie one of my raised-eyebrow looks, but she didn't notice since she was too busy gawking at the bronze statue straddling her motorbike. All right, I admit it. Jessie was gorgeous. A super-hot, olive-skinned, green-eyed beauty with a killer body. No wonder I'd never introduced her to Lizzie. Jessie whipped off her helmet and swaggered our way, flashing that dangerously sexy grin of hers.

"Well, well, if it's not O'Conner," she said.

"Well, if it isn't Barnett. What the hell are you doing here?" Jessie and I stared each other down like it was high noon at the OK Corral.

Lizzie cleared her throat. "Isn't anyone going to introduce me?" She looked back and forth between Jessie and me. When neither one of us made a move, Lizzie extended her hand to Jessie, who reached for it without taking her eyes off me.

"Lizzie, this is Jessie."

"I've heard so much about you." Lizzie held onto Jessie's hand longer than necessary.

"All excellent, I'm sure." I rolled my eyes with enough flare that I hoped Jessie would notice. "It looks like you girls got yourself into a predicament. Are you okay?" Jessie looked at me with what actually seemed like concern.

"Lizzie bumped her head, but we're fine," I replied. "Aside from being stuck in a ditch, that is."

"You sure you're okay?" Jessie placed her hand on Lizzie's arm, which was all it took for her to morph into a teeny-bopper. Lizzie fluffed her hair, giggled, and twisted around like she needed to pee. Seriously? I thought she was smart enough not to fall for Jessie's obvious charisma like every other lesbian in LA did.

"Barnett, what are you doing here?" Even though I already knew the answer, I wanted confirmation.

"Well, after I told you about Clarissa's retreat, I thought what the hell. That sounds like fun. Three weeks away from manic LA to spend time with a bunch of lesbians in the beautiful red rocks of Sedona. Count me in!"

"Goody! It should be way cool!" Goody? Way cool? Was Lizzie fifteen years old or thirty?

Blistering, stagnant air surrounded me as the sun beamed down. I attempted to take a deep breath, forcing hot air into my lungs. My face felt flush and my blood pressure soared as my agitation grew, which wasn't entirely weather related.

"You mean the Beverly Hills P.D. can actually do without you for three weeks?" I asked.

"Oh, you're a police officer?" Lizzie expressed so much enthusiasm that even she must have heard how fake it sounded. Apparently, she was not only a teenager but had Alzheimer's as well, since I know I'd told her before that Jessie was a cop.

"Yeah, she's a *Beverly Hills* cop." I knew Jessie assumed everyone thought Beverly Hills police officers did nothing but help Paris Hilton find her lost dog and maybe took a slap or two in the face from a temperamental actress stopped for speeding. I also knew how much she wanted to be with the LAPD. Not that I was mean-spirited, but I had to break up the love fest between Lizzie and Jessie. And fast.

Jessie sneered before nervously looking around in the knee-high grass growing in the ditch. She picked her legs up high and tiptoed out of the weeds to stand on the asphalt.

"Why don't you girls come over here? Snakes love tall grass. And ditches."

"You mean to tell me that big, bad Officer Barnett is afraid of snakes?" I loved to tease her.

"Just the poisonous, deadly ones, O'Conner." Jessie seemed anxious as she peered into the ditch. She actually looked pretty adorable when she wasn't so cocky. "Summer is a haven for rattlers in Sedona. You know, the poisonous ones?" Jessie threw me a venomous look. That was enough for Lizzie to dart out of the ditch and stand next to Jessie...unnecessarily close to Jessie. I opted to stay in the ditch.

"So, what happened here?" Jessie asked.

"We almost hit a deer. And obviously ended up in a ditch in the process," Lizzie said.

"Yeah." I butted in before Lizzie could say anything about me grabbing the wheel. "But I'm about to call AAA. They should have us out of here in no time. Thanks for stopping, but I'm sure we can handle it from here."

Lizzie gave me a don't-be-so-rude look, which I ignored.

"You have cell service out here?" Jessie asked.

"Of course." I looked at my phone. No bars. Damn T-Mobile.

"Lizzie has an iPhone. We'll call from hers."

"I'll wait with you until AAA shows up," Jessie offered.

Before Lizzie could say, "Aw, that's so sweet," which I could tell she was about to do by the look on her face, I said something about it being too hot and that we'd wait it out in the air-conditioned car. And really, Jessie couldn't do anything anyway. We needed a tow truck, not a biker chick. Reluctantly, Jessie agreed and said she'd head to the lodge, but not before Lizzie squealed, "It was so nice to finally meet you" followed by a beauty-pageant wave if I've ever seen one.

❖

After the tow truck pulled us out of the ditch, we were back on the highway. As Lizzie drove, I silently stewed about Jessie showing up unexpectedly. She wasn't part of my plan, and I certainly didn't need the competition. If I'd known beforehand that she'd be attending, I would have suggested Lizzie and I vacation somewhere else.

Lizzie suggested we find a bathroom pronto, and I couldn't have agreed more. I'm usually particular about the cleanliness of public restrooms, but I needed to go so bad I could have cared less if I'd had to use a smelly Port-A-Potty in the middle of a cactus grove. Ordinarily, when it's that bad I'd just go on the side of the road, considering traffic was light, but all that talk about snakes put me off the idea. Swinging the car into a Snack 'n Stuff, Lizzie and I rushed in frantically looking for the restroom, hoping to find more than one stall.

"Bathroom?" I asked the cashier.

"Customer only," she responded.

"What?"

"You gots to bees a customer to use our facilities." She actually said "gots to bees" but then said "facilities" like we were in some fancy, smancy place. I slapped a pack of Red Rock Gum—the nearest thing to where I was standing—on the counter. After paying the woman, we headed to the "facilities."

Since we'd been on the road for seven hours, Lizzie and I decided to take a break and stretch our legs. While she was perusing the snack portion of Snack 'n Stuff, I checked out the stuff. Red Rock T-shirts, a replica of Bell Rock inside a snow globe (except it had specs of red dirt instead of snow), green alien keychains with SEDONA—WE WERE HERE written on them, and tons of other... well, stuff. Spotting a rack of CDs, I noticed one in particular: a road-trip mix. How cool was that? I purchased the CD without Lizzie noticing. It seemed like a fun thing to surprise her with and a chance to show my playful, spontaneous side.

Actually, I'd been told I don't have a spontaneous side, but that didn't come from Lizzie. That came from Patty, who was my last girlfriend, and then Celia, the one before that. Pretty much every woman I'd ever dated threw that up in my face at some point during the lesbian-drama ending of a relationship. They usually yelled "and you're about as spontaneous as an ant!" right before slamming the door on their way out. What does that even *mean?* Admittedly, I'd made some bad choices in girlfriends in the past, but those days were gone. Dating Lizzie would change all that.

I'll never forget the first time I met Lizzie. It was about a year ago when I was sitting in my cubicle at work slaving away on quarterly sales reports. Tim from Private Client Services walked up behind me. I knew it was him from the smell of Aramis. I was under a major time crunch and hoped that if I ignored him, he and his scent would disappear. Instead, he cleared his throat and said, "Malley?" Damn. Couldn't the man take a hint?

"Hey, Tim, I'm really busy right now. Can this wait until after lunch?" I kept my back to him.

"This will just take a minute. I'd like to introduce you to our new employee."

Oops, I felt embarrassed for being so rude. "Oh, I'm sorr..." I stopped mid-sentence because I'd spun around in my chair and was staring at the face of an angel. Fluorescent lighting beamed down on her golden spun hair at just the right angle to create a halo effect. The fairness of her features contrasted to her deep, kind, cinnamon-colored eyes.

"Malley, this is Elizabeth. She's our new senior portfolio manager. We're lucky to have her. She comes from J.P. Morgan. Malley is sales analyst for our Sales and Marketing team."

"You can call me Lizzie." She had the sweetest smile I'd ever seen. Grasping her outreached hand, I knew immediately we'd be best friends.

CHAPTER TWO

THE TEAL ARCHES

W hy do you hate Jessie so much?"
I practically choked on my McDonald's Caesar salad. Feigning a crouton mishap, I downed Diet Coke to kill time until I knew how to answer Lizzie's question.

We were driving through Sedona on the way to the Rainbow Lodge when Lizzie said she was starving. Considering all I'd eaten so far was a pack of Red Rock gum, I agreed to getting some chow.

"Are you still on Weight Watchers? What can you eat?" Lizzie asked.

"Yeah, I have an app with the point values of hundreds of restaurants. I should be able to find something." Grabbing my cell phone, I starting punching in restaurant choices. The thing about Sedona, though, is that it has very few chain restaurants. Normally, that would be a big appeal, but not when you're counting Weight Watchers' points to the tee.

It's not that I was fat. Well, not too much anyway. I had about fifteen pounds to lose. I was attractive, mind you, with blond hair in a cute pixie cut, bright-blue eyes most people would kill for, and a cute baby face that made me look younger than my thirty-two years. After deciding to pursue Lizzie after she finally dumped Heather, I got back on Weight Watchers because I knew Lizzie was attracted to slim women.

"Mmm, how about a bakery?" Lizzie rolled down the window as we both inhaled an intoxicating sugary scent wafting from the cutest bakery I'd ever seen. Even though I probably gained ten pounds from the fragrance alone, I took another deep, slow breath. I could practically taste Grandma's butterscotch cinnamon bun melt in my mouth.

"What an adorable bakery," I said.

Lizzie looked at me sideways. "Not that again, Malley."

"What?" I feigned ignorance. "It's just a pipe dream. Like I'd really quit my job and open a bakery in West Hollywood."

"It's not that it's a bad idea, but it's so risky. Businesses are closing down all the time. And you have such a stable job. You've been there almost ten years."

God, had it been that long? Lizzie was right, I know. But it was still a nice dream to have every once in a while.

"Hey, since when did McDonald's paint their *M* teal?" Lizzie asked, changing the subject.

"Didn't you know? This is a great Trivial Pursuit question. The only place in the world that doesn't have golden arches is… drum roll, please…you guessed it, Sedona!"

"Wow. I didn't know that."

"We should take a selfie in front of the teal arches," I said.

"And I hate to say it, but I could eat here if you wanted. Their salads aren't too bad, and I know the point values." Lizzie pouted but pulled into the parking lot anyway.

"Good God, it's hot here," she said. "Let's take our picture before my face melts off."

Lizzie and I put our heads together as I held out my phone and snapped the photo in front of the teal arches. Looking at the picture, I couldn't help but marvel at how good Lizzie and I looked together. Like a real couple. We were so freaking adorable that I planned to frame the snapshot when I got home. I suppressed a nervous giggle and grinned widely at the thought of Lizzie and me dating. It could actually happen. And in as little as a few weeks.

So there we were, eating salads, when Lizzie scrunched her eyebrows together and asked the question that made me drink a gallon of Diet Coke.

"Why do you hate Jessie so much?"

"I don't hate her, per se."

"Well, you definitely don't like her."

"I told you about Jessie before. She's an obnoxious playgirl who probably only dates airhead models who wear no bigger than size zero. She struts around the apartment building in her tight uniform just to show off her ass and her gun."

"Mmm…she could arrest me anytime. I'm ready for my strip search, Officer." Lizzie coyly shrugged. "Sorry, guess I've been a little horny since I threw Heather out."

The thought of Lizzie being horny made me incredibly hot. And being in the middle of a family restaurant with screaming kids isn't the place to get hot.

"Anyway," I said, trying to divert my mind from Lizzie being strip-searched. "Jessie thinks she's all that and a bag of chips."

I'd heard that phrase on the Jerry Springer show one day when I was home sick and thought it was hilarious. So much so that I told Lizzie about it the next day at work, and we routinely said it when describing a conceited person who thought they were better than everyone else. I then broke into a five-minute soliloquy about how annoying Jessie was, like playing Melissa Etheridge at top volume when she knew the walls were paper-thin and I lived right next door. And really, Melissa Etheridge? How clichéd was that? And once when she was working out in the gym, I was pretty sure I saw a tattoo on her lower back when she bent over to pick up a dumbbell. Lizzie knew how much I hated tattoos, so I didn't even need to explain why that irked me so much.

"I don't get it," she said, shaking her head. "I know you. You're not a judgmental person. There must be some other reason Jessie ticks you off so much."

"She's annoying as hell!" That came out a little louder and higher pitched than I'd intended. With her mouth wide open, Lizzie jerked her head up from her Southwest Salad.

"Oh. My. God. You have a crush on her!"
A torrent of emotions passed through me all at once. Shock. Confusion. Speechlessness. One not-so-great thing about me is that when I get flustered all I can do is shake my head, blink wildly, and flail my arms around.

"This is so classic. There's a fine line between love and hate, Malley. The sparring is like foreplay." *Foreplay?* "You've seen romantic comedies," Lizzie said. "Boy meets girl. They clash for whatever reason, and then halfway through the movie Meg Ryan and Tom Hanks kiss, realize they're in love instead of hate, and live happily ever after."

"You are soooo wrong, Lizzie. You have no idea how wrong you are." I was inches away from telling her why, but the timing wasn't right. I didn't want to ruin my well-thought-out plan by blurting out my love for Lizzie when I was blinking nonstop and waving my arms around like a crazy person.

"Trust me," I said, "you're totally wrong about Jessie."

Lizzie shook her head. "Methinks she doth protest too much," she whispered, and I pretended not to hear.

I'll admit that when Jessie moved next door six months ago, I thought she was drop-dead gorgeous. We bumped into each other as I was coming out of my apartment and she was moving into hers. Her muscular arms were straining from carrying what appeared to be a heavy box, and she was panting in a way that turned me on. When she peered over the box, I was met with the most beautiful emerald eyes I'd ever seen. At the risk of sounding ridiculous, all of my vital organs—essentials such as breathing and heart beating—stopped with that one look. Maybe it was wishful thinking, but Jessie seemed as mesmerized as I was. It wasn't just that she was beautiful. In a way, Jessie seemed familiar, like we'd met before. That wasn't possible, though, because I would have remembered her eyes for sure. So I thought maybe she was an actress and I'd seen her on TV. We were in LA, after all.

"Hi," she said. "I'd shake your hand, but…" Jessie cocked her head toward the box in her arms. I loved her voice. Sort of raspy and breathy, but in a sexy way, not in an out-of-shape-smoker way. I blinked rapidly and reminded myself to breathe.

"Let me help you with that," I offered. Taking the key dangling from her fingers, I unlocked her door. I glanced around the apartment, looking for a missus or, God forbid, mister. No one in sight. And no ring on the appropriate finger. Things were looking up.

"Please, come in," Jessie said. She put the box down and extended her hand. "I'm Jessie."

"Hello. I'm Malley." Was it my imagination, or did she just check out my ring finger?

"Malley. That's an unusual name. I like it."

A goofy grin flashed across my face. I really needed to work on my flirting skills. "So, where are you moving from?"

"Long Beach. I love it there, but this is so much closer to work."

"Where do you work?"

And that's when everything came crashing down. Any hopes of a romance were killed within the next two seconds.

"I'm a police officer with the Beverly Hills P.D."

Damn. Out of all the thousands of careers in the world, she'd have to be a cop. Well, it was a nice fantasy while it lasted. She was totally out of my league anyway.

"Ah. It was nice to meet you, Jessie." I made a swift, ungraceful exit, tripping over her box before darting down the hall. Real smooth. As I walked to the elevators, I considered friendship with Jessie but quickly tossed that unrealistic notion aside. The thought of trying to be friends with a woman I was just moments ago lusting over would never work. I'm serious when I said my heart actually stopped beating.

Instead, I chose the immature route and attempted to keep my distance from Jessie, which was difficult living next door. I played it cool and detached when we'd run into each other around the apartment complex. It didn't take long for her to take the hint. At first, I felt bad about it. She seemed nice enough. But then it got to where every time we interacted, we'd usually end up in an argument, with me wanting to throttle her. But now that I was in love with Lizzie, maybe Jessie and I could be friends after all. Maybe.

❖

My face was probably as red as Bell Rock. I'd been stewing for at least five miles about how Lizzie could possibly think I had a crush on Jessie. Foreplay? Me and Jessie? Was she kidding? We were like oil and water.

By mile six my heart rate was almost back to normal as I caught glimpses of Cathedral Rock in the distance. I'd forgotten how breathtaking Sedona was. My first time there was after my dad got a job in Phoenix and we drove up one Saturday, not knowing what to expect. Most of the drive was through desert with nothing but rocks and cacti for miles, with the wind whipping up mini tornadoes of dust. It wasn't until we got closer to Sedona that my eyes popped out of my head.

"Malley, honey. Up ahead is Bell Rock." My mom pointed, which was completely unnecessary since it would have been impossible to miss. A ginormous blood-red, intricately carved rock towered over our blue Ford. No sooner had we passed Bell Rock than we came upon an equally ginormous structure with even more varied carvings and formations. Pretty soon we were completely surrounded by oddly shaped mountainous rocks, painted in striations of red and pink.

The best part of that trip was when my dad and I hiked to the Kachina Woman. After all those years, I never forgot about the disappearing Indian, and I still had the heart-shaped rock. Every now and then I slipped it into my pocket to use as a touchstone. It seemed to calm me when I needed it most. I'm not sure why, but my dad and I never shared that experience with anyone. Not even my mom. It was sort of a mysterious thing, with a disappearing Indian and all, so I guess we wanted to keep it to ourselves. Or maybe we were afraid no one would believe us.

"Are you okay?" Lizzie's voice brought me back to the present. I considered telling her about the Indian and the heart rock. If I were to share it with anyone it would be her. But I didn't. It didn't feel right.

"Yeah," I said. "Just breathing it all in."

"It is beautiful," she replied. We rode in silence a few more miles, enjoying the scenery.

"My mom's excited to meet you," I said. "I'm glad we're going to take a day and drive up to Oak Creek Canyon."

"How's she doing?"

"She's coping. It's hard, you know? But she loves living in the cabin."

"You know, Malley, if you ever want to talk."

"I know. Thanks." But talking about it was the absolute last thing I wanted to do.

Chapter Three

Unlucky Number Seven

Y ou're number seven." A tall, thin woman wearing an outfit straight out of an L.L.Bean catalogue shoved a rainbow keychain in front of me.

Tentatively, I took the keychain, which had a key dangling from the end. "And what's a number seven?"

The woman responded in one long, run-on sentence without taking a breath. "I'm sorry. I'm Clarissa. You must be Malley. Jessie told me what happened and that you'd be late, so I went ahead and picked a key for you. And you're number ten." She handed Lizzie a key with the same rainbow keychain.

"Just what do key number seven and ten do?" I asked, suspicious.

"They let you see who you're rooming with."

She sprinted to the porch of what appeared to be the main cabin of the Rainbow Lodge. Clarissa stood before twenty or so lesbians who were chatting and laughing outside in the near darkness. Wait. What? I was rooming with Lizzie for three weeks, not some random lesbian I didn't even know. That wasn't part of the plan. Not that I intended to sleep with Lizzie, although I certainly wouldn't turn her down if it came to that.

Clarissa clapped her hands to get everyone's attention. "Now, ladies, I know most of you came here with a friend you'd like to room with, but part of this retreat is about discovering new things about yourself, and you'll never do that if you do the same things you've always done. Over the next three weeks you'll accomplish feats you never thought possible, like complete a treacherous hike or even calm your mind with meditation. I'll cover more of what you can expect during orientation tomorrow morning, but for right now I'd like you to find the woman with the same number key as you and say hello to your roommate."

Lizzie shrugged. "I guess what she said is true. We'll never have new experiences if we don't try something different."

"Yeah, but it's not like we've ever roomed together. That was going to be different." I jutted my bottom lip out in a pout. It had been a long, hot, crazy day, and the last thing I needed was some wilderness chick putting a kink in my plan. I sighed loudly, not even trying to hide my frustration.

"Hey there, looks like I'm lucky number ten." A husky woman with a heavy Texas accent dangled her keychain in front of Lizzie. She looked like Humpty Dumpty with short, spiky hair.

"Yeah, looks like." Lizzie peered at me sideways with a furrowed brow.

"I'm Rhonda." The woman shook Lizzie's hand so hard her head bobbed up and down uncontrollably. "Wow, you are one hot chickadee." Rhonda slowly licked her lips.

Ugh. When Lizzie looked at me with fear in her eyes, I headed straight for Clarissa.

"Excuse me, Clarissa?" I tapped her bony shoulder.

Swinging around she almost knocked my eye out with her clipboard. "Malley!" She smiled broadly with a twinkle in her eyes. "I'm sorry things are so crazy. I was looking forward to meeting you. You're just adorable. Jessie talks about you all the time." *Why would Jessie talk about me? And just what had she been saying?* "Have you found your number seven yet?" Clarissa flashed a wide grin.

"No, but that's what I want to talk to you about. See—"

"I'm so glad you decided to come to the retreat. Jessie told me you have an office job. Working with numbers or something?

Well, this will be an incredible getaway for you." I flinched when Clarissa grabbed my chin and studied my face. "Jessie told me you have fair skin, and she wasn't kidding. Now, sugar, be sure and put lots of sunscreen on in this Arizona heat, or you'll be redder than the rocks." She cackled loudly like that was the funniest thing ever. What was she talking about, and why would Jessie tell her about my fair complexion? I shook my head from her grasp and tried to get us back on track. "Clarissa, this rooming situation—"

"I'm so sorry, sugar, but Edwina's waving me down. We'll have plenty of time to talk tomorrow." She was off in a flash, wildly swinging her clipboard at someone I assumed was Edwina. I walked back to Lizzie, defeated.

"Doesn't look like it went so well," she said.

"No, but I'm not giving up. Where's Rhonda?"

"Over there bragging to her friends that she gets to room with me." Lizzie scrunched her face like she was sucking on a sour candy. Did it make me a horrible person that I was glad at how unhappy Lizzie was about the arrangement? I liked that she wanted to be with me instead of Rhonda. As disappointing as this situation was, it could have been so much worse. The second number-ten key could have belonged to some hot lesbian.

"So where's your number seven?"

"I have no idea." I glanced around the yard, squinting in the darkness at the remaining women. "She's probably in the cabin using up all the hot water. Look, I'm going to talk to Clarissa first thing tomorrow and get this straightened out. Will you be okay with Rhonda for one night?" Before Lizzie could answer, I heard Jessie's voice behind me.

"Ladies, I'm so glad to see you made it safely." As I turned around, my heart betrayed me by pounding out of my chest. Damn, if she didn't look good. Smooth olive skin, shoulder-length shiny dark hair, and killer green eyes that sparkled in the moonlight. Not to mention the snug, white tank top that hugged all the right curves, and cutoffs that displayed long, lean legs. Usually, I'd say something smug, but all I could do was stare. I was aware of how sexy Jessie was, but sometimes she'd catch me off guard and take my breath away.

"Hi, Jessie. It's great to see you again." Lizzie flipped her hair back in a classic Cher move. Standing close behind Jessie was a powerhouse broad dressed in a black business suit and high heels. Not exactly wilderness attire. The woman placed her hand on Jessie's lower back. She looked about ten years older than me and a hundred times sexier.

"Oh, this is Nicole," Jessie said. "Nicole, this is Malley and Lizzie."

"So this is the next-door neighbor?" Business-suit broad raised an eyebrow and extended her hand in a limp handshake that gave me the creeps. She wiped her palm on her skirt before running it through her luxurious brown hair, causing thick, wavy locks to fall seductively around her perfectly sculpted cheekbones. She batted long eyelashes, which I was fairly certain were fake, as she looked down on me. And speaking of fake, I don't think anyone's breasts could possibly be that substantial *and* buoyant without the assistance of a surgical lift.

"Nicole's a lawyer from Phoenix. We just met tonight."

Lawyer? Why did I suddenly feel inferior? And business-suit broad was awfully touchy-feely to have just met someone.

"I was hoping Jessie had the number-three key, but I'm not so lucky." Nicole leaned forward like she was about to plant a wet one on Jessie's cheek, but instead she opted to slip her arm around her waist instead. And I repeat: they just met tonight?

"So, Nicole," I said. "What kind of lawyer are you?"

"Corporate." Okay, a woman of few words. "What's your profession, if I may ask?"

"I'm a...uhh...sales analyst. Lizzie and I work for the same financial-investment company."

Nicole looked about as uninterested as a cat with a bone. "Jessie, darling, I'm going to get settled, but I expect to meet up with you tomorrow. You promised to take me hiking, remember? I'm in cabin three if you need anything tonight." I swear to God the woman actually purred in Jessie's ear.

"Cabin three?" I asked. "Okay, got it. If Lizzie and I need anything we'll be sure and come on over." Business-suit broad swung her head around. If looks could kill, I'd have been six feet under. Without a word she slithered away into the darkness.

"Who wears a business suit to a lodge?" I asked.

"She worked today and just drove in from Phoenix," Jessie said.

"She's awfully forward to have just met you."

"Be nice, O'Brien. She's just being friendly." Jessie cocked her head and looked a little irritated with my assessment of her new friend.

"I'm totally nice. Didn't you think she was forward?" I asked Lizzie.

"Most definitely. In a sultry, sexy sort of way."

"So have you found your roommate yet?" Jessie asked, completely changing the subject.

"Lizzie got Rhonda over there." I pointed to a group of women. "She's the scary-looking one with the crew cut and oversized Texas Longhorns T-shirt."

"Oh, sorry about that, Lizzie."

"It's just for one night. I'll get it straightened out tomorrow," I said.

"And where's your roomie?"

"Don't know. Don't really care, 'cause by tomorrow night Lizzie and I'll be rooming together. What about you?"

"Not sure yet. Been trying to track down the other number-seven key."

Lizzie looked at me with her mouth wide open. That's when it hit me. Number seven. No way. I must have looked like that deer we almost hit.

"Did you say seven?" I held up my rainbow keychain as Jessie's smile lit up the night.

"Well, I'll be. You just can't seem to stay away from me."

"Wait a second," Lizzie chimed in. "You get Jessie and I get Rhonda, the bull-riding butch?"

"Wait...this is perfect," I said. "Jessie can switch rooms with you. You'd switch with Lizzie, wouldn't you?" I conjured up the most pathetic, pleading look I could muster. Jessie's smile dropped. "I...I don't think I can. Clarissa takes these rules awfully serious."

"You'd throw Lizzie into Rhonda's den when you know you could handle her ten times better than Lizzie could? You're a cop, for Christ's sake. She wouldn't try anything with you." I wasn't giving up that easily.

"I'm sorry, but Clarissa would never go for it," Jessie said, slowly backing away. "I'm going to head to the cabin. I'm really sorry." Jessie sprinted across the lawn, like she couldn't get away fast enough.

I couldn't help but notice her toned, muscular legs as she darted away. "I'm definitely talking to Clarissa tomorrow," I said, never taking my eyes from Jessie as she disappeared into the darkness. "Definitely."

❖

Pine needles. That's the first thing I smelled when I opened the cabin door. It was cuter than I expected, with a rustic feel and extremely wood intensive: wood floors, wood walls, wood beams. A small nightstand separated two beds, and a huge panoramic aerial photo of Sedona hung on the wall. There was a mini-fridge and a small round table with two chairs. The bathroom door was closed and the water was running, so I figured Jessie was showering, which sounded like a divine idea.

It had been a long day. I wanted nothing more than to stand under the spray of hot water relaxing my tired muscles and hopefully relieving the dull headache that had started the moment Jessie held up her number-seven key. As I laid my suitcase on the bed and started unpacking, the bathroom door opened, releasing a mist of steam. Jessie was fanning the door back and forth, wearing nothing but a towel wrapped around her. Water droplets slid down her bare shoulders from her damp hair.

"Oh, hey, I didn't know you were here. Just letting out some steam."

"Great, you probably used up all the hot water."

"Don't worry, princess. I left plenty for you." Jessie brushed her teeth and then closed the door as she dressed.

Of course she'd look adorably sexy in her pjs as she sauntered out wearing a gray cotton tank top and shorts. She must have put her shirt on without drying off completely because it clung to her wet skin, revealing erect nipples. Not that I was looking.

"I can't believe you won't switch rooms with Lizzie." Maybe if I scolded her I could stop wondering what was under that thin material that was see-through when she stood in front of the lamp. Geez, get a grip.

"If you want to switch rooms you can be the one to convince Clarissa. Not me."

"Fine. I will. ASAP," I said.

Jessie lay down on her bed, put her hands behind her head, and watched me unpack. I always felt self-conscious when she stared at me, which seemed to be quite often when we were together. It was like her intense green eyes were trying to penetrate my soul with just one look. It was unnerving.

Carefully, I folded a shirt and laid it in the top drawer, which I'd claimed as my own. Even though I planned to be in Jessie's cabin only one night, I hated living out of a suitcase. I lifted a hefty cookbook out of my bag and placed it on the nightstand in case I couldn't sleep and needed something to pass the time. I regretting doing so the minute I plopped it down. I know some people think it's weird that I read cookbooks instead of novels, and I was sure Jessie would be one of them.

"What's that?" she asked, pointing at the book. "You read cookbooks?" Okay, here it comes. The teasing. The snickering. "Do you cook?"

"I bake," I replied, smoothing out the wrinkles in the shorts I planned to wear the next day.

Jessie grabbed the book, flipping through the pages. "What do you bake?"

Hmm…maybe she wasn't going to tease me after all.

"My signature item is a butterscotch cinnamon bun. It's a recipe my grandmother and I concocted. I used to love to help her cook."

"Sounds delicious. Maybe you could make it for me sometime." Jessie put the cookbook back on the nightstand.

"Maybe," I replied, knowing that was probably a lie. "Hey, where's your luggage? And how'd you bring suitcases on your motorcycle?"

"I shipped some things to Clarissa beforehand."

"So this wasn't really a spur-of-the-moment trip, was it? You knew days ago you were coming?" I eyed Jessie suspiciously, as she'd never said a word to me about attending the retreat.

She didn't reply but instead reclined against the headboard and closed her eyes. Looking at Jessie, I admired—and was a little envious—how beautiful she looked without makeup. Her olive complexion was flawless. That woman's face didn't have one pore. She was perfect. In contrast, I had light freckles to cover up and looked ghastly without at least a little makeup. Jessie's eyes popped open, startling me. I looked down, busying myself with some all-important sock folding.

Closing my empty suitcase, I stuffed it in a corner. "Aren't you going to unpack?"

"I will in a minute," she mumbled.

"I hope you have an iron, because if you wait much longer your clothes will be wrinkled."

"Fine," she said. Sighing loudly she swung her long legs out of bed. Jessie grabbed her suitcase and dumped her clothes out. Then she stood and stared at the pile before scooping it in her arms and stuffing everything into the bottom drawer.

"Oh yeah, your clothes won't be wrinkled now."

"You worry too much, O'Brien." Jessie sat up in bed and clicked on the TV.

"I love this movie," she said as her face lit up. "It's *An Affair to Remember* with Cary Grant and Deborah Kerr. Have you seen it?"

It was a black-and-white 1940s type movie that didn't look familiar. "No, I'm not much into old flicks."

"Seriously?" she asked.

"Yeah, the characters always fall in love too fast. It's not believable."

"So you don't believe in love at first sight?" Jessie reduced the volume, seemingly interested in my response.

"Of course not. Do you?"

"Mmm...maybe."

"I'm gonna take a shower," I said. "I'll leave you to your unrealistic romance."

Closing the bathroom door, I wondered if Jessie was an incurable romantic. Surely not. She didn't seem the type. Although maybe she was one of those hard-on-the-outside, mushy-on-the-inside types. But then again, a romantic wouldn't leave her wet towels on the floor and toothpaste splatters on the mirror. Could she have been any messier?

I must have stood under the showerhead for thirty minutes. The pulsating water on my skin felt divine as it washed away the events of the day. I was a prune but felt completely renewed as I stepped out of the shower. Tomorrow was a new day. I'd remedy the rooming situation, and Lizzie and I would start a wonderful vacation together.

When I opened the bathroom door, flickering light from the TV screen illuminated the room. Jessie had turned off all the lights in the cabin and was propped up with pillows, half asleep.

"Cute," she muttered, casting droopy eyes my way. Looking down at the lacy pink tank top and striped shorts I was wearing, I ran my fingers through my half-dried hair.

"Thanks," I said. I'd planned to entice Lizzie, not Jessie, with my nightwear. If Jessie liked it, then maybe Lizzie would, too. Sitting on the edge of my bed, I texted Lizzie to make sure she was okay. After I was satisfied Rhonda wasn't attacking her, I grabbed the three-week retreat schedule.

"What's that?" Jessie asked.

"The itinerary. Just looking at what's up for tomorrow."

Jessie leaned over and snatched the paper out of my hands.

"Hey!"

"You highlighted, underlined, and put notes in the margins?"

"I like being organized." I grabbed the paper back before the grin on her face turned into outright laughter. Even though I desperately wanted to review the itinerary, I suggested we get some shut-eye. Snuggling into bed, I pulled the covers tightly around my neck and sighed contentedly, relaxing into the mattress. Flashing lights from the TV screen flickered across my closed eyelids as voices from distressed lovers filled the cabin. Knowing I'd never fall asleep under these conditions, I sat up and looked at Jessie. She was slumped in bed with her eyes closed.

"Barnett!" No response. "Wake up!" Silence. "There's a snake in your bed!" Nothing. The TV remote was balanced on her chest, rising and falling with her breathing. I wasn't going anywhere near Jessie's chest, so I grabbed a pillow and flung it at her. It smacked her right in the face.

"What the fuck?" She sat up, shaking her head. "Did you just throw a pillow at me?"

"Turn the freakin' TV off."

"I'm watching it."

"You were sleeping." I sighed dramatically. "Come on. I'm exhausted and I can't sleep with Deborah what's her name crying her eyes out."

Jessie felt around the bed for the remote, which had toppled off her chest. "It's Deborah Kerr," she said as she grabbed the remote control. Poising a finger on the power button, she gave me a dirty look before clicking it off.

Immediately, I almost asked Jessie to turn the TV back on as blackness filled the cabin. I was used to city lights coming in through my apartment blinds, and at the very least the numbers on my alarm clock illuminated half my bedroom. This was downright eerie.

"Barnett?"

"What?" She sounded groggy and irritated.

"Why did you tell Clarissa I have a fair complexion?" The thought popped into my head and was out of my mouth before I could stop myself.

"What are you talking about?"

"Clarissa said you told her I have fair skin. Why would that ever come up in conversation?"

Several seconds of silence passed, and I wished I could see Jessie's face. Instead, nothing but velvet blackness filled the room.

"I don't remember ever telling her that."

"Oh. Just seemed like an odd thing for her to mention. Good night, Barnett."

"Good night, O'Brien," Jessie said, sounding more awake than before.

Chapter Four

Meet 'n Greet

Eager to get to orientation and see Lizzie, I was up early. When I opened the bathroom door after fixing my hair and putting on a little makeup, I was surprised to see Jessie sitting in bed writing in a notebook. Her hand was flying across the page so fast I wondered if her handwriting would even be legible. When she saw me standing in the doorway, she abruptly stopped writing and tucked the notebook under her leg, looking slightly embarrassed.

"Morning," she said. "You're up early."

"Yeah, I want to check on Lizzie. And I'd literally kill for a cup of coffee right now."

"I can make some." Jessie jumped out of bed and went to the small coffee pot on top of the mini-fridge. Before I could tell her not to bother, she'd ripped open a package and poured grounds into the filter. The aroma smelled heavenly. Not that I'm a coffee addict, but not having slept very well I was looking forward to a caffeine kick. The bed was comfortable enough, but it takes me a while to feel relaxed in a new place, and having Jessie three feet away didn't help.

I sat at the table as Jessie grabbed two cups from the cabinet and scurried around the kitchenette gathering cream and sugar. I had to admit it was thoughtful of her to brew me some java.

Admittedly, Jessie could be nice sometimes. I took a whiff of what smelled like a French-roast blend, which practically melted me in my chair because it smelled so divine.

"I make the best java this side of the Mississippi," Jessie said proudly as she put two steaming cups on the table. She stood over me with her hands on her hips, apparently waiting for my review. As I cradled the mug in my palms, a warm feeling overcame me. It felt nice to be sitting together in a cabin in the woods holding a warm drink made especially for me. After blowing the coffee a bit to cool it off, I took a sip and couldn't help but scowl at the bitter liquid.

"Ugh, this is awfully strong," I said. Jessie looked as though I'd slapped her across the face. "I probably just didn't put enough cream in it." Taking another sip, I tried not to grimace. The last thing I wanted to do was hurt her feelings, but from the wounded look on her face I was pretty sure I had. Jessie plopped into the chair opposite me. "Did you sleep well last night?" Changing the subject was the way to go.

"Not bad. I kept rolling over on the remote, though." Jessie arched her back and rolled her shoulders.

"You slept with the remote? Were you afraid I'd steal it?" I chuckled.

"No. I couldn't find it with all the covers and pillows, and it was pitch-black in here." Jessie looked irritated. Maybe we weren't morning people. Attempting to communicate with her in the early hours probably wasn't the wisest choice.

Looking over the rim of my cup at Jessie, I couldn't help but smile. She stared at me, furrowing her brow.

"What?" she asked.

"It's just...your hair...it's doing some...things." I waved my hand toward her head. She looked adorable with droopy eyes, rumpled clothes, and tousled hair, like a kid who'd just jumped out of bed, excited to watch Saturday-morning cartoons. Jessie quickly ran her fingers through her hair, attempting to fix the chaotic strands. "It's cute," I said. "It's...the windblown look."

Jessie's body tensed as she straightened her posture. She looked like an overly starched dress shirt, stiff and ready to snap at any moment. "Well, we can't all be as perfect as you, with your pressed clothes, Photoshopped complexion, and picture-perfect hairdo." I was a little taken aback by her reaction. I hadn't meant it as an insult.

"I didn't mean…" I started to explain, but the sour look on Jessie's face turned me off. I swear if she'd had her gun handy she would have shot me.

"Well, you could certainly learn a thing or two from me, Officer Barnett." And with that, the cozy scene turned bitterly cold.

❖

"What *is* that?" I asked.

"Hell if I know." Lizzie moved an unidentifiable object around with her fork. "Someone said this was scrambled tofu and this is tempeh bacon, whatever the hell that is."

"Oh yeah. I may have forgotten to tell you they serve vegan meals here."

"Yeah, I think you overlooked that part of the brochure." Lizzie gave me a playful shoulder bump. Waiting for orientation to start, I scanned the room, which was filled with women munching down on breakfast. Jessie was nowhere in sight. I did feel sort of bad about storming out of the cabin and slamming the screen door like a five-year-old.

"Aren't you going to eat anything?"

"I had a protein bar. Weight Watchers, you know. How was your night?"

"I didn't sleep much. Rhonda snores like a baboon."

I smiled to myself, knowing I didn't snore in the least. Lizzie was going to love being my roommate for the next few weeks… and for many years to come if things went as planned.

"Did I just hear my name?" Rhonda startled us from behind as she pulled out a chair, scraping it along the floor. She plopped down next to Lizzie, who scooted her chair closer to me since Rhonda had clearly invaded her personal space. "What the hell is this?" Rhonda peered into her plate of unidentifiable objects. "It's a vegan breakfast," I said.

"Ugh, this looks like some kind of healthy California crap. I figured Arizona would be a meat-and-potatoes sort of place." Rhonda stuffed a fork-load of...something...into her mouth.

"Ladies, ladies, may I have your attention, please?" Clarissa tapped a cup against her clipboard in an attempt to rally the troops. "I hope you're enjoying breakfast." I heard a few groans but didn't think they were audible to Clarissa. Out of the corner of my eye, I saw Jessie walk in and take a seat. She folded her arms across her chest, stretched out her legs, and slumped down. I watched her for a while until she turned and held my gaze. Quickly, I averted my eyes back to Clarissa.

"...should have in front of you a schedule, but I'd like to cover some of the activities over the next three weeks..."

I could still see Jessie out of the corner of my eye. She continued to stare at me long after I turned away. I straightened my posture, feeling self-conscious about being observed.

"...yoga, massage, meditation, and several guided hikes. No activity is mandatory, of course. I'd like you to participate in anything you desire. This is your time to relax, rejuvenate, and make some new friends. After breakfast we're having a meet 'n greet in the lounge of the main cabin. And later this afternoon we have our first guided hike on Baldwin Trail around the base of Cathedral Rock. Please feel free to come to me with any questions or requests. My door is always open."

"Okay, this is the perfect time for me to talk to Clarissa about the rooming situation," I said to Lizzie.

"What rooming situation?" Rhonda asked through a mouthfull of food. Gross. She didn't even attempt to cover her mouth when she spoke. Ignoring Rhonda's question, I practically sprinted to Clarissa.

"Hey, Clarissa, do you have a sec?"

"Malley! Good morning. Did you get some breakfast?"

"No, I'm fine."

"You have to eat something. Are you going on the Baldwin Trail hike?"

"Um, I'm not sure yet. Listen—"

"Well, you need to power up. It's a four-mile hike and you'll need your strength."

"So about the roommate—"

"Oh, I do hope you like your cabin. Listen, sugar, I need to organize a few things before the hike this afternoon. Grab some breakfast and I'll see you in a bit." Clarissa and her clipboard were gone in a flash. So much for that open-door policy.

❖

"Hi, I'm Sam." A cute blonde thrust her hand toward me.

"I'm Malley." We shook hands, smiled, and then stood awkwardly staring at each other until another lesbian walked up to introduce herself, thereby relieving the current lesbian to move on to someone else. This meet 'n greet wasn't all it was cracked up to be.

"Oh, so you're a heart," Cally, or Carla, or someone like that said.

"Huh?"

"Your name badge has a heart on it." Clarissa had requested that we wear dorky name badges and draw a symbol under our name that represented what we wanted to accomplish during the next three weeks. Lizzie drew a peace sign and I drew a heart. Cally, or maybe it was Carla, who had horrible penmanship, had a yin-yang symbol.

"Balance, huh?" I asked.

"Yeah, are you into New Age stuff?"

"No, not at all. But that's a popular symbol, so I've seen it before." Awkward silence before she nodded and moved onto someone else. Scanning the room, I spotted Lizzie talking to Jessie and Nicole. I hesitated to join them but thought it might break the ice between Jessie and me since she seemed to still be sulking about my coffee and hair comments. Plus, I was beyond curious to know what symbol she'd drawn on her name badge.

"Hi, everyone." My eyes darted to Jessie's badge just as she checked out mine. Weird. We both had the same symbol, except she had two intertwining hearts instead of one. Wishing I'd thought of the same thing, I wanted to edit my version. Hers encapsulated more of what I wanted to accomplish with Lizzie.

Nicole caught me staring at Jessie's badge. Speaking of Nicole, she was wearing an off-white silk blouse with polyester black pants and high heels. Something more suited for the courtroom than a wilderness lodge. Everyone else was in shorts and sandals.

"So, uh, Nicole." I literally bit my tongue to keep from commenting on her attire. "You should check out Carla, or maybe it's Cally, over there. She drew the same symbol as you did." Completely ignoring my comment, Nicole slipped her hand around Jessie's waist and whispered something in her ear. Jessie's expression was passive as she nodded a few times. Nicole walked away without even so much as a see-you-later to Lizzie and me.

"What was that about?" I asked.

"What?" Jessie said.

"She completely ignored Lizzie and me, and what was with all the secretive whispering?"

"Nicole was actually pretty nice," Lizzie said. "Well, until you walked up."

"Nice? And oh my gosh, what's with that outfit?" Jessie tilted her head and stared at me. "What?" I asked, playing dumb. Jessie shook her head and walked away. Obviously, I was the only one who thought Nicole was an uptight seductress.

"Hey, girls," Rhonda said. Even Rhonda had better fashion sense than corporate-lawyer chick. Well, maybe not better, but more appropriate. "Yawl going on the hike later today?"

Lizzie forced a smile. "We might."

"So Rhonda," I said. "Where are you from?"

"Born and reared in Waco, Texas. That's outside of Dallas."

"Waco. Wasn't there some weird cult suicide there years ago?"

"Yeah, some wackos, not to be confused with Waco." Someone should really tell Rhonda it's not attractive to snort when laughing. "You ever been to Texas, Lizzie?"

"No, never have."

"You should check it out sometime. Cowgirls can be a lot of fun." Rhonda nudged Lizzie with her shoulder.

"That's something to think about," Lizzie responded.

"So what's with that Nicole chick?" Rhonda asked. "Does she have a pencil stuck up her ass or what?"

"I know, right? And she hangs all over Jessie like they've known each other for years."

"I thought they were together. As in, you know, together, together." Rhonda circled her thick hips around, ending with a quick thrust forward. I supposed that was to indicate some sort of sexual move. It probably should have concerned me that Rhonda and I had the same taste in women. We both had a thing for Lizzie and despised Nicole. But I didn't really want to think about that when we were on a roll.

"They just met last night," I said.

"Grrr...what a cougar. And what's with that outfit?"

"Exactly!" I said.

Lizzie sighed and walked away as my new best friend and I dissed Nicole.

Chapter Five

Cathedral Confessions

We were totally lost and it was all Jessie's fault. Lizzie and I had decided to go on the Cathedral Rock hike and gathered with everyone at the Baldwin Trailhead, which was less than a mile from the lodge. With water and granola bars in our backpacks, we headed down the dusty trail, Clarissa leading the way. I'd planned to clear the air with Jessie about our silly misunderstanding that morning, but she took off like a jackrabbit.

"I didn't know this was a race, Barnett." I was out of breath after jogging to catch up with Jessie, who hurried down the trail. My stout legs were taking two steps to her one long stride. "Hey, could you slow down? I thought we were supposed to be following our fearless leader."

"I know these trails better than Clarissa does." Jessie stomped red dirt with her hiking boots. Contemplating how to make up with Jessie, I considered saying something like, "I didn't mean to hurt your feelings about the ghastly coffee you made, and I wasn't making fun of your goofy hair." But actually saying it out loud would have made our misunderstanding sound all the more immature. Instead, I wimped out and didn't say anything, using the silence to catch my breath…and catch glimpses of Jessie.

Damn if she didn't look good. Since my personal goal was to stay away from her as much as possible around our apartment complex, I rarely had up-close contact with her—unless it was when I snuck peeks at her doing crunches in the gym while I was on the treadmill. She had long, lean, muscular legs, and sculpted tan arms. And her butt was just begging for me to take a squeeze to see how firm it was. Not that I go around checking out women's rear ends, but I was walking behind her since she was trucking it down the trail, so my eyes were naturally drawn to that area. Too bad Jessie was a cop. I wondered if things would have been different between us if she'd had any other career.

"So, where'd you get the name Malley?"

It took me a minute to realize Jessie had asked me a question. She slowed down until I caught up and we were walking side by side. Now maybe I wouldn't be fantasizing about squeezing her rear end.

"I was named after my grandmother. On my dad's side. What about you? Is your name short for Jessica?" I realized Jessie and I didn't know much about each other.

"No, it's Jessie." She took a deep breath and paused. "I was named after my brother."

"Your brother? Wasn't it sort of confusing having two *Jessies* in the family?"

"He died when he was five. I came along a year after that. My parents are sort of New Age hippie types and said it was quite possible I was his reincarnated soul." She gave me a sideways glance to gauge my response.

"Interesting." But I really thought it was weird. "How did he die?"

"He was born with a rare form of brain cancer. They said he wouldn't live past one, but I guess he showed them."

"Oh, how sad. That's horrible. I'm so sorry, Jessie." The word Jessie hung in the air. It sounded odd. It was the first time I had called her Jessie and not Barnett.

"Your parents must have been so distraught. How does someone get over something like that?"

"I think their spiritual beliefs helped a lot. They believe everything happens for a reason. When I was older, one of my aunts told me that my dad started writing after the accident."

"Your dad's a writer?"

"Yeah, he writes self-help books."

"That's so cool. I guess I pictured him as a police officer like you."

"Hardly." She chuckled. "My parents are anti-gun and violence."

"Do you write?" Jessie glared at me. "It's just that you were writing in a notebook this morning." Silence. "Never mind, it's none of my business."

"So what about your family?" Jessie asked, getting the spotlight off her.

"Not much to tell. I'm an only child. My mom lives in Oak Creek Canyon. Lizzie and I are going to see her one day this week or the next."

"Where's your dad live?"

I always dreaded that question and never knew quite how to respond. "Up there." I pointed to the sky and kept walking, a lump in my throat. Jessie stopped. I wanted to keep going, keep moving. Instead, I turned around to compassionate green eyes.

"It's okay. It's been a little over a year now." But it wasn't okay and never would be, no matter how long it had been. And then came the customary sympathy, which I dreaded because it always made me want to cry.

"I'm so sorry. I just...I don't know what to say. What...how did it happen?"

"It's not something I really want to get into right now."

"I'm sorry. No, you're right." We continued on the trail in silence. The healthy thing to do would be to talk about my dad's death, but I rarely did so except with my mom. She was the only person who understood, the only person who could console me, if that was even possible.

As with most trails in Sedona, the terrain was rocky. I stared at my hiking boots as I trekked, careful not to twist an ankle stepping on a rock. Eventually, it leveled out and we were walking in red dirt. I caught a whiff of something, eucalyptus maybe, as we meandered through trees. Most people think Sedona is all desert, but it has lots of trees and a clear stream that flows from Oak Creek Canyon to Sedona. Feeling the warmth of the sun, listening to the songbirds, and stretching my legs in a now-reasonably paced hike since Jessie had slowed down, made me glad I was communing with nature instead of stuck in a cubicle at work.

"Hey," Jessie said, kicking up a cloud of red dust as she stopped. "This side trail winds up Cathedral Rock all the way to the top. You game?"

"Is it safe? The others won't know where we are."

"Yes, it's safe, and we'll probably be back down before Clarissa and the group even reach this point."

"It looks steep." I gazed up at the narrow, rocky trail.

"Where's your sense of adventure, O'Brien? You worry way too much, you know."

"I do not! I'm…responsible."

"Well, I'm not passing up a chance to see Sedona from the top of Cathedral Rock." Jessie started up the path, stopped, and turned around. "So you coming or what?"

Taking that as a dare, I said, "I can handle anything you can dish out, Barnett. Let's go." And with that we were climbing up the huge rock.

After a strenuous uphill hike, we were rewarded with a stunning 360-degree view of Sedona. Magnificent red-rock formations towered around us, some as far as a mile away. Inhaling deeply, we savored the clean air as opposed to the LA smog we were accustomed to. Jessie sat on a flat, wide rock and patted the place beside her. Not wanting to get red dust on my backside, I hesitated but then decided to live dangerously.

"I'm glad we came up here," I admitted. "It's gorgeous."

"See what happens when you take a chance?"

"Well, this trip is all about taking chances for me." Jessie peeled her gaze away from the view to look at me, silently urging me to continue. "It's just…I have things I want to accomplish the next three weeks." I traced a finger through the red dirt, not surprised to see I'd drawn a heart.

"Such as?"

"Just…things." Knowing Jessie, she wouldn't let up, and I regretted saying anything.

"Could you be a little more evasive? You mean like walking an inch outside of the crosswalk, or eating dinner at seven p.m. instead of six, or not wearing socks with your sneakers and risking blisters?"

"Noooo," I said, annoyed by her teasing. "For your information, I plan to take a major risk in the romance department." I straightened my posture, jutted out my chest, and looked right at her.

"Oh?" Jessie was definitely intrigued. "Romance, huh? Who's the lucky girl?"

"I'm not telling you before I even tell her."

"Let me get this straight. She doesn't know you have the hots for her?"

"The hots? Yeah, that's romantic."

"Come on, who is it? Rhonda? Nicole?" I rolled my eyes at her lame guesses. "Lizzie?"

I never was good at lying, so I didn't say anything, which was a dead giveaway.

"It *is* Lizzie. Huh. Guess I shouldn't be surprised." Jessie gathered a handful of red pebbles, allowing them to fall to the ground through her fist. "So, are you in love or what?" Jessie looked at me out of the corner of her eye.

"Yes, and don't say a word to anyone. Seriously, Jessie. This is too important and I shouldn't have said anything." I looked directly into her eyes, needing confirmation that she understood.

"No, of course not," she said. "Wow. In love. So, when will you tell her?"

"At the end of the retreat. Actually, that's why I wanted to ask Clarissa about switching rooms. I'd planned on Lizzie and me spending time together. Nothing against you, you know?"

"Yeah, no, of course. But why wait until the end of the retreat to tell her?"

Reflecting on Jessie's question, I didn't have a good answer. Why *would* I wait? It's not like Lizzie would suddenly fall in love with me during the next few weeks. Either she'd know if she wanted to date me or not. I was afraid of rejection for sure, but there seemed to be some other nagging reason I couldn't put my finger on.

"I'll have to ponder that," I said.

Jessie stared at the ground, her clinched jaw jutting out. Apparently out of questions, she reclined on the rock, closing her eyes. I'm not sure how long I sat there going over the pros and cons of telling Lizzie how I felt sooner than I'd planned. Maybe I should. After all, nothing was standing in my way.

A loud clap of thunder that caused Jessie and me to jump interrupted the silence. "Uh oh," she said. "We better head back down." Jessie bolted to her feet.

"Rain? But it's not even in the forecast." I frowned at the charcoal-gray sky that hung over Cathedral Rock.

"Did you check the forecast?"

"Well, no," I said, feeling suddenly unprepared. Gathering our water bottles and backpacks we headed downhill.

It didn't take long before dark, ominous clouds filled the sky and one fat raindrop plopped on my nose. Jessie picked up the pace as I tried my best to keep up. Within minutes, light rain turned into a downpour, followed by another round of thunder. I wasn't used to the sound of thunder, or even rain for that matter, living in Southern California. I'd heard about Arizona monsoons and how they came in bursts. I hoped they disappeared just as quickly. The red dirt turned to sludge as we hiked down the trail. Visibility was limited, and I'd long ago given up trying to cover my head, resigned to the fact that we were getting drenched.

Jessie, several yards ahead of me, stopped in the middle of an intersection with two separate paths trailing off in different directions. As I walked up behind her, she took off on one trail, with me heading down the other. Realizing we were going in opposite directions, we both stopped and looked back at each other.

"It's this way," she yelled over the thunder.

"No, it's this way."

"I know these trails, O'Brien. It's this one."

"No it's not," I yelled back. "I remember passing this oak tree with a cactus underneath."

"Come on, we're getting soaked here. Follow me." Jessie started walking, obviously expecting me to follow like a little lost puppy dog.

"Barnett!" I yelled as loud as I could, which was enough to stop her. "You're the most stubborn, pigheaded woman I've ever met! You're not even willing to consider that you might be wrong." Jessie stomped toward me until she was inches away from my face.

"What?" she yelled.

"You heard me. Pigheaded!"

"Oh my God!" She threw her hands into the air, lifting her face to the rain. "If that isn't that the kettle calling the…I mean the…can calling the…wait, no…"

"I think you mean the pot calling the kettle black." I couldn't help but grin.

"Exactly! You're not only stubborn but completely exasperating. What's with you? You've had it in for me from the first moment we met. Why do you hate me so much?"

"I don't hate you." Far from it.

"Well, you certainly don't like me."

"Do you really want to have this conversation in a rainstorm?" Jessie's hair was plastered to her head as droplets of water rolled down her face. She glared at me for what felt like several minutes, seemingly considering whether she wanted to continue her line of questioning.

"Fine," she said, breaking eye contact. "You're more than welcome to take the wrong trail, but don't expect me to come looking for you when you get lost."

Red-hot anger rose to my cheeks. She really would leave me, wouldn't she? Silently, I weighed my options. I wasn't *completely* sure I knew which path to take. Just pretty sure. So, I figured if we went her way, then it was a win-win situation. One, if we got lost I could forever hold it over her head with a well-crafted story of "Remember that time in Sedona when you..." Or two, if she was right, we wouldn't make the headlines of the *Sedona Sentinel* as TWO LOST LA LESBIANS DROWN ON WILDERNESS HIKE.

"Fine!" I yelled. "But if you're wrong, I swear..." Jessie stomped away through mud puddles before I could finish my sentence.

After about twenty minutes of tediously hiking through rain that stung like pinpricks, Jessie had to know we were on the wrong trail. We were lost, going in the opposite direction of where we should be heading. Just as I was about to yell out to her, my hiking boot caught on a rock, sending me flying forward and landing face-first in a sea of mud. Intense pain shot through my knee and up my leg. Jessie swung around and sprinted to my side.

"Are you all right?" She crouched beside me, lifting my head so I wouldn't drown in a puddle. "Can you move?" I tried to get up but was stopped by a stabbing pain in my knee. Jessie helped me into a sitting position. I was completely covered in red mud, head to toe. "Are you hurt?"

"My right knee's killing me," I said. "I think I landed on a rock."

"We need to get out of this rain so I can take a look. Can you stand?"

I didn't respond because I was too busy biting my tongue trying not to cry out from the stabbing pain.

Jessie pulled me up and helped me limp to a grove of trees, which acted as a semi-roof from the rain. She lowered me into a sitting position with my back against a tree trunk. I was shivering from the shock of the fall and the cool breeze on my wet skin, so Jessie wrapped me tight in her arms, pulling me into her chest.

"You're freezing," she said, trying to create friction to warm me by rubbing my back. Was that the scent of lavender? How could she smell so good after hiking all day and getting caught in a rainstorm? I inhaled her intoxicating scent. Jessie gently rocked me as I felt her heart pounding against my cheek. It was a nice place to be. Safe and warm.

"Are you okay?" She sounded worried.

"I...I don't know. I'm muddy."

"This is no time to be worried about wrinkled clothes," she said with a half-smile.

As though suddenly realizing we were embracing, Jessie quickly released me and backed away, leaving me suddenly cold. Her eyes contained a mixture of fear and embarrassment. We stared at each other until I grabbed my knee, which was throbbing.

"Oh my gosh, you're bleeding." Jessie stretched out her shirt and put pressure on my knee. I couldn't help but grimace when she pressed harder. "I'm sorry, Malley, but we need to stop the bleeding." She continued applying pressure, covering her T-shirt in blood. When she was fairly certain the bleeding had stopped, Jessie examined my knee. "The cut doesn't look too deep, so I don't think you'll need stitches, but your knee's already swollen and bruised. Does anything else hurt?"

"No. I'm pretty sure I didn't twist or break anything."

"I should be more prepared. It's never safe to go hiking without a first-aid kit. And a flashlight." Jessie nervously looked around. Not only was it dark from the thunderstorm, but it was also getting late. We'd stayed on Cathedral Rock longer than intended, and taking the wrong trail had put us way behind.

"This is all my fault," she said. "We should have stayed with the others. It wasn't safe to come up here by ourselves. And now you're injured." Jessie looked at me with concern. "If I wasn't so stubborn, and...was it pigheaded?...well, we wouldn't be lost... and on the wrong trail." That last part had to hurt.

"Jessie," I said, putting my hand over hers. "I'm glad we came up here. I wouldn't have missed that gorgeous view for anything. Really."

Jessie lowered her eyes to my hand, which covered hers. She stared at it for several seconds. Did she want me to yank it away? Maybe she was uncomfortable. We'd never been this physically close before. It should have felt odd, I know, but it didn't. It felt natural.

"I think I should call for help. It's getting dark and you can barely walk." Jessie pulled out her cell phone and held it up, trying to get a few bars. "Listen, the rain has let up a bit. I'm going to hike a little higher to see if I can get cell reception."

"You're leaving me?" I suddenly felt five years old.

Jessie put her hand on my shoulder. "I'm just going to see if I can get a signal."

"Stay with me." I scooted closer to her. There was something about being wet, cold, lost, and hurt that made me feel incredibly vulnerable. Normally, when I felt afraid I'd dig out the heart rock the Indian gave me by the Kachina Woman. Holding it in my palm or clutched to my chest always comforted me. But the rock was at home in my top drawer, so I had to resort to Jessie for comfort.

"Come here." Jessie slipped her arm around my shoulder, pulling me close. I smelled the calming lavender again. "I won't leave you. I promise."

As much as I hated the thought of Jessie being a cop, I bet she was a good one. I could picture her embracing a little lost boy, talking to him sweetly, making him feel safe. Or reassuring a frightened car-wreck victim. She had a way of making a person feel protected and comforted.

After holding me for not nearly long enough for my taste, Jessie looked down to meet my eyes. "Do you think you can walk? We can't stay here all night. It's not safe."

She was right. We had to get back to the lodge before nightfall. Regretfully, I released my hold on Jessie, finding it surprisingly sad to think I'd never have another opportunity to be that close to her again.

❖

"Oh my God! Where were you?" Clarissa and Lizzie said in unison as they bolted off the porch of the main cabin when they saw Jessie and me coming down the path. Even though my knee had throbbed the entire way, I managed to limp with Jessie as my crutch. At this slow hiking pace, it took us hours to reach the lodge, but we did so just after night fell.

I'm sure we were quite a sight to Clarissa and Lizzie. I was hobbling and covered in mud. Jessie had blood all over her shirt. And we were both drenched and smelling like wet puppy dogs. We probably looked like we'd just stepped off a battlefield.

"What happened? I was about to call 911!" Clarissa swung her phone at Jessie.

"Why didn't you answer your cell? I called and texted a dozen times!" Lizzie yelled.

"Oh my God, you're hurt." Clarissa eyed Jessie's blood-stained shirt.

"Actually, Malley is the one who—"

Lizzie grabbed my shoulders, fear in her eyes. "You're hurt?"

"Listen," I said, feeling the need to calm the two hysterical women. "We're okay. I hurt my knee, but I'm fine. We lost track of time and weren't expecting a thunderstorm. It wasn't anyone's fault." I looked at Jessie, who had a hopeless, apologetic expression.

"We were worried sick," Clarissa said.

"I'm taking you inside right now to take care of that knee." Lizzie grabbed my hand, pulling me along. Jessie and I looked back at each other as two frantic women dragged us in different directions.

❖

I slowly creaked the cabin door open, trying not to wake Jessie. The lamp between the two beds clicked on. "Sorry if I woke you. Lizzie didn't want to let me out of her sight. I took a shower there and she loaned me something to wear. All I want to do now is sleep for twelve hours." I collapsed into bed.

"Yeah, I'm exhausted, too. How's your knee?"

"Hurts, but it's fine."

Jessie clicked off the light and I heard her turn over in her bed. I still wasn't used to the darkness of the cabin at night.

"So, did you tell her?" Jessie asked.

"Tell who what?"

"You know. Tell Lizzie how you feel."

"Oh no. Rhonda was there, and it's been a crazy day as it is." I did wonder why I hadn't opened up to Lizzie. She was being a loving, compassionate nurse, tending to my wound, holding my hand and telling me how scared she was something had happened to me. Rhonda was only in the room a short time before she went outside to smoke with the chimney gang, as we called them. I kicked myself for passing up the perfect opportunity.

"What is it that you love about her?" The anonymity of the darkness must make it easier for people to ask questions they wouldn't normally ask in the daylight.

"About Lizzie?" I asked, yawning. "We're very much alike. We get along really well and enjoy doing the same things. She's considerate and smart and fun. And very beautiful, of course. I don't know. It's hard to put into words."

If Jessie said anything more, I didn't hear, because I was sound asleep within minutes.

CHAPTER SIX

THE SEDONA PATIENT

Bang. Bang. Bang. Would someone stop that banging? Some people are trying to sleep around here. I squinted at the clock. 11:11 a.m. That couldn't be right. More banging. Was that my head pounding or was someone knocking at the door?

"Malley?" Lizzie creaked the cabin door open as I propped myself up on one elbow. Oh. My. God. I felt like a train had hit me. Not only was I not used to hiking six miles, mostly uphill I might add, but the fall had strained every muscle in my body. "I'm sorry to wake you, but I wanted to make sure you're okay."

"Is it eleven?" I rubbed my face with my hands. "I haven't slept this late since I was a teenager on the first day of summer."

"Are you in pain? Does anything hurt?"

"All of me hurts." I collapsed onto the bed, staring up at the ceiling. Lizzie leaned over me, concern etched on her face.

"You look like hell."

Great. Just the impression I wanted to make on Lizzie. She laid the back of her hand on my forehead as though checking my temperature. As much as I loved Lizzie doting on me, I wanted to get her out of the cabin ASAP, considering I probably looked like the bride of Frankenstein.

"I'm okay. Just really sore. I need a hot shower and some breakfast...or I guess that would be lunch." I rubbed my itchy eyes, which I imagined were bloodshot. My head spun around like a tilt-a-whirl as I sat up in bed.

Lizzie put a hand on my shoulder to steady me. "Are you sure you're okay?"

"Yeah, I'm fine," I said after my head stopped spinning. I held Lizzie's gaze, hoping she'd believe me and scram. "I'm just going to hop in the shower. I'll meet you in the dining room in about half an hour."

Lizzie squinted at me for several seconds before nodding and heading for the door.

My sore muscles relaxed a bit after a steamy shower, but I winced in pain when I forgot about my knee and rubbed it while drying off. Coming out of the bathroom, I looked around the empty cabin. Where was Jessie? Knowing her, she'd probably gotten up early, gone for a jog, and was now taking a five-mile hike. The heel.

After lunch, I had no interest, or physical ability, in participating in yoga or hiking or any of the other activities highlighted in my schedule. Lizzie and I took a slow-paced walk around the grounds and found a cute pond with koi fish. It had a small waterfall and was surrounded by pine and oak trees, which provided much-needed shade from the heat. We spent the afternoon sitting on a bench chatting about everything from work to how happy she was to be away from Heather.

The day was definitely looking up. I hadn't spent much time with Lizzie since arriving at the lodge. I missed her. We saw each other at work every day and had established a routine of meeting for coffee before starting the workday. Schedule permitting, we always had lunch together, and sometimes we'd go out for drinks after work if she was mad at Heather and didn't want to go home.

When I got back to the cabin later that day, Jessie was sitting at the table writing in a notebook. As before, she immediately stopped writing, closed the journal, and tucked it away.

"Hey," she said. "How are you feeling?"

"I felt like total crap this morning but a little better now." I walked to my bed with a slight limp, trying to hide how much my knee ached.

Jessie approached, sitting on the bed beside me. "Let's see that cut." She gently lifted the bandage. Normally the invasion of personal space would surprise me, but I think she felt responsible for me getting hurt and wanted to help. "This is getting infected, Malley. I'll get some hydrogen peroxide and antiseptic."

Jessie went into the bathroom while I checked out my knee. Ew, it was looking bad.

"You need to leave the bandage off to let it air out," Jessie yelled as she washed her hands. I was pretty wimpy when it came to pain so I was already wincing when I saw the handful of supplies she brought out of the bathroom.

"Where'd you get all that stuff?"

"From my first-aid kit. The one I *should* have taken on the hike." Jessie knelt beside me and poured hydrogen peroxide on my wound, which immediately foamed. Then she lightly dabbed antiseptic on it. "There," she said, sitting back on the bed next to me. "That should do it. Are you sore?"

"You could say that," I said with a chuckle. In a surprising move, Jessie put a hand on my shoulder, massaging tense muscles. It felt so good I didn't even think to protest.

"Malley, I just wanted to tell you I'm really sorry for getting us lost, and I'm so sorry you got hurt."

I heard words and knew I should probably respond, but all I could think about were Jessie's hands, which were now on the back of my neck, kneading tender muscles. Closing my eyes, I melted under the warmth of her touch. I didn't dare move, for fear she might stop. Was Jessie a closeted massage therapist? 'Cause she certainly knew what she was doing. She sensed exactly where I wanted, and needed, her touch the most. The pressure she applied was the perfect mixture of strong yet tender. Jessie's fingers slid from my neck into my hair, massaging my scalp. Chills ran through my body as my pulse raced.

My eyes flew open when I realized I'd been moaning, which sounded sexual in an embarrassing sort of way. Jessie stared at me with a mixture of desire and confusion in her eyes. Instinctively, my eyes dropped to her lips, which were slightly parted. I'd never noticed her mouth before, how her bottom lip jutted out a bit in a sexy pout and how utterly kissable her lips looked. I gazed into her eyes again and saw only desire, the confusion seemingly gone. Was I crazy to think Jessie was about to kiss me? As she inched closer and tilted her head, my breathing became shallow at the thought of her lips on mine.

A knock on the door broke the hypnotic daze. Jessie's eyes widened and she drew her head back sharply. We stared at each other until the next knock was accompanied by a creak of the door.

Jessie moved back onto the bed as Lizzie poked her head into the cabin. "Hey, I just wanted to check on the patient."

I was still staring at Jessie, unable to think or speak, my heart pounding. What exactly had just happened? Were we actually going to kiss?

"Um, she's better, I think." Jessie's voice sounded hoarse.

"That's good to hear." Lizzie entered the cabin and walked to the bed. "Malley, you're awfully flushed. Are you sure you're feeling okay?"

"Am I?" Placing my hands on the sides of my face, I felt the heat. I glanced back and forth from Jessie to Lizzie. It wasn't that Jessie and I had almost kissed that bothered me so much. It was that I wanted her to kiss me…desperately…that made me feel incredibly guilty with Lizzie so near. Really, though, it wasn't my fault. Jessie had started it with all that shoulder-rubbing stuff.

"Do you feel up to seeing the sunset tonight? I heard there's a great view from Airport Road."

I stared at Lizzie, dumbfounded, thinking about what would have happened had she not walked in.

When I didn't respond, Jessie chimed in, saving me from the awkward silence. "Yeah, the view from there is awesome. It's a popular spot so you should go early."

"Great," Lizzie said. "Do you want to join us? You can show us where to go."

"Sure." Jessie looked at me timidly. "If that's okay."

"Yeah," I said. "Of course."

"Malley, are you sure you're okay?" Lizzie asked.

"Just…a bit heated is all."

❖

"Why in the world did you suggest she come along?" Lizzie and I were sitting in her car waiting for Jessie.

"You said it was okay. Besides, I'd like to get to know Jessie better." Lizzie squirmed in the driver's seat, staring straight ahead. She was up to something. I could feel it. "What?" she asked, innocently batting her eyes. "Look, you said you didn't have a crush on Jessie, so is it so wrong that I might be interested in her? Would you mind?" Lizzie played with her car keys, which dangled from the ignition, avoiding eye contact.

My jaw went limp as my mouth opened wide. Lizzie and Jessie? I'd been standing in line behind Heather for a year. There was no way I'd let Jessie cut in front of me. "I don't think you and Jessie would fit very well together."

"Why do you say that? I know you don't like her very much, but she seems nice. Not to mention gorgeous. Maybe she'll be my rebound fling."

Of course. How could I be so foolish as to overlook the rebound theory? Everyone knew the first relationship after a major breakup was doomed from the beginning. And Lord knows I didn't want to be Lizzie's transitional girlfriend. I wanted our relationship to last, white picket fence and all. For a second, I considered urging Lizzie to go out with Jessie, but then reconsidered. Jessie was a catch. It was too much of a gamble.

"Anyway," I said. "I think you might have some competition." I pointed at Jessie, who was followed closely by the snow queen— my new nickname for Nicole.

Lizzie grunted and started the car as I fumbled with SiriusXM, looking for a good station. The Coffee House. My favorite. They played mellow, singer-songwriter tunes. Jessie and the snow queen opened the door and scrunched into the backseat.

"I hope you don't mind, but I thought Nicole might like to come along."

"The more the merrier," Lizzie said through clenched teeth.

"Where to?"

"I can drive if you'd like since I know where to go," Jessie offered.

"That'd be great." Lizzie hopped out of the car and switched places with Jessie before I could even blink. Jessie gave me a quick glance before putting the car in reverse. I stared at her perfect profile. Perfect eyes. Perfect nose. Perfect lips. Lips that I'd imagined kissing me less than an hour ago. I blinked rapidly, attempting to rid myself of the image.

"I haven't driven a car in a while, but I promise to be careful," Jessie said. She seemed nervous pulling onto the highway.

"Ah yes, you're a motorcycle chick, aren't you?" Lizzie said.

"Motorcycles are so sexy," Nicole purred. Subtly was not her strong point.

"Hey, what are you doing?" I asked. Jessie was punching buttons on the radio. "That was Norah Jones. I like that song."

"Let's find a better station."

"There's nothing better than The Coffee House, Barnett."

"Here. This one's good."

Siriusly Sinatra? Jessie had to be pulling my leg or trying to annoy me on purpose.

"You'd choose Frank Sinatra over Norah Jones? Lizzie, back me up here."

"Actually, I kind of like that song." Lizzie was no help.

"He has a sexy, sultry voice," Nicole said. Was everything sexy to her?

"Well, I picked the station first." I punched in The Coffee House. Jessie furrowed her brow and looked at me longer than she should have, considering she was driving. "Everybody knows the passenger gets to pick the music anyway."

"Who says?" Jessie asked.

"It's a rule. It's…uh…it's in the *California Driver Handbook.*"

"It is not." Jessie punched in Sinatra. I punched in Norah. Sinatra. Norah. Sinatra. Norah.

"Hey, you two. You're going to break my radio," Lizzie said. "Let Jessie pick the station, and you can choose the music on the way back. God, just like kids."

Jessie smirked and punched in Sinatra. "Fly Me To The Moon." Exactly where I wished I was instead of in a car with those three.

Airport Road was much like every other highway in Sedona: narrow, winding, and climbed in elevation. Jessie was right. It was a popular spot at sundown. We parallel-parked along the side of the road since the parking lot was packed. Hiking uphill we reached the overlook, which had a view of Sedona surrounded by mountainous rocks.

"Wow," we said in unison. The sky was streaked with a gorgeous array of reds and oranges. It looked like a painting. The red rocks turned pink in the changing light. As the sun dropped, the sky evolved into a mixture of blue and purple with a little orange still mixed in. Now I understood what all the hype was about when it came to Sedona sunsets. It was something you had to experience in person.

Lizzie moved closer to me as the wind picked up and blew a warm breeze our way. It was such a romantic setting I couldn't resist slipping my arm around her waist, and surprisingly she didn't give me a weird look. This was heaven. A breathtaking sunset and Lizzie close to me.

Nothing could have brought me down in that moment, except for Nicole, who was practically mauling Jessie. She was standing behind Jessie with her arms wrapped around her, smashing her breasts into her back. They looked like conjoined twins. I couldn't understand what Jessie saw in her. The only positive was that the sickening sight seemed to turn Lizzie off on the idea of dating Jessie. Apparently, she was already taken.

The sun set much too quickly for my taste. I could have stared at the vibrant landscape forever and vowed not to miss another Sedona sunset.

As we pulled up to the lodge, I cringed, remembering I still hadn't sorted out the roommate situation. Not only was I wasting time on my Get Lizzie plan, but being around Jessie was doing strange things to me. It was crazy to think I'd actually wanted to kiss her. Lizzie was the one I wanted, not Jessie. Switching rooms would be my number-one priority...if I could ever pin Clarissa down long enough to bring it up.

❖

Jessie and I were in our respective beds that night where it felt easier to bring up certain topics in the dark. Well, everything except for our almost kiss. I didn't want to think about that, much less talk about it.

"You and Nicole seem to be getting along well. You think you might hook up with her?"

"I'm not here to hook up."

Why had Jessie drawn two intertwining hearts on her name badge if she wasn't looking to meet a woman? At the risk of sounding like we were in junior high, I had to gauge Jessie's interest in Lizzie. "What if a beautiful woman, let's say Lizzie, wanted to go out with you? What would you do?"

"I'd say no thanks."

Propping myself on my elbow, I looked toward Jessie's bed even though all I could see was total blackness. "Seriously? I can understand turning down Nicole, but Lizzie?"

I heard Jessie shift in her bed, her voice louder so she must have been facing me. "You don't like Nicole very much, do you?"

"I don't even know her," I said. "She seems pushy. And I'd bet my life she was one of those popular kids."

"Popular kids?"

"You know. Oh, wait…you were probably one of them as well, huh?"

"You mean popular in school?" Jessie chuckled. "Hardly. I was a total geek. Glasses, braces, and I was a chubs."

"No way. You're putting me on."

"Seriously. You're talking to the president of the science club. I didn't even have a date until my senior prom, and it was with my best friend, Allan, who also happened to be gay. We just weren't out yet."

"Wow. I'd have never guessed."

"There's a lot about me you don't know."

"Apparently." I lay back in my bed and closed my eyes. "Good night, Barnett. And Norah's ten times better than Frank," I whispered.

"Good night, O'Brien." I heard the smile in her voice.

CHAPTER SEVEN

COFFEE TALK

L ittle did I know that "free day" in the lodge schedule meant Clarissa was in Flagstaff for an all-day meeting, so I couldn't talk to her about switching rooms. With that plan shot to hell, I suggested that Lizzie and I go sightseeing to get a little time to ourselves. Just the two of us.

This was one of the reasons I loved Lizzie: she was even more organized than I was. Planning ahead, she had bottles of water and healthy snacks in a cooler and a Sedona guide map highlighted with the most popular scenic spots. She'd make an awesome girlfriend. I'd read an article once that said kissing your best friend was like kissing your sister. It said that friends could have comfortable, long-lasting relationships, but that the passion was usually absent. But I didn't agree. Not that I'd ever kissed Lizzie, but I was sure we'd have passion. How could there not be passion with someone as awesome as her?

"Malley, go to the yellow sticky note in the guidebook." I reached into the backseat, grabbing the book while Lizzie drove through town. "There's a hike Rhonda was telling me about. It's a steep climb, but it ends in a rock formation shaped like a woman."

"A woman?" I raised my eyebrow.

"Yeah, an Indian name or something. It's in Boynton Canyon."

"Kachina Woman." I read the book but didn't need to do so. I knew what woman Lizzie was talking about. My heart sank. How could I talk Lizzie out of seeing a rock shaped like a woman? What lesbian wouldn't want to see that? The last thing I wanted to do was dredge up memories of me and my dad in Boynton Canyon and do something stupid like start crying at the top of the ridge. So, I did the only thing I could think to do in a pinch. I lied.

"Rhonda told me about that as well," I said. "She also said she was going to hike up there this morning." I felt bad for lying, but I knew that would turn Lizzie off right away.

"Oh. Well, maybe we can go later. I've had my fill of Rhonda the past few days. Speaking of roommates, how are things going with Jessie?"

Why did I suddenly feel guilty and defensive? It's not like Lizzie was a mind reader and knew I'd been fantasizing about Jessie kissing me. And it's not like I purposefully fantasized. I tried to forget about our almost-kiss, which was increasingly difficult every time I looked at her lips.

"What do you mean?"

"You two getting along?"

"I guess. Yeah, actually she's not as bad as I thought she'd be." Lizzie stared at me as we sat at a stoplight. I looked straight ahead, never taking my eyes off the red light, as though it were the most captivating thing in the world.

"Well, I'd rather room with Jessie than Rhonda any day. She's so gorgeous, I wouldn't even care if she snored."

A vision of Jessie and Lizzie making out flashed through my mind. They were sitting on my bed when Jessie tilted her head, leaned forward, and pressed her pouty lips against Lizzie's mouth. A pang of jealousy ripped through my gut. The thing was, though, I wasn't sure if I was jealous of Jessie...or Lizzie.

"Malley? What do you think?"

"What?" Had Lizzie just asked me something?

"I said do you think Jessie and Nicole are dating?" I knew where this line of questioning was going.

"Uh…yeah, I'm pretty sure they are." I was on a roll. Two lies in under five minutes.

"Hmm…how about we grab some coffee and decide what we'd like to do today?"

"Sure," I said. "How about that bakery we saw driving into town?"

As Lizzie pulled into the parking lot, I saw a yellow motorcycle parked in front. Hopefully someone in Sedona owned a carbon copy of Jessie's bike. No such luck. When Lizzie and I walked into the super-cute bakery we saw Jessie sitting in a booth sipping a cappuccino and writing in a notebook. Was Sedona so small that I couldn't even get away from her for one day? Lizzie made a beeline for Jessie before I could suggest we hide at a corner table. Jessie slipped her notebook into her backpack and motioned for us to sit. Lizzie slid into the booth with me beside her.

"Fancy meeting you here, Barnett," I said. "What are you writing?"

"Nothing important. What are you two up to today?"

"We were thinking about going to Chavez Ranch. There's a great view of Cathedral Rock from there," Lizzie said.

"I've had enough of Cathedral Rock. Right, Malley?" Jessie grinned as her eyes met mine.

I blushed at the recollection of being wrapped in her arms in the rain, feeling protected and cared for. I'd never smell lavender again, or get caught in a rainstorm, and not think about Jessie. As though reading my mind, her eyes darted downward, a hint of red touching her cheeks.

"Malley?" I turned to Lizzie, who was staring at me. "I said how's your knee doing? Where's your mind today?"

"Oh, it's much better. Thanks." I stole a quick glance at Jessie, who was studying her clasped hands as though she'd never seen them before.

"What can I get you?" We glanced at a waitress standing by our table. Lizzie and I ordered coffee, which seemed to annoy the waitress, who was probably thinking we wouldn't leave much of a tip for a small order. After turning, the waitress stopped abruptly and spun around to face Jessie. "I just wanted to say that was a really nice thing you did earlier. Most people wouldn't bother."

"It was nothing." Jessie shrugged.

"It was something, and for that I'm giving you a free refill." She took Jessie's cup and walked back to the counter.

"What was that about?" I asked.

Jessie shrugged again, looking embarrassed. "Nothing." When I raised my eyebrow, Jessie rolled her eyes, knowing I wouldn't let it go. "There was this homeless guy sitting in a booth counting his pennies for a cup of coffee, so I bought him breakfast. No biggie."

"That was really nice of you," Lizzie said.

It *was* a thoughtful thing to do. Honestly, it probably wouldn't have crossed my mind to do that. I think most people would have ignored the guy. Maybe she was mushy under that hard cop exterior after all.

While Lizzie and Jessie chatted about Sedona hot spots, I scoped out the bakery. It was a small place but decorated in soothing pastel blues and greens. They served coffee and pastries of every kind. I'd always dreamed of owning a place just like this, a charming boutique where people could sit for hours drinking coffee and partaking of delectable desserts. I even knew what I'd name my place. Fun Buns. That's what my grandmother used to call our butterscotch cinnamon buns, which would be my signature item.

"Malley? Earth to Malley." Malley. That's me. I looked at Lizzie as she laughed. "Daydreaming, were you?"

"Sorry, I guess I was."

"You're not fantasizing about opening a bakery again, are you?" Lizzie asked.

"No...well, maybe. I was just looking around the place."

"You want to open a bakery?" Jessie asked.

"Malley has a great job. And it's stable. She'd be crazy to give that up," Lizzie said.

"But if it's her dream then—"

"Dreams don't pay the rent, and California isn't cheap, as we all know. Besides, businesses are closing down all around us."

"Still, though, she should give it some consideration. At least check out the possibility."

I looked back and forth from Jessie to Lizzie as they talked about me like I wasn't even there.

"Malley can bake, that's for sure, but owning a business is a whole other deal," Lizzie said.

"She can't live in fear." Jessie tapped on her chest three times as she said, "She should follow her heart."

It's a good thing they were acting as though I were invisible, because I'm sure my mouth was wide open. That was exactly what the disappearing Indian had told me by the Kachina Woman right before he tapped on my chest three times.

Chapter Eight

A Kiss is Just a Kiss

I had Clarissa cornered. She was sitting behind her desk in her office, and I was standing in front of the door so she couldn't escape unless she crawled out the window.

"Clarissa, this has been such a wonderful vacation so far." Buttering her up was the way to go. "Everything's so well organized. But I do have one request."

"Of course. Just name it."

"Lizzie and I want to room together. While I totally support your ingenious idea of mixing people up, pairing Jessie and me isn't going so well."

Clarissa's smile faded. "You and Jessie aren't getting along?"

"It's not that we don't get along. It's more that Lizzie and I wanted to spend some quality time together."

"Oh. Well, I wouldn't want to force anything on you." Clarissa looked terribly disappointed, which made me feel like crap.

"It would be better all the way around, I think, if we switched rooms." I flashed my most genuine smile. "Like now. As in by tonight."

"I see. Well, does Jessie know?"

"Yeah, and she'll probably be happy to get rid of me."

"I hate to hear that, but if this is what you want, just give me some time to talk to Rhonda to see if she objects to switching, and I'll let you know."

Rhonda. Damn. I forgot about her. The last thing she'd probably want to do was leave Lizzie's side. Still, though, things were finally looking up.

❖

Jessie eyed my suitcase as I packed. "What are you doing?" "I talked to Clarissa about switching rooms, and she didn't throw a fit like you claimed she would. She's discussing it with Rhonda right now." I felt a little sad about leaving, surprised that I had enjoyed spending time with Jessie. But I had to get my plan with Lizzie back on track, and being close to Jessie wasn't part of that plan. I certainly didn't want to risk any more almost-kisses.

"Oh." Jessie looked like she'd just lost her puppy.

"It's nothing against you. Really." I placed my hand on her arm.

"So, you're still going through with your plan?" Her eyes were a dark, cold teal.

"Of course. Why wouldn't I?"

"You and Lizzie don't seem to...fit."

"What are you talking about? We're best friends. How much better can we fit?"

"That's what I mean. You're *friends*." Jessie paced back and forth, her body tense.

"That's the whole point of this trip, Barnett. I plan to be *more* than just friends. What's your problem?" I wasn't sure where Jessie's agitation was coming from.

"I don't have a problem. I just...I think you're making a mistake. Like you warned me about hooking up with Nicole."

"Oh my God, you're not seriously comparing Lizzie to Nicole, are you? That's ludicrous." I wasn't sure what we were arguing about, but that statement seemed to enrage Jessie all the more.

"So you wouldn't have a problem with me hooking up with Nicole?"

"No…yes…I mean, what? I don't care what you do." That was perhaps a little white lie, because the thought of Nicole and Jessie together made me ill.

Searing pain shot through my fingers. I hadn't been paying attention to what I was doing and had inadvertently smashed my fingers in my suitcase. What a klutz.

"Holy shit!" I screamed. Collapsing on my bed, I cradled my hand. "Damn, that hurt."

"Let me see." Jessie grabbed for my hand, but I pulled away. "This is all your fault, you know."

"Just give me your hand." Jessie laid my hand in her palm and examined my throbbing fingers, which were already swollen and turning blue. She immediately went into the kitchen, returning quickly with ice wrapped in a towel. "This is going to be cold, but you need to get the swelling down." Jessie sat on the bed next to me, carefully wrapping my hand in the towel.

"Christ, I can't believe I did that." Intensity from the pain made me nauseous and brought tears to my eyes. "I'm such an idiot."

"You're not an idiot. Does it hurt?"

"Hell yeah." The ice quickly numbed my fingers, which helped with the sting.

"I'm…sorry," Jessie said. She studied the print on my bedspread, avoiding eye contact.

"It wasn't your fault. I wasn't paying attention to what I was doing."

"That's not what I meant. You know, sorry for grilling you about Lizzie."

"It's okay," I said, although I was clueless about why she'd seemed so agitated. "Sorry you're always having to take care of me. I'm really not accident-prone."

"Lucky for you I've had lots of first-aid training." Jessie smiled as the tension between us seemingly disappeared. "How's it feeling now?"

"The ice pretty much numbed everything, so better. But I bet it'll be hurting like a son of a bitch after it thaws out."

Jessie placed her palm over my wrapped hand and closed her eyes. "Do you know what Reiki is?"

"Ray...what?"

"Reiki. It's a form of healing that works with the life-force energy." Jessie opened her eyes and looked completely serious.

"Life-force energy?" I was cynical but didn't want to hurt her feelings by scoffing at something seemingly important to her.

"All I do is direct healing energy to the injured area. It's harmless. May I?" Jessie motioned toward my hand.

"Sure. Go for it." Sounded weird but couldn't hurt, I figured, and I did trust Jessie.

She closed her eyes, covering my hand with her palm. Her body relaxed as she took a deep breath, letting it out slowly. Jessie asked that I close my eyes as well and release any tension in my body. Within minutes I felt warmth emanating from her hand, quickly melting the ice. Every now and then I'd take peeks at Jessie. I'd always thought Jessie was beautiful, but in that moment she looked stunning. She practically glowed. We stayed in that position about five minutes before she opened her eyes, taking another deep breath. Jessie looked at me, her eyes a sparkling, clear green.

"Your hand felt warm," I said. "Where'd you learn how to do that?"

"My dad is a Reiki Master and he initiated me." Master. Initiated. It all sounded too airy-fairy for me. Carefully, I unwrapped the towel. My fingers were blue but weren't hurting nearly as much. I didn't care if that was because of the ice or the Reiki. I was just glad the pain had subsided.

"It feels better. I don't have to call you Master now, do I?" I smiled.

"I'll settle for Superwoman." Jessie put her hand on my arm. It still felt warm.

Shivers went down my spine as she lightly stroked my skin with her thumb. We stared at each other, neither one of us wanting to turn away. Jessie's eyes dropped to my lips. Was she thinking about our almost-kiss, as I was? I had the answer to my question when Jessie leaned forward, pressing her lips against mine in the hottest kiss I'd ever experienced.

It was tender at first, with light pressure. She nibbled on my lower lip and kissed the sides of my mouth. We parted for a moment, with eyes still closed, then pressed our lips together again. Harder and more urgent this time. The warmth of Jessie's mouth sent electricity coursing through me. We moaned in unison when the tip of her tongue touched mine. Damn, could this woman kiss. The sensation of Jessie's lips, the taste of her, my arousal when she ran her tongue underneath the inside of my top lip sent my head spinning.

In retrospect, I should have pulled away. I mean, what gave her the right to sit there and kiss me like that? But I wasn't exactly thinking straight at the time. The only thought in my mind was how soft her lips felt.

Slowly Jessie lowered me back onto the bed, pressing her body against mine, never breaking the kiss. My hands had a mind of their own. I ran my fingers through her hair, satisfying a long-time curiosity of what her shiny, healthy locks would feel like. It was silky and smooth, just as I'd imagined. I caressed her back and lower to her buttocks, pressing her into me.

Desperately wanting to feel the touch of her skin, I slipped my fingers under her shirt. Jessie moaned into my mouth from the contact. She was so sexy. I could have kissed her forever. And I would have if she hadn't quickly pulled away.

Hovering over me, she stared at me in shock. "Malley," she said breathlessly. "I'm…I'm so sorry. I don't know what happened. It just…I'm sorry. It was a mistake."

A mistake. Yes, of course. A mistake. What else could it be?

"I don't know what I was thinking." Jessie sat up, putting space between us. "Lizzie won't ever find out about this. I promise."

Lizzie. Right. The woman I love.

I quickly sat up, careful not to touch any part of Jessie in the process. I stared at her, not sure what to say, still processing what had just happened. We'd kissed. And not only that, but I liked it. A lot. My eyes darted to Jessie's lips, red and swollen from our mini make-out session. I wanted to brush her lips with my fingertips. I wanted to wrap my hand around her neck and pull her into another searing kiss. With that thought, I bolted off the bed.

"I'm going to get some fresh air." I ran out of the cabin as far away from Jessie as I could get.

Ending up at the pond, I circled the water over and over, mentally chatting with the koi, who opened their mouths wide as if yawning. What in the world had just happened? I kissed Jessie. Or she kissed me. Either way…it was Jessie, for Christ's sake. I hadn't even kissed Lizzie yet. Heat rose within me as I relived the moment. Our bodies intertwined, the feel of her smooth skin on my fingertips, her warm, wet tongue. After just one kiss, I was more than ready to rip her clothes off.

What was wrong with me? I attributed my carnal response to a dating dry spell. Yes, that was it. I just hadn't kissed a woman in a while and had forgotten how hot it could be, although it had never been *that* hot. Jessie's words rang in my ears. "It was a mistake…a mistake…" and one she obviously regretted.

She was the one who kissed me. She made the first move. How dare she do that? Everyone knows you can't kiss someone passionately, lay them back in the bed, and then say it was a mistake.

"You know what I'm going to do?" I asked the koi. "I'm going to tell Lizzie how I feel about her right now. No more pussyfooting around. It's time to put this plan into action!" And before I knew it, I was banging on Lizzie's cabin door.

CHAPTER NINE

GET LIZZIE

A ll right, all right, I'm coming." Lizzie swung the screen door open. "Malley? Why are you panting and sweating?"

I really should have caught my breath before knocking. Sprinting all the way from the pond wasn't such a good idea.

"I...I need to talk to you." Stepping into the cabin, I saw Rhonda sprawled out on the bed watching a soccer game. She completely ignored my silent plea for her to leave but instead turned up the volume on the TV. "Let's go outside."

We walked to a picnic table under a shade tree. Lizzie sat on top of the table and put her feet on the bench. Even though I was pacing back and forth, surprisingly I wasn't nervous. Now that it was actually happening, I felt relieved to get it over with. I paced because I wasn't sure how to begin. Lizzie was quiet as her eyes followed me back and forth.

"Lizzie."

"Yes?"

"Lizzie." I took a deep breath and faced her head-on. "I have something important to say. But what's most important to me is our friendship, so if what I say turns you off in any way, I don't want it to come between us, okay?"

"Malley, you're not making any sense. And you're kinda freaking me out right now."

Okay, not off to a great start.

"Listen, I'll just come right out and say it, but don't feel bad if you turn me down. I would understand." Okay, maybe I *was* a little nervous after all. "Lizzie, I think we're really great together. You're my best friend. I love spending time with you and being with you. You're absolutely beautiful and someone I would be honored to be with. I just…would you ever consider dating me? I've wanted to ask you for so long now, but you were with Heather. So, you know, would you want to? Date me, I mean?" I paused, but then remembered an important addendum. "And I don't mean in a rebound, transitional girlfriend way either. I mean, in a real together way."

Did that even make sense? I regretted not practicing the speech more. Regardless, it was done. All I had to do was wait for the firing squad.

After what felt like an eternity, Lizzie stood and walked around, rustling leaves with her shoes. She looked deep in thought. This couldn't be good. Stopping in front of me, she looked into my eyes.

"Malley, you're my best friend, too, and the thought of us dating has crossed my mind. But as you said, I was with Heather. To be completely honest, I do still think about her sometimes. I know it's crazy. We were never good together. I just want you to know that I'm still healing from that relationship."

"I understand completely. It's okay. Just forget I asked." I stared at the leaves. Lizzie raised my chin with her hand so that we were eye to eye. "It's okay, Lizzie. Really." But please don't say you want to date Jessie instead of me.

"You didn't let me finish. If we go slow and you don't expect too much too soon, then maybe we should explore dating one another."

"Seriously?" I was in shock. The million times I'd visualized that scene it always ended with Lizzie saying no and me throwing up on her shoes. "Wait…was that a yes or a maybe?"

Lizzie smiled, placing both hands on my shoulders. "It's a yes. But we go slow."

"You'd seriously date me? As in together?" It still hadn't sunk in yet.

"You're funny." Lizzie's eyes sparkled as she laughed. "Yes, Malley. I want to go out with you. And I agree completely that I don't want this to affect our friendship. No matter what happens let's always be friends."

This had gone better than I could've ever imagined. I couldn't wipe the grin from my face. Remembering what Lizzie said about going slow, I hugged her tight but refrained from kissing her.

"One other thing," she said. "We better keep the roommate situation as is. That wouldn't exactly be going slow, you know?"

"Very true. Even though we are lesbians and it's our nature, we shouldn't move in together that fast," I said with a smile. "Jessie will just be stuck with me awhile longer."

My heart dropped when I remembered Jessie and the kiss. I wasn't sure why, but I absolutely dreaded telling her that Lizzie and I were dating.

❖

There's a first time for everything, so when Lizzie suggested we check out the meditation class I said I was game. Technically, this was our first date, if you can call meditating together a date. Hand in hand we walked to an array of yoga mats sprawled out under an oak tree. It was late evening so the temperature was bearable.

Feeling Lizzie's hand in mine, I could hardly believe we were dating. I would have pinched myself if I had a free hand. Before we ever reached the yoga mats I saw Jessie leaning against a tree, fixated on our clasped hands. Her intense stare never veered from our intertwined fingers until we got closer and she looked me right in the eyes. Good. At least now I didn't have to tell her. She already knew.

"What's this?" Nicole asked, motioning toward our hand-holding. Something about Nicole struck me as odd, something I couldn't put my finger on. Oh yes, she was actually smiling and looked genuinely happy to see me. That was a first.

Rhonda stomped over. "You two? Together?" She looked less pleased than Nicole.

"I asked Lizzie if she wanted to date me. And she actually said yes." I raised our intertwined fingers, giving Lizzie a light kiss on her hand. "Can you believe it?"

"No," Rhonda said before storming away.

"Why, I think that's wonderful." Nicole beamed. "Congrats, you two." Why the hell was she so happy? I glanced at Jessie, who was still leaning against the tree, her eyes cast to the ground.

Lizzie and I picked out mats side by side. Clarissa put on some New Age relaxation music and asked everyone to take a seat. Nicole grabbed Jessie's hand and led them to mats right across from Lizzie and me.

I'd tried to meditate once or twice before, but with my wandering mind I didn't last more than a few minutes. I hoped this wasn't one of those hour meditations. No way would I last that long. After about ten minutes the spacey music started making me drowsy. In an attempt to wake myself up, I opened my eyes, scanning the crowd. All eyes were closed and no one was snoring. Even Rhonda looked deep in a trance. Obviously, I was among experienced meditators here.

My gaze stopped on Jessie. She looked so peaceful, like a slumbering angel. Heat rushed to my face as I stared at her lips. Lips that I would never be able to look at the same way again. Instinctively I brushed my finger over my bottom lip, mimicking the sensation of Jessie's touch.

As if Jessie sensed me watching her, I noticed her eyes shoot open. My heart lurched. After a few moments, she closed her eyes again, but I kept mine open for the rest of the meditation.

After class, everyone but Jessie hung around and chatted. She headed straight for the cabin without a word to anyone. Since it was getting late, I walked Lizzie back to her cabin. As we both leaned against the front door, I wasn't sure if I should kiss her. I needed clarification on what "go slow" meant. I felt like an awkward teenager expecting her father to start blinking the porch lights any second. Lizzie reached for my hand, which was stuck in my pocket.

"I had fun tonight, Malley. But maybe we could go on a real date tomorrow. Do something fun together."

"Absolutely," I said, still thinking about whether I should make a move to kiss her. I'd dreamed about that moment for almost a year. To actually be in a position where Lizzie and I might kiss was still unbelievable. In that moment, I wanted to kiss Lizzie more than anything. I wanted her to take my breath away. I wanted every nerve in my body to be on fire from her touch. I wanted her to wipe the memory of Jessie's kiss completely from my mind.

Lizzie raised my hand to her lips, giving me a light kiss. Not exactly what I was hoping for, but it was sweet nonetheless.

"Good night, Malley."

I mustered a weak smile and put my hand back into my pocket. Still, I was content. I was dating Lizzie. That was more than I could have ever hoped for.

"Ouch," I whispered as I stubbed my toe on something hard in the dark cabin. Jessie was already in bed, which was a relief. I had no desire to discuss our unexpected kiss or Lizzie. Wow, I'd had two kisses in one day, even if one was on the hand. I was becoming a regular slut, which made me chuckle, because I was anything but.

After a quick shower, I climbed into bed, the same bed where earlier my heart was thumping as Jessie expertly kissed the hell out of me. I didn't want to think about the kiss. Her soft lips. The sound of her voice as she moaned. Nope, I wouldn't think about any of that.

"So I guess you did it." Jessie was hoarse and sounded tired. I immediately knew what she meant.

"Yeah. And she actually said yes. Can you believe that?"

Silence.

"Are you moving out tomorrow?"

"No. Lizzie wants to take things slow, so we'll keep sleeping arrangements as they are."

Silence.

Finally, she said, "Don't forget to put antibiotic on your knee tonight."

"Already did. Good night, Barnett."

"Good night, O'Brien."

CHAPTER TEN

FIRST DATE

Shopping? That's what Lizzie wanted to do on our first official date? When I scrunched my face at the suggestion, she relayed that Heather never took her shopping. So, I unscrunched and off we went, thus proving I was a far superior girlfriend than Heather.

We hit every pottery shop, art gallery, and crystal store in Sedona. Being with Lizzie was always fun, but I guess I'd envisioned something a little more romantic. Like maybe a moonlight hike or dinner by candlelight at a nice restaurant. I guess to me, any low-lit activity equaled a real date. Not trudging down the sidewalks of Sedona going into shop after shop.

By late afternoon my feet were aching when we ended up at Tlaquepaque, an arts-and-crafts village in Sedona. The place was cute, nestled under sycamore trees and along the banks of Oak Creek. Tlaquepaque means the best of everything and was fashioned after a traditional Mexican village. I know because I read the plaque when I wandered outside after getting tired of waiting on Lizzie. She tried on everything in the store…twice, and sometimes even three times. I don't know why, though, 'cause she looked great in everything.

With bags in hand, Lizzie found me sitting by the courtyard fountain. She apologized for taking so long and gave me a peck on the cheek, which made me smile, reminding me that we were dating. Pulling colorful Mexican dresses out of her bags, Lizzie showed off her purchases. She looked so beautiful with the sun shining on her radiant face. I'd never seen her so happy. After the on-again off-again drama with Heather, I was overjoyed at the possibility of getting a chance to make Lizzie happy. She deserved it. I made a vow to myself right then to do everything I could to keep that beautiful smile on her face.

"Why don't we pick up some pizzas on our way back," Lizzie suggested. "I can't possibly eat another course of tofu turkey. We can get Jessie, Clarissa, and some of the girls together."

Spending the evening with Jessie and everyone else wasn't exactly what I had in mind. I'd been hoping we'd squeeze in a romantic dinner alone. But I agreed. Maybe this was part of Lizzie's "go slow" strategy.

Because I called ahead to Clarissa, she already had a selection of soda, beer, and music blaring on the stereo when we reached the lodge. The music selection was eclectic, with everything from disco to country to pop. Several women were there, including Jessie, who looked awfully cute in blue-jean shorts, hiking boots, and a tank top. How could she still be single? Or maybe she wasn't, since Nicole was hanging on her arm like a monkey.

"Hey, you two lovebirds," Nicole said to Lizzie and me. "Did you have fun today?" She must have dipped into the spiked punch one too many times. She'd never been happy to see me before.

"It was great," Lizzie said. "We hit every store in town, I think."

"I thought you hated shopping?" Jessie asked me.

"Not when it's with the right person." I slid my arm around Lizzie's waist. Jessie rolled her eyes.

"I'm going to get some punch," Nicole said. "Malley, do you want some?" It took me a second to realize she was actually talking to me. In fact, I don't think she'd ever said my name before.

"Uh…no…thanks, though." I stared at Nicole as she sauntered to the punch bowl. "What in the world has gotten into her?"

"What do you mean?" Jessie asked.

"She's...nice."

"You're incorrigible, O'Brien. You didn't like her when you thought she was a bitch, and now you don't like her because she's being nice."

Jessie walked away before I could respond.

"I just think it's weird she's being so friendly all of a sudden," I told Lizzie.

When a George Strait song came on, Rhonda dragged a poor, helpless girl to the middle of the room, where they made their own dance floor. A couple more women joined in the dancing, and that's when Lizzie grabbed my hand.

"No, no. I can't dance to this. In fact, I can't dance, period."

"Aw, come on, Malley. Give it a try."

"It's country. Are they two-stepping? I can't do that." I eyed Rhonda, who, I had to admit, had some pretty fancy moves.

"We can dance any way we want. It doesn't have to be the two-step."

I watched as Nicole successfully convinced Jessie to dance. Not wanting to sit there like a sore thumb and watch those two go at it, I figured I'd give it a try. Lizzie pulled me close as we started swaying to the music. Okay, maybe I liked dancing after all.

"See, isn't this nice?" Lizzie whispered in my ear.

"Yeah, I could get used to this." I relaxed as my lips turned upward in a satisfied grin. Lizzie and I were a couple. Actual, real-live, irrefutable girlfriends. It didn't get much better than this. I couldn't even count how many parties I'd been to alone over the past year. It was so much better to be with someone instead of feeling like a fifth wheel. And having that someone be Lizzie made it all the more pleasurable.

My smile dropped when I caught sight of Nicole, who had jammed her thigh between Jessie's legs and firmly planted both hands on her rear end.

"What's wrong?" Lizzie asked. Following my gaze, she looked at Jessie and Nicole.

I shook my head. "She makes such a spectacle of herself. Geez, get a room."

"Look at me, Malley. Why do you care what Jessie and Nicole do?"

"I don't, but she's practically attacking Jessie."

"Jessie's a big girl. She can take care of herself." We both looked at the couple as Jessie pried Nicole's hands from her ass and backed away. They had some sort of exchange we couldn't hear, and then Jessie stalked off, leaving Nicole standing alone in the middle of the dance floor. "There. See? Jessie took care of it."

I watched Jessie as she walked to the punch bowl, scooping red liquid into a Dixie cup. She looked around the dance floor until her eyes met mine. After what felt like several long seconds, she looked away before disappearing into a group of women.

Lizzie and I danced through a couple of songs until I mustered the courage to ask a nagging question. "So…are you sorry I'm the one who asked you out…instead of Jessie?"

Lizzie abruptly stopped dancing and backed away so she could look me in the eye.

"Is that what you think? I wouldn't want to be with anyone else but you."

"Really?" A slow smile crept on my face.

"Yes, really. I'm glad we're dating."

"Good," I said. In a move that would have made even Fred Astaire envious, I pulled Lizzie close to me and whirled her around the floor with grace and flair.

We danced to at least five songs until we took a break to mingle and get something to drink. Rhonda must have taken over as DJ because ten country songs played in a row. Needing a breather away from the twang of the music and the rambunctious women, I stepped out onto the porch as Lizzie chatted with Clarissa. I was surprised to see Jessie leaning against the railing with her arms crossed and staring straight up into the night sky. She seemed lost in thought, so I slowly let the screen door close so as not to startle her.

She seemed unaware of my presence, so I drank in the sight of her. Moonlight shining on her hair, delicate profile, and piercing emerald eyes. She looked like a Greek goddess awaiting her chariot to descend from the sky.

"Hey," I whispered. "Need a break from the cackling women, too?" Jessie continued gazing at the sky.

"We just don't see this in LA."

"What?" I asked, looking up at hundreds of sparkling diamonds against black velvet with a bright full moon hanging overhead. "Oh, wow. We certainly don't."

"You and Lizzie seem happy together," Jessie said, still staring at the moon.

"It's amazing how things have turned out. I think I'm still in shock that she actually said yes."

"I'm glad you're happy. You deserve it."

Jessie's beautiful green eyes locked into my blue ones. My stomach flipped. Ever since that kiss something was different in the way she looked at me. Longing mixed with sadness. Neither of us had mentioned the kiss, but it was always there between us and frequently played in my mind.

Jessie looked past me as the screen door opened. "And speak of the devil," she said. Lizzie wrapped her arms around my waist from behind, resting her chin on my shoulder.

"What are you two talking about?" Lizzie asked playfully.

"Actually how sickeningly happy you two are," Jessie said. "It makes all of us want to barf."

Lizzie laughed and tightened her hold on me.

"Well, I'm calling it a night," Jessie said. She took one last look at the moon amidst sparkling stars before disappearing into the darkness.

In one quick move, Lizzie whirled me around. My face was inches away from hers.

"Thank you for being considerate today, taking me shopping. I know it's not really your thing."

"I want to make you happy. I was glad to do it." Okay, so that was half a lie.

"I know this was only our first date, but you already make me ten times happier than Heather ever did. I have a really good feeling about this." Lizzie motioned with her hand between us.

"Me too."

Lizzie smiled as she ran her hand up and down my arm. Cocking her head to the right, she kissed me without warning. It was so sudden and quick that when we broke apart I wasn't sure it had actually happened.

I'd waited for that moment for almost a year and wouldn't be satisfied with just a peck, so I leaned into Lizzie for another go-around.

It was a light, gentle kiss, not the passionate scene I'd been dreaming about. No fireworks but a nice kiss nonetheless. Again, though, it was a bit on the quick side.

I was about to jump into round three when Lizzie spoke.

"Wow, that was amazing."

Amazing? Really?

Lizzie closed her eyes. "You made my whole body tingle."

Damn, maybe I was better at this kissing stuff than I thought.

Lizzie wrapped her arms around me in a tight hug. "I hate to say it, but it's getting late."

"Yeah, we should get some sleep. Do you want me to walk you to your cabin?" *So maybe I'd have a chance to kiss you again?*

"No, I'll be fine. It's just two doors down. Good night Malley."

I stood on the porch, staring at the full moon. Lizzie and I had actually kissed. I couldn't begin to count how many times I'd dreamt about that moment the past year. Granted, it didn't knock my socks off, but first kisses are usually awkward anyway. Well, except for the one with Jessie, but that was probably just a fluke. The too-die-for smooches with Lizzie would come soon enough.

❖

The great thing about screen doors is that they're porous. So if someone is talking on the porch and you're in the cabin, it's pretty easy to overhear a conversation without technically having to eavesdrop. That's what I told myself, anyway, when I just so happened to be straining to hear Clarissa and Jessie's conversation. Clarissa was asking if Lizzie and I were dating. Why she would care, I wasn't sure. Jessie confirmed that we were but didn't sound very happy about it. Or maybe that was just my imagination. Clarissa said she was sorry, but what would she be sorry about? Or maybe she said one of us was scary? Okay, maybe screen doors weren't such great eavesdropping aids after all.

"So, was that Clarissa you were talking to on the porch?" I feigned ignorance when Jessie walked into the cabin.

"Yeah, she said we're meeting at the Red Rock State Park at two p.m. if we want to go."

"Already highlighted in my schedule," I said with a smile.

"Ah yes, of course. Um, Malley, I think we should talk."

Jessie looked serious. This couldn't be good. I feared she'd bring up the kiss. Personally, I wanted to forget about it and move on. Granted, it invaded my dreams at night, leaving me panting upon waking, but that wasn't something I wanted to discuss. Eventually, I'd forget about the most passionate kiss I'd ever had. I'm sure I would. Eventually.

"Talk about what?"

"Um, about what happened the other day." Jessie pointed to my bed.

Like I wouldn't remember? "Oh. Yeah. It's no big deal. Like you said, it was a mistake." That comment had smarted at the time, and I guess it still did since I threw it back in her face. "It's forgotten," I lied.

"Oh, okay. Yeah. With me too. Forgotten."

Ouch. Not sure why that stung when I'd just said the same thing to her. "Great." I beamed with loads of fake enthusiasm. "See you at the park at two. Be there or be square."

I bounced away like I was riding on a pogo stick. God, I was such an idiot sometimes.

CHAPTER ELEVEN

TWO SNAKES IN ONE DAY

Something was terribly wrong. Jessie was as stiff as an ironing board. Her face was ghostly white and she was sweating and trembling. Women were gathered around her with concerned looks, whispering to each other. Clarissa had a hand on Jessie's shoulder as they stood at the brink of a dry creek bed.

Lizzie and I had lagged behind in the nature walk through the Red Rock State Park. We wanted some alone time to do whatever it was couples do in the forest. Hold hands, pick flowers, whistle with the lovebirds. All the stuff I'd dreamed about doing with Lizzie before we ever came on this trip. But the fear that washed over me when we came upon Jessie and the others disrupted our blissful forest frolic.

Trying to gauge the scene, I slowly approached. "What's going on?" I asked. Inching closer, I saw complete panic on Jessie's face.

"Would you get everyone out of here?" Her voice cracked as she stared straight ahead. She was breathing shallow, and her whole body lightly trembled.

I glanced at Clarissa, who looked like she was about to cry. Lizzie was a big help and told the women to continue on the trail and that there was nothing to worry about, which I was terribly afraid was a lie. Lizzie and Nicole stood beside Jessie as Clarissa pulled me aside to fill me in.

"She's having a panic attack. She refuses to cross the creek bed. Jessie has a fear of snakes. No, actually it's a phobia. It's pretty intense, Malley."

No shit. I'd never seen Jessie like that before. "I don't understand. Did she see one?"

"She thought she saw a rattler slither across a rock just as we came to the creek bed. She freaked."

"So what do we do? I mean, how do we help her?"

"We need to get her away from here. Go back on the path where we came. She'll never cross the creek." Clarissa looked back at Jessie, who resembled a standing corpse. "She trusts you. If we can get her to turn around and go the other way, she'll be okay. Do you think you can walk her back?"

"Yeah, of course. But…what if she freaks out? I don't know how to handle something like that."

"Just talk to her gently, help her relax, and remind her to take deep breaths. Once she gets away from here she'll be okay."

"Yeah, I can do that." I was scared but wanted to do something to help Jessie.

As we approached the three women, Clarissa placed her hand lightly on Jessie's back. "Jessie, sugar, you don't have to cross the creek. Malley is going to hike back with you. I need to catch up to the others, but Malley will be with you every step of the way."

Nicole shot me a venomous look. Her nice girl act was short-lived. I guess she hated me again.

"Hey, Barnett, fancy meeting you here," I said, trying to lighten the mood. "Do you think you can move your legs for me?" Jessie swallowed and looked at me out of the corner of her eye. "If you go with me, I promise not to be a klutz and trip on a rock this time. Although I do think I looked pretty sexy covered in mud. Like one of those hot mud-wrestling babes on Channel 9."

"You would think that," Jessie said, her voice shaky.

"Is it okay if I do this?" Tentatively, I put an arm around her shoulders, which seemed to ease her shivers. "I know you've secretly always wanted to hold my hand, but you really didn't have to go through all this trouble to do so."

"You're so vain." I took one of her tightly clutched hands, lacing my fingers with hers, and felt her body relax a bit.

"Do you think you can turn around?"

Jessie nodded once, still staring straight ahead. After one audible gulp, she shuffled her feet in a circle. Once she'd turned her attention away from the creek bed, her breathing grew deeper.

"Can you take a step?"

Jessie paused before taking a shaky step forward.

"Awesome," I said. "Now can you do that 500 more times?"

Jessie chuckled and took another step.

"We'll be all right," I told Clarissa. "We'll meet you back at the trailhead. You three catch up to the others."

"You're the best. Jessie, I'll see you soon. Malley has my number if anything comes up, but I know you two will be just fine."

Lizzie. I'd forgotten about Lizzie. Looking back, I gave her a reassuring nod before inching down the trail with Jessie wrapped in my arms.

Clarissa was right. Once Jessie was away from the creek, her panic subsided. She was by no means her normal self but considerably better than before. We walked in silence almost the entire way. Every once in a while I'd ask if she was okay, but beyond that she didn't seem to be in the mood for conversation. Realizing I'd been holding my breath, I let out a sigh. It unnerved me to see Jessie like that. She was always so strong and sure of herself.

Once we reached the trailhead, I was glad to see all of the women had already left except Clarissa and Lizzie. Something told me Jessie didn't want an audience. She climbed into the passenger seat of Clarissa's car without saying a word. I hoped she'd be back to her old self by the time they reached the cabin.

Once Lizzie and I were in her car driving back to the lodge, she peppered me with questions. I filled her in as best I could, but she knew just as much as I did. Suddenly remembering how I'd teased Jessie about her fear of snakes when we were stuck in the ditch, I felt horribly guilty. Arguably, I didn't know she had a phobia or suffered panic attacks, but I still felt ashamed.

"Heather has a car just like that. Same color even." Lizzie pointed to a maroon Prius just ahead of us. I grunted, not really wanting to talk about Heather.

"Oh my God. I think that *is* Heather." Lizzie sped up to get a closer look. Oh great. Now she was having mirages of her ex-girlfriend.

"That's not Heather. She wouldn't be in Sedona. You haven't heard from her, have you?" It dawned on me that I'd stupidly never asked that question since they broke up.

"Well...she's called and texted several times, but I haven't responded."

"She has? What did she say?" Why was I surprised? Heather would so do that.

"Just that she misses me and wants to talk." Lizzie slammed on her brakes at a yellow light as the maroon Prius plowed ahead like the driver was on a mission.

❖

Jessie was leaning against the counter sipping a glass of water when I got back to the cabin.

"Hey," I said.

"Hey."

Not exactly an intriguing conversation, but it helped break the ice. Knowing Jessie, I figured she'd be embarrassed about her episode, even though she had no reason to be. In fact, it showed she was actually human and not so damn perfect.

"Thanks," she said. "You know, about today."

"You're welcome. You'd have done the same for me."

Jessie's eyes met mine and she nodded.

"Do you...I dunno...want to talk about it?" I asked.

"Well, I'm sure Clarissa told you everything already."

"Not really. Just that I probably shouldn't offer you snake on a stick as an appetizer." Jessie smiled.

"That would be better than the tofu crap she's serving." Jessie pulled out a chair and sat down. I did the same, taking that as an invitation to talk. "This isn't something I'm particularly proud of. If the guys in the precinct ever caught wind of this, I'd never hear the last of it."

"Jessie, being afraid of something doesn't make you weak. You can't be perfect all the time."

"Look who's talking," she said with a grin. I wasn't sure if that was an insult or a compliment.

"So when did it start? Your fear of snakes? If you want to tell me, that is."

"I remember exactly when it was. I was five years old and we were playing outside with some of the neighbor kids. There was this old jalopy that we used to play in. I don't even know who it belonged to. It didn't run anymore." Jessie took a sip of water and a deep breath. I had a feeling this story wouldn't end well.

"We were playing in the car, when one of the kids found a garden snake. Nothing dangerous, but it was a pretty big one, especially to a five-year-old. Well, he thought it would be hilarious to throw the snake in the car with me and slam the door shut. I freaked. I couldn't get the door open and the snake was going wild, crawling all over me…" Jessie got a faraway look in her eyes, and when chill bumps appeared on her arms I knew she was reliving the moment.

"God, Jessie, I'm so sorry. That must have been terribly frightening for you." My heart ached as I imagined this adorable little green-eyed girl being tortured. I wanted to wrap my arms around her and erase that horrible memory altogether.

"Yeah, kids, huh?" She tried to make light of the experience, but I could tell she didn't mean it.

"This fear doesn't make you less than, you know. You don't let it stop you from hiking or getting out in nature. You're the bravest person I know. You're a cop, for Christ's sake. You risk your life every day."

Jessie's humiliation seemed to lift. I meant every word. I, of all people, knew how dangerous the life of a police officer could be.

Lizzie stuck her head through the screen door. "Am I interrupting anything?"

"No," Jessie said. "We were just talking shop."

"How are you doing?" Lizzie asked Jessie as she walked into the cabin.

"I'm fine, thanks."

"That's good. Um, could I steal Malley for a minute?"

"Of course." Jessie bolted out of the chair. "I need to run by Clarissa's anyway."

I detected something strange in the sound of Lizzie's voice, and she looked like she might barf. She waited until Jessie was out of the cabin before she spoke.

"Heather's on her way here."

"What? Where? Sedona?"

"No, here to the lodge."

"What!? I don't understand. You told her where you were?"

"No! I haven't talked to her since I kicked her out. I have no idea how she found me. She sent a text saying she'd be here in ten minutes."

Ten minutes? Heather? Here? "Wait…I don't understand. Why would she come here?"

"Malley, I don't want to see her."

I grabbed Lizzie's shoulders and looked into her eyes. "You don't have to. I'll get Clarissa to kick her off the property for trespassing."

Lizzie covered her face in her hands.

"I still don't know how she could have found you."

"I swear I didn't tell her where I am."

Lizzie was near tears, so I pulled her into my arms. "It'll be okay," I said, stroking her hair. "You don't have to see her or talk to her."

"But maybe I should," she said through a sob. "Maybe we should talk."

"Helloooo?" I'd know that gruff voice anywhere. "Anybody here?" Heather loomed outside, yelling and peeking in the cabin windows. "Lizzie?"

"That's her," Lizzie said fearfully.

"Listen, you stay here and I'll get rid of her." Shaking my head as I stepped on the porch, I couldn't believe Heather had risen from the dead.

"Heather, what are you doing here?"

"Malley?" She squinted in the sun to get a better look. "Where's Lizzie?"

"I don't know." I put my hands on my hips, locking my knees in a firm stance.

"Don't give me that. You two are joined at the hip."

More than you know, I wanted to say. "Lizzie doesn't want to see you. So you might as well get in your car and head back to LA."

The screen door creaked behind me as Lizzie stepped onto the porch. Great, make a liar out of me. I'd never understood Lizzie's attraction to Heather. Lizzie was refined, professional, and accomplished. Heather was a screw-up who couldn't even hold down a job. Lizzie completely supported her financially when they were together. Not to mention that her personality was about as pleasant as knuckles on a cheese grater.

"How did you find me?" Lizzie asked.

Yeah, I wanted to know the answer to that question as well.

"I saw the picture Malley posted on Facebook."

"What picture?" I said, knowing I was about to catch her in an outrageous lie.

"The one of you and Lizzie in front of the teal arches at McDonald's." Damn social media. I thought the selfie was so cute I couldn't resist uploading it to Facebook. "I Googled teal arches, found out the place was in Sedona, and called every hotel and resort in the area."

I looked apologetically at Lizzie. "I'm so sorry," I whispered.

Heather walked closer, lifting one leg and propping her foot on the porch. "Can we go someplace and talk?" she asked.

Lizzie turned to me with questioning eyes. "It might be a good idea," she whispered.

Even though I wanted to yell, "No! Let's arrest her for trespassing!" it wasn't my place to tell Lizzie what to do. After several contemplative moments I decided to be an adult. "You should do what you feel is right," I said.

Lizzie turned to Heather. "I'll give you thirty minutes, and that's all," Lizzie said.

Heather puffed out her chest and beamed as Lizzie stepped off the porch. I had a fraction of satisfaction when Lizzie met Heather's attempt to put her arm around her with a hard swat to the hand.

Lizzie looked back at me once as I watched my girlfriend of three days saunter away with her ex.

It was getting late and had been way longer than thirty minutes. I waited up for Lizzie as long as I could until sleep claimed me. It was after midnight and Heather's car was still parked where she'd left it hours before. They couldn't still be talking. Maybe they were in Lizzie's cabin? Rolling around in her bed perhaps?

Jessie knew something was up, but I didn't feel like talking about it. I hoped Heather would be gone before morning and this nightmare would be over. Not wanting my imagination to get the better of me, thinking about Lizzie and Heather together…in bed, I lay down and tried to relax. The next thing I knew, Lizzie was shaking me awake early the next morning with news that rocked my world.

"You're what? You can't possibly be serious!" Lizzie was the last person on earth I ever thought I'd yell at. We were standing on the porch so we wouldn't wake Jessie.

"I'm so sorry. This is something I need to do. Please understand, Malley." Lizzie grabbed my shoulders in an attempt to get my attention.

I glared past her at Heather, who was casually leaning against her Prius with a smirk on her face. "So you're really going with her?!"

"Just to her hotel to talk some more. We need to discuss things."

"So what were you doing all night? Weren't you discussing? Or was something else going on?"

"It wasn't like that. Nothing happened. Please try to understand."

"What about us?" I was whining, not even trying to hide how pathetic I felt.

Lizzie's eyes brimmed with tears.

Oh no, she wasn't allowed to cry. I was angry and wanted to stay that way. She wasn't allowed to soften me up with tears.

"I need closure with Heather before I can start something new. We have some unresolved issues. You understand that, don't you?"

What was I supposed to say? No, I don't understand. I want you to stay here with me. Only an insecure, selfish person would say that. And even though I was insecure and selfish, I knew I wouldn't have a future with Lizzie if I fought her on this. I had no claim to her, especially after dating for only three days, and I knew she was right. I took a deep breath and closed my eyes. "How long will you be gone?"

"I don't know. Maybe a couple of hours. I'll text you."

I paused for dramatic effect before saying "fine" but replied in a way that clearly let her know it was anything but.

Lizzie hugged me and kissed my cheek. From the murderous scowl on Heather's face, I'd bet money Lizzie had told her we were dating.

Chapter Twelve

Alien Adventures

I can't fucking believe she left with Heather!" I slammed the screen door, causing Jessie to bolt upright in bed.

"Huh? What? What's happening?"

"This is fucking unbelievable!" I yelled.

"What the fuck's going on, Malley? It's barely past seven, and you don't fucking cuss. The worst I've ever heard you say was damn, and that made you blush." Jessie rubbed her bloodshot eyes.

I stood over Jessie's bed with my hands on my hips, shaking my head. "Get this. Heather, Lizzie's ex-girlfriend, tracked her down, and she just left to go to Heather's hotel room. In her Prius!"

"Ouch. Sorry." Jessie grimaced. "Did Lizzie tell Heather where she was?"

"Well, no. It's not important how she found her." I was kicking myself for posting that selfie on Facebook. The last thing I needed was a speech about it from Jessie. "You're missing the point here."

"So, like...what did Lizzie say?"

"She said they have unresolved issues to discuss."

"Well, that makes sense, I guess."

"You don't understand." I glared at Jessie. "She and Heather have been on and off for a year now. I've been waiting for Lizzie to come to her senses, and she *finally* did by throwing Heather out of the apartment. Lizzie said they were done. Over. She said she wouldn't talk to Heather if she was the last lesbian in LA."

"Huh." Jessie lay back down.

"I gotta get out of here." I paced back and forth.

"Where?" Jessie raised up and propped herself on one elbow.

"I don't care. Just…out. I need to run or punch something or…just get out of this cabin and this place." Anger and fear welled within me, which I desperately wanted to release. I couldn't sit still. If I did, I'd cry, and I'd rather be angry than cry any day.

"Put your swimsuit on," Jessie said, jumping out of bed.

"What?"

"You heard me, O'Brien. You have five minutes to get ready and meet me outside."

"Yes, ma'am," I said with a salute. I had no idea where we were going and didn't really care. I just wanted out.

❖

"There's no way in hell I'm getting on that thing." I pointed to Jessie's motorcycle.

"And just how do you propose we get to where we're going? I don't suppose Lizzie left you her car keys?"

"No. And just for the record we're not mentioning her name again today. So, is this thing safe?"

"Hop on and see." Jessie straddled her bike and handed me a helmet.

Not so fast. We needed some ground rules. She wasn't allowed to speed, and the agreed-upon signal to immediately stop if I freaked out was me knocking on her helmet. In reality, I'd probably grab the handlebars, which would end us up in a ditch, but she didn't need to know that. Once I was perched on the bike behind Jessie, I thought maybe this was what I needed after all. I was in the mood to do something wild and crazy.

"Hold on tight," Jessie said. Wrapping my arms around her waist, I felt her toned abs through her T-shirt. The scent of sweet almonds filled the air, and I realized it was coming from Jessie's hair. Damn she smelled good.

"Malley, I might need to actually breathe, so maybe not so tight?"

"Oh, sorry," I said, loosening my hold just a bit.

True to her promise, Jessie pulled away slowly and drove well under the speed limit. Once we were on the highway, I was astonished by how much fun I was having. When I yelled into her ear to go faster, Jessie immediately complied. The faster we went, the greater the thrill. It was such a rush and surprisingly erotic. Who knew motorcycles could be such a huge turn-on?

My breasts were pressed against her back, which made my nipples harden. The feel of Jessie in my arms mixed with the vibrating sensation between my thighs caused a pounding deep within me. My heart raced and moisture flowed, making me so wet I thought I might slip off the seat. I wondered if Jessie was as turned on as I was.

We flew down a winding highway, which picked up elevation as we rode precariously close to the edge of a cliff. At one point Jessie pulled the bike into an overlook, and we sat speechlessly gazing at the soaring bloodred monoliths surrounding the tiny town of Sedona below. We drove a few more miles as the terrain turned into a pine forest with glimpses of a rushing creek running through it.

When we came to a stop, Jessie laid her hand over mine, which was still wrapped tight around her waist. "Are you okay? How was the ride?"

"How was it?" I gave an extra-hard squeeze before releasing her. "It was amazing! I never felt so…freeeee!" I swung my arms out in a grand gesture as she laughed.

"See, all that worrying for nothing." Jessie dismounted the bike, causing me to suddenly miss the feel of her against me.

"Riding down the highway, with the wind rushing past me," she explained. "That's what I imagine flying would feel like, you know?"

I did know.

"So, what's Slide Rock?" I asked, reading a sign at the entrance of a trail.

"You've never been here before? Well, you'll see."

I followed Jessie down the gravel path, surrounded by scented pine trees. "Oh wow!" My voice echoed through the canyon. Beyond the trees was a glorious sight of an elongated smooth sandstone rock covered with flowing clear water that spilled into a large swimming hole. It was the largest natural water slide I'd ever seen. "Are we sliding down that? Is it safe?"

"You have a thing about being safe, don't you?" Jessie looked at me with a smirk.

"I don't know. Do I?"

I was getting a little nervous about actually sliding down a slick rock into a pool whose depth was impossible to gauge from my current vantage point. I wasn't exactly the daring type, despite recently becoming a motorcycle momma.

"You loved the motorcycle ride. Just give it a chance." Jessie whipped off her T-shirt and shorts. Oh, wow. I was hoping I hadn't said that out loud. Jessie looked amazing. She caught me staring at her gorgeous physique in a red bikini—possibly with my mouth wide open and drooling. Quickly, I looked away while blushing. Yeah, I was smooth.

"So...you...uh...work out, huh?"

Jessie smiled broadly. "Some. Now get your clothes off." Realizing how that sounded, she blushed. "I mean, you know, take your shirt and shorts off."

That didn't sound much better.

Enjoying her embarrassment, I couldn't resist prodding her a bit. In the most seductive growl I could muster, I said, "And after I take all my clothes off, Officer Barnett, just what would you like me to do?"

In retrospect, that wasn't such a good thing to say since it conjured up images of Jessie laying me on the red rocks and having her way with me. We stood and stared at each other for much too long. My heart thumped wildly as I replayed our sensual kiss.

"So, uhhh…what do we do with our stuff while we're swimming?" I asked

It took Jessie longer than normal to respond. "We…uhh…can leave them here."

Jessie turned her back as I took my shirt and shorts off. I was disappointed that I didn't look anywhere near as sexy in my swimsuit as she did. With fifteen pounds to lose I didn't dare go near a bikini, but instead stuck with a safe black—for slimming purposes, of course—one-piece. At least this suit made my breasts look amazing. The push-up support lifted these babies, which created some enticing cleavage, if I must say so myself.

When I was done, Jessie turned around and looked directly at my chest, quickly up to my eyes, then at my chest again before averting her eyes to the ground. Why, I do believe she was checking me out.

The ginormous natural rock slide required that we hike uphill for what felt like miles. Once we reached the top, we sat on the highest point to catch our breath. It was a beautiful view, and I would have been satisfied to sit up there all day. Did we actually have to slide down this thing to have fun? Was that really necessary?

"Okay, what you want to do is lie down and keep your body straight as a board," Jessie explained. "Don't try to sit up and slide because you might tumble over and hit your head."

Oh my. I resisted the urge to ask again if it was safe.

"I'll go first and then you follow after I've reached the bottom so we don't run into each other. See you downhillllll!" Jessie screamed the entire way down the rock slide before splashing into the waterhole. It looked like a bumpy, rough ride.

"That was amazing!" she yelled from below.

Sitting alone at the top, I was seriously rethinking this whole rock-slide thing.

Sensing my reluctance, Jessie yelled, "You can do this, Malley. Just relax and let go."

The word "go" bounced off the canyon walls. Let go. That wasn't exactly one of my strong points. I inched down the rock a little, and then a little farther, until the force of the rushing water carried me away before I was ready to let go on my own. I screamed my head off the entire way. Jessie was waiting in the waterhole to catch me as I came plunging down.

"You did it!" she said. "So what'd you think?"

It took me a minute to catch my breath and stop my head from spinning. This was even more of a rush than the motorcycle ride. "Let's go again!" I yelled. Jessie threw her head back in laughter while playfully splashing me with water.

We spent most of the day cooling off in the swimming hole and going down the slide until we were too exhausted to hike up the hill again. When we weren't doing that we were soaking up the sun. The pulsating heat on my body felt divine. I looked at Jessie, who was lying beside me with her eyes closed, wondering if she was enjoying the day as much as I was. I hadn't had so much fun since I was a kid and didn't even think about Lizzie and Heather once.

Jessie's bronzed arms and legs were glistening with coconut suntan oil. As much as I tried not to stare, I let my eyes roam down Jessie's body. It would have seemed so natural to lightly run my fingers down her arms and lay my hand over hers. Or teasingly trace figure eights inside her thigh—with my fingers or tongue, I couldn't decide which.

What was I thinking? This was Jessie, after all. That damn kiss had started it all. It had turned me into a horny teenager.

❖

Jessie sat up and towel-dried her hair. "How about we go to the Red Planet? I'm starving."

"I'm hungry, too, but I'm not sure about the Red Planet." It was a cute, funky diner with an outer-space, alien theme. "I like it, but it's not in my Weight Watcher's app."

"And why does that matter?"

"I'm on Weight Watcher's and I want to stick to my daily points."

Jessie dropped her towel and looked at me. "Why are you on a diet? You don't need to lose weight."

"Are you kidding? I need to lose at least fifteen pounds, if not more."

"You look beautiful. You're just the right size." Jessie looked down, embarrassed by her admission.

I was in shock. She seemed serious, but I found it hard to believe that someone as perfect as Jessie would think I looked good, much less beautiful.

"They have healthy stuff there, too," she said. "It's not all burgers and fries. You don't have to stick to the exact points this one meal, do you?"

After some consideration I figured I could be a little flexible, especially since the most I'd eaten all day was a couple of granola bars. So off to the Red Planet we went on yet another thrilling motorcycle ride.

The diner was decorated with flying saucers, an eight-foot-tall stuffed alien sitting at the bar, and everything space-related under the sun. A young, attractive waitress, wearing a Welcome Earthlings T-shirt, brought us two waters in glasses shaped like the moon. Normally, a waitress would give us some time to ponder the menu, but this one stood right by our table—her eyes glued to Jessie.

"What do you suggest?" I asked. She might as well be of some benefit if she was going to just stand there.

"Whatever you want," she said seductively. Her eyes never left Jessie, who was scanning the menu. "The spaghetti and space meatballs are to die for." She leaned over Jessie, jutting her boobs out and pointing to the item in her menu.

"So I guess there really is water on the moon," I said as I took a sip out of my moon glass. No one got it.

"I think I'll take the Flash Gordon Veggie Burger. No fries. And water's fine." Jessie closed her menu.

"Anything else?" The waitress batted her mascara-caked eyelashes. "I'll bring you whatever you want."

"No, I'm good with that, thanks."

"Alrighty then," I said. "I'll have the Cosmic Cobb Salad with the Green Alien Goddess Dressing. And water's fine for me, too."

"Be back in a flash," the waitress said. She emphasized "flash" as a cute play on words from what Jessie had ordered. After taking our menus, she practically mowed down a wandering toddler as she backed away, because she was too busy staring at Jessie.

"Oh. My. God."

"What?" Jessie looked around the restaurant. "What is it?"

"That waitress was totally coming on to you."

"What? Get out of here. She was just being friendly."

"Friendly, my ass. She was all over you and completely ignored me. You seriously didn't notice that?"

Jessie frowned and shook her head like I was insane. Was it possible she could really be that clueless? I figured people like Jessie fell in love with themselves every time they looked in the mirror.

"You must know you're smoking hot, Barnett."

Jessie rolled the saltshaker between her palms. "You're imagining things." She grabbed the pepper shaker, making sure the cap was screwed on tight.

"I never see you text or call anyone. No hot chick waiting back in LA?" I asked.

"No one special."

Well, that was vague. "Ah, so, hundreds, not just one?" I raised an eyebrow, very much wanting to know the answer to that question.

"No. In fact, I haven't had a date in over a year."

"Seriously? No way. I'm sure Nicole would jump at the chance to go out with you."

"She's not my type."

"So what's your type?"

Jessie looked at me and held my gaze just long enough to make me wonder for a minute if I was actually her type.

"I don't really have one. I'll just…I'll know she's the one when I meet her." Jessie didn't avert her eyes from mine.

"So tell me about your last girlfriend."

"Ah, now that's a relationship I'd rather forget. We dated six months. She was an actress. *Very* dramatic, to say the least."

"What was your longest relationship?" I asked.

"That would be Annie. We were together three years."

"Did you know she was the one when you met her?"

"No. I don't think I've met the one yet." Jessie glanced around the restaurant and looked suddenly uneasy.

"So what happened?"

"There's not much to tell. It was a nice relationship while it lasted, but we were more like best friends than we were lovers. I think that's why we stayed together so long. There wasn't anything fundamentally wrong with the relationship. We got along great, had fun together, but it just lacked...passion."

"Who ended it?"

"I did, but it was mutual in the end. We're still friends. What about you? Is Lizzie the one?" Jessie took a sip of water, looking at me over her glass.

"I think so. I hope so. I haven't had very good luck in relationships. I've made some unwise choices, you could say."

"Maybe you just haven't met the one yet, either." Jessie looked directly into my eyes.

It was one of those intense stares that left me wondering what she was thinking. My phone beeped and vibrated on the table. A text from Lizzie. My heart sank. I was afraid to open it.

"From Lizzie?" Jessie asked, surely reading the dread on my face.

"Yeah. I'm not sure if I want to read it."

"It might be good news. You'll have to read it sooner or later."

"You're right." I swiped my finger across the screen to open the text, which said, "Sorry I left so suddenly. Will call soon. I do care about U. XXOO." I closed my phone and sighed, taking a swig of water.

Sensing the plummet in my mood, Jessie tried to change the subject. "So you've been here before?"

"Yeah, with my parents. I was about fifteen, so a long time ago. My dad would love that I rode a motorcycle today."

My smile faded with the mention of my father. Even though he'd been gone a year, I still found it hard to believe he'd actually died. A hard lump formed in my throat and tears threatened, but I held them back.

"Did your dad like motorcycles?" Jessie asked.

"Yeah, he rode one every day. My mom refused to let him take me for a ride. He and I had some pretty dangerous adventures together when I was a kid, most of which we never told my mom about."

"So you were an adventurous kid? That surprises me. I mean, you seem to want to play it safe."

"Well…I've become more careful in my old age." Or maybe I should have said fearful.

"You must have loved your dad very much," Jessie said.

Oh no. We weren't going there or else I'd cry for sure. I nodded and was never so happy to see our flirty waitress as when she walked up with our orders, but not without giving Jessie a wink first.

Chapter Thirteen

Surprises

To end our adventurous day at Slide Rock, Jessie and I sat on the porch of the main cabin with Clarissa, enjoying a star-filled Sedona night. It was the first time we'd sat still all day. I was exhausted and knew I'd be sore in the morning, but it had been worth it.

"Did you like the rock slide?" Clarissa asked as she squeaked back and forth in her rocking chair.

Jessie chimed in before I could open my mouth to respond. "She loved it. Just like a little kid, begging to slide one more time." I couldn't help but grin at her enthusiasm.

"I wouldn't go that far," I said. "But yes, I did enjoy myself."

"I figured Jessie would be the one you'd have to pry away. When we were kids, the Slip 'n Slide was her absolute favorite."

"You two have known each other since you were kids?"

Clarissa stopped rocking, her eyebrows furrowed in a frown. "Jessie and I are sisters."

"Wait a minute. Clarissa is your *sister*?! You never told me that!" I slapped Jessie on the arm. "I thought when she called you sister at the pizza party she meant in a lesbian-sisterhood sort of way."

"I never told you? Hmmm…I thought I had."

"No!"

"That's Jessie for you. Withholding information," Clarissa said as she glared at Jessie. The obvious discomfort between the two of them made me think Jessie was withholding more.

"How could she not tell me that?" I mumbled to myself. Clarissa must have been at least ten years older than Jessie, but I didn't want to assume anything. "So you're really her sister?"

"Yeah," Clarissa said with a chuckle. "Flesh-and-blood sisters."

"Well," I said, rubbing my palms together. "This changes everything. Now you can give me all the dirt on Jessie."

"Hey now." Jessie leaned forward, grabbing my wrists. "That's not fair."

"Of course it is." I let out an over-exaggerated evil-witch laugh.

"Now, now, kids. Don't argue." Clarissa laughed. "But I do have a hankering for some ice cream. Jessie, why don't you go to the kitchen and dig some out of the big freezer? Wouldn't you like some ice cream, Malley?"

"Oh, yes," I said, playing along. "I'd love some."

"You two just want to get rid of me so you can gossip. Fine. I have nothing to hide." Jessie stood, stretching her long legs. "You behave." She pointed a finger at Clarissa, giving her a stern look, which made me think she actually did have something to hide. This was going to be fun.

Once Jessie was out of range, I got down to business. "So what was Jessie like as a kid?"

"Pretty much the way she is now. She liked being adventurous, taking chances. But she had a calm side to her as well, and a strong connection to nature. There's a lot more to Jessie than meets the eye."

"Yeah, I'm slowly learning that. So you're the oldest?"

"By nine years. My mom had several miscarriages between me and Jessie."

"It was just the three of you?" Clarissa stopped rocking and raised an eyebrow. "You, Jessie, and little Jessie?"

"She told you about that? I'm surprised. She never mentions him to anyone. It was so hard on my parents and they did the best they could, but giving her the same name as little Jessie was a lot to put on a kid."

"When did she come out and how did your family handle it?" It dawned on me that we were at a lesbian function. "Are you..."

"No, I'm not a lesbian. I have a boyfriend in Sedona. I'm straight but not narrow," Clarissa said with a wink. "Many years ago after Jessie told me she was gay, I started hosting these lesbian retreats twice a year. I saw how so many places didn't accept the gay community, and I wanted to do something to show my support."

"That's wonderful. I'm sure she appreciates that. And your parents were okay with her being gay?"

"Oh yes. They're completely non-judgmental."

"Jessie said they weren't overjoyed about her career choice."

"That's true, but more than anything they wanted her to be happy, so they settled into it."

"Don't you worry about her being a police officer? I mean, it's so dangerous."

"I did at first, but we can't let fear rule us. Life is short. I'd rather her do something that she loves than be stuck at a job she hates just because it's safe."

"Still, though, anything could happen and she could..." I didn't want to imagine the worst.

"All right, you two." The sound of Jessie's voice made us both jump. "Stop talking about me."

"You're so vain, Barnett. We weren't talking about you," I said.

"Yeah, yeah, so who wants ice cream?"

"Not me, I'm on a diet."

"Me either," Clarissa said. "It's too late to eat."

Jessie looked adorable with a blank, confused expression as she stood cradling a big carton of quickly melting ice cream.

"Well, I'm off to bed," Clarissa said.

As we both stood, I gave her a kiss on the cheek. "Thanks for the chat," I whispered in her ear.

"Anytime," she said with a warm smile. "Good night, little sis. You girls be good." Clarissa wiggled her eyebrows and disappeared inside.

"So what did you two talk about?" Apprehension filled Jessie's eyes as she fidgeted with the carton of ice cream.

"Nothing incriminating. I really like Clarissa. She's wise."

"So she really didn't talk about me?" Jessie looked nervous.

"Relax. She didn't give away any of your precious secrets. I can't believe you didn't tell me she was your sister. Just what else are you hiding?"

Jessie lowered her eyes to the ice-cream carton. "I should get this into the freezer before it melts all over the porch. I'll see you in the cabin."

Jessie left me standing on the porch, wondering if I'd ever get to know the real her and surprised by the fact that I desperately wanted to do so.

Walking back to the cabin I kicked myself for forgetting to ask Clarissa a burning question I had about Jessie. What in the world did she write in that notebook of hers?

❖

When I reached the cabin, Lizzie was sitting on the porch. I wasn't sure if I should hug her or slap her.

"Can you talk?" Her eyes were swollen and red, like she'd been crying for twelve hours straight.

"Of course." My tone sounded colder and more formal than I'd intended. Sitting beside Lizzie on the step, a million questions ran through my mind, but I waited for her to speak.

"Malley, I'm so sorry about all of this. I had no idea Heather would want to come back." So Heather wanted to get back together. No big surprise there. "But that doesn't mean I don't care about you."

"Why did you say you wanted to date me if you have unresolved feelings for Heather? Why would you kiss me and pretend like we were dating?"

"I wasn't pretending. I want to be with you. I just…I'm confused. Please. Just give me some time to sort things out."

"You said I make you ten times happier than Heather ever did. Doesn't that count for something?"

"Of course. I'm not saying I'm going back to her. I just…I need closure."

Lizzie looked so sad as tears brimmed in her eyes. It broke my heart. As she pulled me into a tight hug, a part of me wanted to pull away, but a larger part could never resist Lizzie, especially when she was in pain.

"So what happens now?" I asked.

"I came back to see you…and to get a few things. I don't even have a change of clothes with me."

"So you're going back?!" I raised my voice. "To her hotel room?"

"Just for a bit. It's important that you know she hasn't touched me, and we're certainly not sleeping together."

That *was* one of the things I wanted to know, but her reassurance didn't ease my mind any less.

"Will you wait for me? I mean, until I figure things out?"

"Of course. God, Lizzie, I've waited for you for a year. I'm not going anywhere."

"I love you, Malley." Lizzie pulled me into another tight hug.

I already knew Lizzie loved me. But I didn't know whether it was a friendship or romantic love.

I don't know how long I sat on the porch, mulling over all Lizzie had said, before Jessie walked up.

"Where's Lizzie?" Jessie sat beside me. "I saw you two talking and didn't want to disturb you, so I took a walk."

"She left again. Going to Heather's hotel room."

"They're back together?"

"She said they're not, but she needs closure or something like that. I don't know." I put my elbows on my knees, resting my chin on my fists.

Jessie laid her hand on my back. "I'm sorry, Malley."

"I'm exhausted," I said, standing up on the steps. "You coming?"

"In a minute."

Opening the cabin door, I turned back to Jessie. "Lizzie did say she loved me. That's something at least."

Right before closing the door, I could have sworn I heard Jessie say, "Who wouldn't love you?"

CHAPTER FOURTEEN

THE CIRCLE OF ENLIGHTENMENT

From the moment I walked into the meeting room of the main cabin, I regretted being there. Nothing good ever comes from a bunch of chairs arranged in a circle. It's like stopping to talk to the person with a clipboard standing outside the grocery store. You just know it's something you'll end up regretting. It'll either cost you time or money or both.

Jessie had talked me into this. She said it would do me good and take my mind off Lizzie. Why I ever listened to her, I don't know. She was snuggled in bed watching *The African Queen* while fighting off a cold. She'd been sniffling all day, so I'd ordered immediate bed rest. Playing nurse, I gave her a couple of aspirin and took her temperature, which was a little high. Then I made her some hot tea and found one of her favorite movies to watch on TV. I guess I did have care-giving instincts after all.

I usually steered clear of sick people, but for some reason I enjoyed doting on Jessie. She looked pathetic, with droopy eyes and a red nose from blowing it so often, and she sounded eerily like Snuffleupagus from *Sesame Street*. I didn't like the thought of her feeling crummy and wanted to make it all better. I wish I'd listened to my instincts and not left her alone, because right now I'd much rather be nestled next to Jessie watching Humphrey

Bogart pull leeches off of his legs. I'd choose leeches over this scene any day.

I entered the meeting room and sat in one of the chairs. So as to avoid eye contact with anyone, particularly Nicole, I focused on the candle perched on a table in the middle of the circle. Rhonda walked in, eyed the joint, then turned to leave, but ran directly into Clarissa, who guided her back into the room. I couldn't blame Rhonda for wanting to escape. This scene was screaming sharing-is-caring big-time.

"Thank you all for coming tonight." Clarissa clasped her hands together with a big smile plastered across her face. "I'll briefly explain a few ground rules and then we'll get started." Clarissa fanned her arms around the circle of chairs. "This is…the Circle of Enlightenment."

I stifled a giggle because of the way she paused for dramatic effect and whispered "Circle of Enlightenment." Like it was some sort of mystical place just because she lit a candle and arranged some chairs in a circle.

Clarissa walked to the center of the circle, grabbing a stack of cards next to the candle. Was she going to tell our fortune or maybe deal out a hand of poker? Maybe this was like Vegas. What happened in the circle stayed in the circle. Okay, I admit it. I was in an ornery mood. I sat up a little straighter in my chair and scolded myself. Pay attention, Malley. You might actually learn something.

"These are crystal cards." Clarissa held up the card deck and twirled around for everyone to take a gander. "Each card has a picture of a crystal, along with questions that pertain to the crystals' properties. I'll walk around the circle where you'll each randomly pick a card." Clarissa smiled. "Of course, though, nothing is ever actually random."

My heart started beating wildly and I felt flushed. What card was I going to pull? What would the questions be? Would I have to answer them out loud to the group?

"After you pick a card, place it upside down in your lap and don't look at the crystal picture or questions until it's your turn to speak." So this *was* about sharing!

"When it's your turn, flip your card over, read it aloud, and spend about ten minutes sharing any thoughts or feelings that come up for you." Ten minutes? I did the quick math in my head. Good gosh, we'd be here for an hour and twenty minutes.

When Clarissa reached me, my hand quivered as I pulled a card from the deck. I so wanted to turn it over. I needed time to prepare my response. This was like being asked to give a speech and not even knowing the topic beforehand. When Clarissa got back to her chair she asked, "Now who would like to go first?"

I wasn't surprised when my hand shot up. It's not that I was eager to share, but I had to get this over with as quickly as possible. No way could I sit still in my chair with that card turned over, waiting until it was my turn.

"Malley, wonderful." Clarissa beamed as all eyes turned toward me.

Flipping over my card, I winced. I quickly scanned the available topics I could relate to the card, aside from the very obvious one that I was most certainly not going to discuss in this so-called Circle of Enlightenment.

"Um, it's an Apache tears crystal card. And it asks if I'm grieving the loss of someone or something, and if I'm allowing myself to mourn and cry." The others in the circle let out a collective "ahhh." For a split second, I was almost happy Lizzie had left with Heather so I'd have something to talk about instead of my dad.

"Well, I'm not sure what to say. I think you all know that Lizzie and I were together for a bit and then she left with her ex-girlfriend. So, I'm sure this card relates to her and that I shouldn't try to hide my sadness." Was that ten minutes long? I guess not, because everyone was still staring at me, waiting for me to continue. I had to think fast. Apache. Tears. All I kept picturing was that commercial where the Indian was crying because of the environment or litter or something.

"Sooo," I said, "um, I know opening up is something I'm not very good at, and I don't like crying in front of people...and... uh...if you make me talk anymore you might really make me cry so I'll just shut up now."

A few women snickered, including Clarissa. Phew. I was off the hook. My heart rate returned to normal.

Rhonda was the next victim.

"Well," Rhonda said, "I have no idea how to pronounce this." Clarissa popped out of her chair and looked at Rhonda's card.

"That's rhodochrosite."

"Thanks." Rhonda exhaled a nervous laugh. "It asks if I believe I'm magnificent and if I allow myself to be who I truly am."

Rhonda was motionless as she stared at her card. I felt bad for her. This Circle-of-Enlightenment thing sucked.

"I can pretty much say I've never felt magnificent. Not by a long shot." Rhonda chuckled, but we didn't join in. She continued talking, never looking up from her card. "People don't seem to take kindly to obese people, you know? Like, sometimes when they look at me I can see the disgust and judgment in their eyes. They don't think I can see it, but I can. I don't see why my weight should matter to anyone. I'd be the same person inside even if I was a size four. It's like they don't want to get to know me. They just see my size."

I felt like crap. The first time I met Rhonda all I saw was her weight and all I heard was her thick Texas accent. I hoped she hadn't seen the judgment in my eyes.

"And I rarely feel like I can be who I truly am. Except maybe in a place like this." Rhonda shrugged. It was one of those moves I'm quite familiar with, one I used often. It's meant to convey that what was said was no big deal, which doesn't really fool anyone.

"My family isn't exactly okay with me being a lesbian. The only way I can be in their lives is if I don't talk about it. Normally I'd just say fuck it and be outta there, but…I wouldn't ever get to see my niece or nephews again…or my mom and dad." Rhonda's voice cracked.

Everyone was motionless and silent. I'm usually not one to notice these things, but the energy in the room had visibly shifted. We could all relate. If not with the weight issues, then being accepted by our family.

"Thank you for sharing, Rhonda," Clarissa said.

Maybe it was because what Rhonda said made me feel weepy, but when it was Nicole's turn, I actually made a point to listen with some interest and compassion.

"Ah, Dalmatians are my favorite species." Nicole smiled. "I got Dalmatian jasper. The card asks…the card asks if I'm having issues with loyalty and if I'm building relationships with trustworthy and reliable people." Nicole took a deep breath. "I guess your comment that nothing is random is accurate," Nicole said to Clarissa.

"Not sure where to begin, but I was married to the love of my life for five years. She was everything I ever wanted, until a year ago when I found out she'd been having an affair with one of our best friends." Nicole looked at her card, seemingly transported back to that time in her life.

"It was such a shock. I had no idea. God, I felt like such a fool. They'd been sleeping together for six months. Six months and I didn't have a clue. I kept her dinner warm and stayed up until she got home from those so-called late nights at the office. *C'est* la vie." Nicole sighed.

"But, you know, everything happens for a reason, and maybe I pulled this card to remind myself to be more discerning next time and choose a trustworthy partner."

All at once it hit me. Nicole wanted Jessie because as a police officer she was the ultimate symbol of reliability and truthfulness. Nicole was throwing herself at Jessie because she was lonely, sad, and desperate for someone to protect her from ever getting hurt like that again. My realization didn't mean that Nicole was now my new BFF, but it did help me understand her better.

By the time we got around to all the women, it was getting late and everyone was emotionally drained.

"Well," Clarissa said, "this has been such a wonderful, enlightening evening, and I feel so much closer to all of you. Thank you for your honesty."

Clarissa's last words jabbed me in the heart. I regretted not being completely honest with the group. Guess I had a ways to go before I was enlightened.

CHAPTER FIFTEEN

THE NAKED, BRONZE STATUE

Talk about awkward. And stimulating.

Waking up at six a.m., I tossed and turned, trying to go back to sleep until finally surrendering and getting out of bed. Jessie was sleeping peacefully. I considered waking her up but thought she might still need rest because of that nasty cold. Not wanting to disturb her by making coffee or anything, I decided to take a walk.

The cool early morning breeze brushing against my skin felt glorious. Sedona in the summer wasn't known for its cool breezes except in the wee hours of the morning before even the snakes and lizards woke up. Pine needles crunched under my Nikes as I looked up at the looming ponderosa-pine trees.

I'd halfway listened when Clarissa explained the history of the ponderosa pine when we first arrived at the lodge. Just the word "history" had made me want to tune her out. But I did hear her say that when a ponderosa pine's young—if you can call a hundred and twenty years old young—the bark's black, but then it turns yellow with age. Actually, the tree sheds its black bark over time, revealing an inner glow of yellow. It's called a black-bark and then a yellow-bark tree. Guess they weren't very creative back then.

Maneuvering through the pines like it was an obstacle course, I searched for a glimpse of yellow bark. My nose found it before my eyes did, as the scent of butterscotch made my mouth water.

I glanced around to make sure no one was spying on me, then wrapped my arms around the trunk of the tree, hugging it tight. I felt a little foolish at first. I wasn't exactly the tree-hugging type. I hoped this didn't mean I'd have to start wearing hemp T-shirts and moccasins, and write a "Go green" blog. Sticking my nose in a crevice of the bark, I took a big sniff. That was something else I remembered Clarissa saying. The smell from pine trees doesn't come from the needles. It comes from the bark. And the yellow bark is known for its sweet smell, like sugar cookies baking in the oven. To me, though, it smelled like grandma's butterscotch cinnamon buns, the ones we spent hours making together when I was a kid. I wrapped my arms around the tree tighter and pressed my cheek against the bark, hoping the scent would rub off like a perfume that would stay with me for the rest of the day.

When I got back to the cabin Jessie was still curled up in bed. Or at least I thought she was since I saw a big mound of covers. Lesson number one: don't assume anything. When I opened the bathroom door, Jessie had just stepped out of the shower. I froze. She froze. I stared. She gulped. Oh. My. God. She was a perfect, bronze statue. A naked statue. Like something you'd see at the Huntington Museum. Her smooth skin glistened as a lone water bead rolled down her collarbone and into the crevasse of her breasts. Her naked breasts. Her perfect naked breasts. Instinctively, I licked my lips. I think she did the same, but it was hard to know when my eyes refused to leave her enticing mounds of flesh. Seriously? Enticing mounds of flesh? Did I just think that?

I should have shut my eyes, apologized, and exited as quickly as possible. But none of those options entered my mind. My thoughts were more around the nature of tracing the water bead's path with my fingertips encircling Jessie's breast around and around until her knees buckled beneath her. My blood pressure soared, and I was quite possibly in the stroke danger zone as heat inflamed my cheeks. My breathing grew jagged, making me light-headed.

I blamed my reaction on that kiss Jessie and I had shared. It brought up emotions and desires I shouldn't be feeling where she was concerned. If she'd never kissed me the way she did, I bet this bathroom scene would have gone an entirely different way. I would have taken one quick look, said something witty like "Nice jugs," then promptly closed the door. While I could explain my reaction to seeing Jessie naked, what I didn't get was what she did, which was absolutely nothing. She stood there, as naked as could be, and let my eyes devour her for as long as I wanted. She didn't try to cover up or say anything or make a move. It was almost like she wanted me to look at her.

If I hadn't been dizzy, I probably would have stared at naked Jessie all day. Fearing I might faint, I blinked rapidly three times before closing the door. I never took my eyes off the bathroom door as I slowly backed away. Something hard hit the back of my calves and I plopped down on the edge of my bed, still staring at the door.

Well, this was awkward. I wasn't sure what the proper protocol was in this situation. If I'd had the Internet handy I'd have Googled "What to do if you see your friend naked." The way I saw it, I had two options. I could scram, avoid all future eye contact with Jessie, and hope she never brought up the subject. Or I could sit there, like an adult, and wait for her to come out of the bathroom so we could discuss what had just happened. Surprisingly, I chose the latter... surprisingly, because I usually preferred avoidance.

Jessie didn't take time to dry her hair before emerging from the bathroom, but thank God she did have the sense to put some clothes on. My stomach churned and my insides quivered. Jessie, on the other hand, looked completely calm.

"So," she said, "that was...interesting."

"Yeah." It didn't so much come out as a word but more of a nervous chuckle. "Um, I'm sorry I walked in on you. I thought you were still in bed."

"That's okay." And it actually did seem okay with her. She didn't look the least bit self-conscious. Jessie sat beside me on the bed, a little too close for my taste, considering moments ago I was ogling her naked breasts.

"Is that butterscotch?" Jessie leaned closer and breathed in deeply.

"Yeah, I was...well...near the yellow pines this morning."

"Clarissa said they smell like sugar cookies, but I think they smell like butterscotch."

"I couldn't agree more," I replied.

Sitting on the bed, feeling the warmth of Jessie next to me, I wondered how I could possibly ever look at her again and not visualize her perfect, naked body. As with our kiss, I'd just have to put it out of my mind, forget it ever happened. But considering I was doing a pretty crappy job of forgetting that kiss, I figured I might be in big trouble here.

CHAPTER SIXTEEN

GHOST TOWN

You did what?" Jessie clicked off the TV and sat up in bed. She looked at me like I had three heads.

"I said I've invited Rhonda and Nicole to go with us." I slid an iron back and forth over my shirt, not daring to look at Jessie.

"What's with the change of heart?"

"Maybe the Circle of Enlightenment workshop got to me." That wasn't a complete lie.

"Sounds like I missed some class."

Jessie had suggested we check out Jerome, which was a ghost town about twenty-five miles outside of Sedona. I couldn't really blame her for being shocked about inviting Rhonda and Nicole. It's not like I'd been silent about expressing my opinion of those two, especially when it came to seductress Nicole. But that was before the Circle of Enlightenment...and before I saw Jessie naked. Maybe they'd act as a buffer between us, or at least distract me from visualizing Jessie's wet, naked body.

"You never told me what crystal card you pulled." Jessie yawned fiercely, like a lazy lion, before stretching her arms out and placing her hands behind her head. She closed her eyes, relaxing in her bed.

"Did you not sleep well?" *Lord knows I didn't after that peep show.* I scanned Jessie's tan, muscular legs to her breasts, which were straining against the words "Just Do It" written across her T-shirt. Gee, thanks for the visual, Nike. Let's just say the slogan didn't conjure images of Jessie running the LA marathon. Rather, it was more along the lines of a between-the-sheets sport.

Jessie's eyes popped open, causing me to avert my gaze downward while rapidly ironing.

"I slept fine. Now what card did you pull?"

"The Apache tears crystal. It was about grieving the loss of something. I talked about Lizzie."

"Ah, of course." Jessie yawned again, closing her eyes.

"I know you weren't feeling well that night, but it's not fair I got stuck in the fiery circle of hell and you got off scot-free. We all had to bare our souls."

Jessie opened her eyes, looking directly at me. "Ask me anything. I'll bare my soul right now."

The only question that popped into my mind was one I dared not ask. *Did you really think our kiss was a mistake?* Instead, I played it safe. "What's your tattoo say?"

Jessie looked perplexed. "When did you—"

"Slide Rock. Little red bikini. Remember?" Not to mention the many times I checked her out in the gym when she bent over to pick up a dumbbell, but she didn't need to know that.

"Right. It says YOLO."

"What does that mean?

"Seriously? You've never heard that before? It stands for you only live once."

"I thought you believed in reincarnation." I unplugged the iron, standing it upright.

"I do, but that's not the point of the tattoo. It reminds me to live in the moment, enjoy life, and take risks. Maybe you should get one."

"Me? I don't do tattoos." I chuckled.

"Then crochet it on a pillow if you have to, but I think it would be a good message for you to remember."

"Thanks for the suggestion but my life is peachy as it is."

"It's just that—"

Rhonda burst through the door without knocking. "I'm ready to see some ghosts and goblins," she said, rubbing her palms together.

"It's not that kind of ghost town," Nicole said, strolling in behind Rhonda. She looked bored and irritated already. She'd deemed herself the Jerome authority since she'd visited it all of two times. Speaking of Nicole, she was wearing brown knit pants, a Pebble Beach Resort golf shirt, and dressy shoes not suitable for walking around a ghost town. Did this woman not even own a pair of shorts and sneakers?

Jessie, on the other hand, had on khaki shorts that hugged her rear end just right without being too tight in a trashy way, a bright-red tank top, and hiking boots. I don't know why, but Jessie looked so much cuter in hiking books than anyone else I'd ever seen. Maybe it was the way they made her look a little tough and rugged. Like she could walk through snow, rain, and even fire to rescue me...or anyone, not just me, of course. That, coupled with the way the red tank top complemented her olive complexion, caused me to gawk at her more than I should have. Knowing what Jessie looked like under that little tank top didn't help matters either. I knew how smooth and toned her skin was. I knew she had a small birthmark right above her belly button and that her breasts were firm and perfectly shaped. Those were things I shouldn't know about a friend, and I certainly shouldn't be salivating while thinking about them.

We piled into Rhonda's Jeep, with me in the passenger seat and Jessie and Nicole in the backseat. I'd actually suggested that they get in the back together. I didn't realize it at the time, but my subconscious plan for the day was to throw Nicole and Jessie together as often as possible. If they hooked up, then Jessie would be off-limits, thus causing me to stop fantasizing about her. What can I say? It wasn't one of my best-thought-out plans.

As Rhonda steered her Jeep down the highway, we spotted Jerome in the distance. It was a town strikingly high in the sky and built precariously close to a cliff. Were we seriously going to drive up that steep, narrow incline with our lives in Rhonda's hands?

Rhonda grabbed the guidebook and started reading aloud. "'Jerome was established in the 1800s and was a popular copper-mining town.'"

I grabbed the book from her. "I'll read. You drive," I said. "'During its prosperous copper-mining years, the town had 15,000 residents and was named the wickedest city in the West. During those days, residents overdosed on opium, died in mining accidents, murders, suicides, and other unnatural, unexplained events. Today, the town is known to be filled with wandering spirits.'" I read that last part in an eerie, twilight-zone sort of voice.

"It's an artists' community," Nicole said. "They have cute shops and galleries. I've never seen a ghost there."

"Well, that's not what the guidebook says." I gave her a sideways glance.

We were all silent as Rhonda's Jeep strained up the incline that led to Jerome. I saw houses built on stilts, which looked like twigs, overlooking cliffs. Those wouldn't last one rainy season in Los Angeles. The houses would be sliding down the mountain in no time. As we got closer to Jerome, I was sorry to see that Nicole was right. This didn't look like any ghost town I'd ever imagined. Where were the abandoned buildings? Where were the rolling tumbleweeds? Where was the crazy old prospector with tales of ghosts that go bump in the night? This didn't look anything like the ghost town the Brady Bunch encountered on their way to the Grand Canyon. Instead, it was filled with quaint coffee shops and artists' galleries. Unbeknownst to us, it was the weekend for the Jerome Artwalk, so we saw scads of arts-and-crafts displays up and down Main Street. It looked as busy as the Third Street Promenade in Santa Monica.

The first thing we did was thank Rhonda for not driving us off the cliff. And second, we got something to eat at a sandwich shop, which sat next to the Sweet Treats bakery. Ever since I started contemplating opening a bakery, it was funny how I'd see one everywhere I went. From what I could tell, by glancing in the door as someone was walking out, it was decorated in bright primary colors and smelled like apple pie. The customer had a big smile on his face as he exited. That's what I wanted. A happy customer coming out of my super-cute bakery, except mine would smell like butterscotch cinnamon buns.

After lunch we strolled down Main Street, looking at paintings, photography, and crafts of all kinds. I walked close to Rhonda, and on the opposite side of Jessie, hoping that would give Jessie and Nicole time to chat. Jessie had looked at me suspiciously in the restaurant when I stepped in front of her to slide into the booth next to Rhonda so she'd have to sit by Nicole. I was certain she didn't know what I was up to, but I had to be smart about playing matchmaker. Jessie was pretty sharp.

At one point, when we were looking at gorgeous, vibrant photographs of Sedona by some famous photographer, Jessie walked behind me to peer over my shoulder. She was so close I could feel the heat from her body. When she leaned in closer, her hip grazed my leg, which sent electricity shooting to my toes. I had to physically pinch myself to keep from leaning back into her so I could feel all of her against me. Mentally, I cursed Lizzie for leaving with Heather. This was all her fault. If she'd stayed at the lodge we'd be dating and I'd be getting chills from her touch instead of Jessie's.

"Hey, look. There's a ghost tour." Rhonda pointed to a sign that read SPIRITS OF JEROME TOUR—TAKE AT YOUR OWN RISK.

"I'm in," Jessie said. "Malley, how about you?" Actually, I did want to go on a ghost tour, but this was my opportunity to throw Jessie and Nicole together.

"No, I'd rather check out this store." I pointed at the nearest establishment within range of where we were standing.

"You want to go into the Sacred Circle? Seriously?" Jessie looked at me in disbelief.

"Sure. Rhonda will come with me."

"No way," Rhonda said. "I had enough sacred circles with that Circle of Enlightenment crap the other night."

I pulled on her sleeve, practically dragging her down the street. "You and Nicole check out the ghost tour and we'll meet up here in an hour." I didn't give anyone a chance to protest. The only person who looked happy was Nicole.

"What the hell, Malley? I wanted to go on a ghost tour."

"This is better. You won't see all this on a tour." Sandalwood incense assaulted us as we opened the door to the Sacred Circle. It was packed with shelves of books, rows of hundreds of crystals, and items that were completely foreign to me.

"I'm going to see if I can catch up to Jessie and Nicole."

I grabbed Rhonda's arm to stop her. "Hey, look, you can get a psychic reading. You can't come to Sedona and not get your fortune told." I could see a spark in Rhonda's dark eyes. I had her. "I'll even treat you." I really had her now. "Go sign up over there."

With Rhonda out of my hair and away from Jessie and Nicole, I perused the store, ending up in the book section. I scanned all the weird metaphysical topics before suddenly stopping at one title: *Sedona's Kachina Woman*. After grabbing the book I began to flip through the pages and found crisp, colorful photographs of Boynton Canyon. My heart ached when I saw a photo of the Kachina Woman. The last time I saw her was with my dad.

"Can I help you find something, young lady?" A voice startled me back into reality. "I didn't mean to scare you."

"It's okay," I said, catching my breath. "I was just deep in thought." I turned around to a middle-aged man with a ponytail and wearing a tie-dyed T-shirt. He looked like he'd just come from Woodstock.

"Ah, the Kachina Woman," he said, looking at the book in my hand. "Have you been there?"

"Yeah. But it was a long time ago."

"It's a magical, sacred place," he said.

"Magical?"

"We've had reports of mysterious, mystical happenings in Boynton Canyon. If you believe in that sort of thing," he said with a wink.

"What sort of mysterious things?" I asked, remembering the disappearing Indian.

"Oh, I've heard tales of miraculous healings, both physical and emotional. People say the Kachina Woman protects everyone who enters the canyon, and if they reach the top of the trail to stand by her side, she'll give them what they desire and need the most."

"You mean like making a crippled person walk?" That was a stupid example since a crippled person would have difficulty climbing up the steep, rocky trail.

But the guy didn't blink. "Anything's possible. I heard once that a blind man came down the trail with his vision fully restored."

"No way." I didn't want to sound skeptical, but that was a little far-fetched.

"That's what I heard," he said. "There's also a tale that an Indian spirit roams the canyon, acting as the Kachina Woman's aide. He makes himself visible just long enough to deliver a sacred gift to someone." Goose bumps appeared on my arms as chills ran down my spine. The hippie narrowed his eyes as he looked at me. "Have you ever seen anything strange in Boynton Canyon?"

"No," I said, much too quickly. "Well, maybe. I'm not sure. It was a long time ago."

The man stared at me for several seconds. "Well, you should go up there again if you get a chance. Let me know if you need help finding anything." His voice trailed off as he walked away.

My entire body felt limp. Could that actually be true? Had my dad and I really encountered an Indian spirit who acted as the Kachina Woman's right-hand man? And was the heart rock a gift from the Kachina Woman? Hundreds of questions were running through my mind, so much so that I obviously hadn't heard Rhonda calling my name.

"Malley! Over here!" Rhonda waved me toward her. Still in a daze, I put the book back on the shelf and commanded my Gumby-like legs to take several steps forward.

"The nice woman here has been waiting. You said you'd pay."

"Yeah, right. Sorry." I looked at the receipt Rhonda handed me. It took me a minute to comprehend what I was seeing. "A hundred and fifty dollars!? What the hell, Rhonda!" I looked at her in horror.

"You said I could get a psychic reading."

"Yeah, but good Lord. A hundred and fifty dollars? I didn't expect you to break my bank account." Rhonda shrugged. "Good God. Did the psychic predict you'd win the lottery? 'Cause if so, I expect this money back. Good Lord."

"Just pay the woman, Malley," Rhonda said, clearly exasperated.

"Sorry," I told the cashier. "I wasn't expecting it to be quite this much." She didn't look fazed. I'm sure I wasn't the first person to freak out over the price.

"Damn, Rhonda. You at least owe me a grande, venti, big-gulp-sized latte after that." As we exited the store, I stopped abruptly on the sidewalk.

"What?" Rhonda asked.

"Look." I pointed across the street.

"Ohhh. Awkward."

Looking at a display of handmade necklaces were Lizzie and Heather. Seeing them together was like a big slap across the face. Not wanting them to spot us, I ducked behind a monstrous landscape mural of Bell Rock, dragging Rhonda with me. I peered at the couple over the frame.

"This is real mature," Rhonda said. "Why don't you go talk to her?"

"No way. Anyway, I want to spy a little to see how they act together. Lizzie said they weren't being physical in any way."

"Yeah, right. She's staying in Heather's hotel room and they're not doing the dirty deed."

I sneered at Rhonda. Actually, after watching them together I was fairly certain Lizzie wasn't bending the truth. They weren't laughing or smiling or touching in any way. In fact, Lizzie seemed sad, and Heather looked like she was ready to punch something. At one point Heather said something to Lizzie, who shook her head no, which caused Heather to stomp down the street. Lizzie sighed, then trekked after her.

Rhonda and I stepped out from behind the mural. Even though they weren't the picture of a blissful couple, seeing Lizzie with Heather was still a shock to the system. Lizzie wasn't holed up in Heather's hotel room screaming obscenities at her. They were out and about, spending time together at the Artwalk.

If that didn't make me feel crappy enough, seeing Nicole and Jessie walking toward us with intertwined arms turned my blood to ice. Now they looked like a happy couple. As they approached, Nicole threw her head back in laughter at something Jessie had just said.

"Malley, are you okay? You look like you've just seen a ghost," Jessie said.

"The ghost of Lizzie," Rhonda whispered.

"Oh," Nicole and Jessie said in unison.

Suddenly, I felt very lonely. Lizzie was with Heather, and I'd thrown Nicole into Jessie's arms. Not that I wanted Jessie anyway, but still. All I was stuck with was a hundred-and-fifty-dollar bill for a psychic reading, and I didn't even have a clue as to what my future held.

CHAPTER SEVENTEEN

COPS AND COOKIES

I'm sorry, Mom, but something came up and I won't get out to see you."

"But you're so close, honey. Can't you get away for just an afternoon?"

My heart melted. Hearing my mom's voice on the phone made me miss her all the more. It doesn't matter how old a person gets. There's nothing like a mother's embrace—and homemade white-chocolate macadamia cookies.

"I'll come soon. I promise."

"I was so looking forward to seeing you and meeting Lizzie." The only good thing about not seeing my mom was that I didn't have to explain why Lizzie wasn't with me.

Jessie had come into the cabin and was standing behind me. I wondered how much of my conversation she'd overheard.

"Listen, I have to go, but I love you and I promise to see you soon. Bye."

"Was that your mom?" Jessie asked.

"Yeah." Tossing my phone on the bed, I walked to the coffee pot and poured a cup.

"Why aren't you going to see her? You said she lives in Oak Creek Canyon?"

"Keep up, Barnett. My girlfriend left in the only means of transportation I had, and even though my mom is cool with the gay thing, I don't think I want to invite her to a lesbian lodge."

"Keep up, O'Brien. I have transportation." Jessie dangled her motorcycle keys in front of my face.

"Your bike? I don't think so."

"You loved the ride, remember?"

"My mom would have a heart attack if I came riding up on a Harley."

"It's not a Harley." I was desperately trying to think of a good excuse for Jessie not to drive me. For some reason, I felt uncomfortable with her meeting my mom and being at the cabin.

"It's sweet of you to offer, but it's fine. I'll see her some other time."

"Don't be so stubborn. Look, I've been wanting to go on the West Fork hike, which is by Oak Creek Canyon. I'll drop you off at your mom's, then pick you up later. It's a six-mile hike. I won't be done anytime soon."

Hmm…that might actually work. Grabbing my phone, I hit the speed dial. "Mom? I'll be there this afternoon."

My heart ached at the sight of the cabin. It was the first time I'd been there since my dad died. My parents had purchased it as a getaway when we lived in Phoenix. We spent holidays, vacations, and sometimes even weekends there. A few months ago, my mom decided to make the cabin her permanent home and sold their house in Phoenix. I think because it held some of our happiest family memories.

My mom bolted out of the door the moment Jessie and I pulled up. I should have known she'd be anxiously waiting. She stopped abruptly when she saw the motorcycle, but then ran and hugged me while I was still sitting on the bike.

"Malley! I'm so glad you're here! And this must be Lizzie."

"No, this is Jessie. Jessie, this is my mom."

"You can call me Angela." She gave Jessie a hug like they were old friends. "Jessie, huh?" My mom eyed me suspiciously.

"She's just dropping me off. She's on her way to a hike and will pick me up later."

"Nonsense. You girls both get in the house. I just baked some macadamia cookies."

"With white chocolate?" I felt like such a kid, but I really wanted to know.

"Of course, honey."

"That's very generous, but I'm sure you and Malley would like some time alone," Jessie said.

"I'd love to get to know any friend of Malley's, so I insist."

Jessie gave me a helpless look and I shrugged, knowing there was no arguing with my mom.

The cabin was exactly the same. The fact that very little had been changed since I was last there was both comforting and sad. I couldn't help but think of my dad, picturing him sitting in his reading chair with his right leg crossed and a pipe in his mouth. He was never the calm, relaxed type except when at the cabin.

The scent of freshly baked cookies brought my attention back to the present. The kitchen, where my mom had led us, smelled heavenly. Jessie and I both inhaled deeply.

"Mom, it smells sooo good in here. My mom bakes the best cookies ever."

"If they taste anywhere near how they smell, I'm in for a treat." Jessie gave her a wink, causing her to beam.

Watching mom stack cookies on a plate, I noticed that she looked older than the last time I'd seen her. It made me melancholy to think about her aging. She was all the family I had left. As devastating as it was when my dad died, I didn't know how I'd handle losing my mom. I'd feel like an orphan. Death was such a major thing. One minute you're talking and laughing with someone, and then the next they're gone.

"How'd you two meet?" My mom placed the plateful of cookies in the middle of the kitchen table where Jessie and I sat.

"Actually," I said, eyeing the cookies, "Jessie's my next-door neighbor."

"Is she now? Well, you two must be good friends."

Before Sedona, I wouldn't have described Jessie and me as friends. After the past few days, though, I felt connected to her.

"You girls help yourself to some cookies."

"Well," I said. "I'm supposed to be on a diet."

"Malley Florence O'Brien, you do not need to be on a diet."

Jessie grinned at me with a twinkle in her eye. Oh great, now she knew my middle name.

"I don't know why girls these days all want to be rail thin. What's wrong with a little meat on your bones?"

Jessie chimed in. "That's what I said. I told Malley she doesn't need to lose weight."

"All right, you two. You convinced me." Jessie and I both snatched a cookie and took a bite at the same time, moaning in unison as the sugary confection melted in our mouths.

"Oh. My. God." Jessie said with a mouthful. "This is the best thing I've ever tasted."

"Told you so," I said.

My mom smiled, obviously enjoying our compliments. "Well, you girls eat up. The doctor won't let me eat sugar so I can't have any."

"These are *so* going back with us." Jessie pulled the plate toward her.

"What's this about the doctor, mom? Are you sick? God, you're not diabetic, are you?"

"No, no, honey. I just need to cut down on the sweets. That's all. Don't you worry."

But I was worried, which didn't go unnoticed by Jessie. She looked at me with understanding eyes, as though instinctively knowing what I was thinking. My gaze followed my mom as she flitted around the kitchen, wondering if she was indeed okay, as she claimed.

"Jessie, has Malley made you her famous butterscotch cinnamon buns?"

"No. She hasn't. I forgot you promised to make me some." Jessie put her hands on her hips, pretending to be irritated.

"She and her grandma came up with the recipe when Malley was about ten years old. They never told a soul what the ingredients are."

"It was more Grandma's doing than mine. I have to admit, though, they are pretty amazing."

"Have you thought anymore about opening a bakery?" Mom asked.

"No, well, yes. I mean, it's not like it'll actually ever happen. It would be a crazy thing to do. I can't just quit my job and start a business I know nothing about."

"Why not?" Jessie asked.

"Because…it's irresponsible."

"You have that nest egg your father left you. He'd want you to use it for something that would make you happy."

"That money's for the future. I don't want to blow it on a pipe dream."

Jessie peered at me hard from across the table.

"So, Mom, is the creek dried up or did you get much rain this year?" I asked, changing the subject.

"Oh no, we got lots of rain. You should take Jessie out back and show her around the property while I clean up."

"Let us help," I offered.

"No, no, I'll be done in a minute."

Jessie and I grabbed a few more cookies and headed outside and down the path to the creek. Everything was vibrant green accented by bright-yellow wildflowers. Jessie bent down, picked a flower, and slipped it behind her ear. She looked like a Hawaiian princess. "Your mom's great," she said as we continued walking.

"Yeah, she's something else."

"How long has she lived here?"

"Only a few months. We've had this place since I was a teenager. It was our vacation home when we lived in Phoenix. My dad loved it here."

"I can see why. Is it hard being here with him gone?"

"Yeah." That damn lump in my throat again. When I didn't say anything further, Jessie took the hint that this particular topic of conversation was closed. We walked the remaining distance in silence until reaching the crystal-clear creek. Having the same idea, Jessie and I sat on a rock and took off our sandals, putting our feet in the cool water. Jessie inched closer until our shoulders were barely touching.

Having her near made my heart beat faster. I resisted the urge to put my arm around her shoulders. Warmth radiated through my heart as I recalled Jessie's arms protectively wrapped around me after I fell on the hike. She'd made me feel warm and safe.

I hated to admit it, but I'd grown to like Jessie. A lot. I didn't want to like her. I preferred it when I thought of her as a conceited, annoying womanizer. It was safer, and far less frightening, that way.

"Tell me what you like about baking," Jessie said.

I took a deep breath, contemplating the question. No one had ever asked me that before, and I found it difficult to put into words.

Jessie turned and looked at me as I gazed at the stream. "Malley?"

As I looked at Jessie, our eyes locked. We were sitting so close I could see gold specks in her green eyes. What was the question again? Oh yeah, baking. Reluctantly, I broke our gaze and returned my attention to the stream so I could concentrate on a response.

"It brings me joy. It's about creating a sweet, delectable, mouth-watering treat out of nothing. Do you know what I mean? When all these random ingredients are separate they have little meaning, but when combined in just the right order and amount, they come together to create something wonderful. This probably doesn't make any sense, does it?"

"No, it does. Go on." Jessie stared at my profile as I spoke.

"I think the joy really comes from seeing the delight on someone's face when they take that first bite. Their eyes get bigger, they stop breathing for a second, and I know in that moment I helped bring a little happiness into their lives. My grandmother used to say that baking opens the heart. Not only for the person devouring one of her cinnamon buns, but for her as well. God, that sounds corny."

"Not at all. It sounds wonderful."

Jessie continued to look at me, but I didn't dare turn my head and get lost in her gold-speckled green eyes.

❖

When Jessie and I got back to the cabin, my mom was relaxing on the couch in the living room. "How'd you like the creek?" she asked Jessie.

"It's beautiful. I could stay here forever."

"Well, you're welcome back any time."

"I might just take you up on that." And with just one wink and a killer smile, Jessie had my mom giggling like a teenager. Apparently, even she wasn't immune to Jessie's charms. Few women were.

Jessie looked around the cabin. "Where's the—"

"Bathroom?" I asked, reading her mind. "It's right through that door."

After Jessie disappeared, my mom jumped off the couch and pounced on me. "So are you and Jessie dating? What happened to Lizzie? I like Jessie, honey. She's good for you. I can tell you two really care about each other."

"We're just friends, Mom."

"No, no, it's more than that. A mother knows these things. I see the way you two look at each other. You belong together."

"That's not going to happen. Ever. It can't. And besides, we're just friends." I walked to the window, rubbing the drapes between my fingers. "Are these new curtains?"

"You're just like your father," my mom said with a chuckle.

"What do you mean?"

"If he didn't want to discuss something he'd change the subject."

"And would it work?"

"Not in the least. So, about you and Jessie..." My mom stopped when we heard the bathroom door open. I gave her a sly smile before excusing myself to the bathroom.

I could hear muffled voices through the door. It warmed my heart at how kind Jessie was being to my mom. Not that I expected anything less, but sometimes her gentleness surprised me.

When I came out of the bathroom, Jessie was in the living room looking at a photo of my dad. I knew exactly which one it was.

She looked at me, then back at the picture, and then at me again. "I didn't know your dad was a police officer."

"Oh yes," my mom said. "He looked so handsome in his uniform." She wistfully gazed at his police-academy photograph.

"Why didn't you tell me?" Jessie asked, her eyes filled with confusion and empathy.

"Just never came up." I shrugged like it was no big deal. "Like you didn't tell me Clarissa was your sister."

"That's not the same thing."

We stood in front of my dad's photograph for several uncomfortable minutes. Jessie glared at the photo, my mom's eyes misted over, and I desperately prayed that the subject of his death wouldn't be our next topic of conversation.

Breaking the tension, I wrapped my arm around my mom and walked her to the couch before disappearing into the kitchen to make us some tea.

"Do you need help?" Jessie's voice came from behind me.

"No, I'll just put some water on to boil. We don't have to stay much longer. I know you wanted to hike today."

"I've enjoyed myself. I like your mom a lot. Very different from mine. More...I don't know...domestic. More like I'd imagine a mother would be."

Jessie stood close behind me while I put a kettle on the stove. I could feel her breath on my neck.

"You know, Malley—"

"Look, Jessie, just let it go." It didn't take a psychic to know what she was about to say. "Let's just go and have a nice cup of tea with my mom. Okay?"

"Sure. I understand."

I could feel Jessie move away from me. I did a sideways glance to make sure she was gone before I allowed a tear to roll down my cheek.

CHAPTER EIGHTEEN

THE GRIM REAPER

Jessie asked the dreaded question, the one I always hated attempting to answer. We were almost asleep and she still hadn't mentioned anything about my dad being a cop. I thought I was in the clear.

"Malley? How'd your dad die?"

For several seconds, I considered faking sleep. Avoidance was usually my tactic anytime the question arose.

"It's late. Can't we talk about it another time?"

"I'd say yes if I thought you actually would."

She had me pegged. Knowing Jessie, she wouldn't let up. Now was as good a time as any to tell her. When it's pitch-black, where it's so much easier to open up.

"He was killed on duty. He and his partner stopped a guy for speeding. My dad approached the driver's side and his partner took the passenger side. The moment my dad walked up, the guy pulled out a gun and shot him between the eyes."

I did it. I told her. It was done. Spurting out the information like that wasn't as bad as I thought it would be. I was able to detach emotionally and focus on the facts. That's all she needed to know. Light filled the cabin as Jessie clicked on the lamp between us. I laid my arm over my eyes, attempting to block out the light...and Jessie.

"It's fine, Jessie. It was June third of last year, so over a year now." *So please turn off the light and go to sleep.*

I heard Jessie get up and felt the indention when she sat on my bed. Afraid to look at her, I kept my eyes closed, silently praying she'd leave me alone.

"Malley, I'm so sorry. I don't know what to say." Jessie's voice was quiet, almost a whisper. "It must have been devastating for you and your mom. I can't even imagine."

Acid bubbled in my stomach, up my esophagus, and into my throat, leaving a bitter taste in my mouth. Instinctively, I clinched the sheet. I felt a warm hand over my fist as Jessie lightly stroked my skin until I relaxed my grip.

"Please look at me." I allowed Jessie to lift my arm, which was still covering my eyes.

I took a deep breath before looking at the most beautiful, compassionate face I'd ever seen. The emotion in Jessie's eyes undid me. I couldn't hold back the hot tears that sprang to my eyes and rolled down my cheeks. Once I got started, I outdid Niagara Falls. A year of pent-up emotions gushed out all at once. I didn't even recognize the guttural howls as my own voice. Curling into a ball, Jessie lay beside me, embracing me. She didn't try to hush me or say that everything was going to be all right. All she did was hold me, which was exactly what I needed.

Just when I thought I was done crying, the faucet would turn on full blast again. Jessie tightened her grasp as I shuddered. I'm not sure how long I cried, not sure how long Jessie held me. Strangely, though, I didn't feel embarrassed. I didn't feel like a blubbering fool.

As the sorrow settled within me, the tears began to subside. I felt completely exhausted, like I'd just run a marathon. After a deep, shaky breath, I sat up in bed, and Jessie kept one arm protectively wrapped around my shoulders. I drew my knees up to my chest, hugging them.

"When my mom called, the minute I heard her voice, I knew. All she said was 'Malley, something happened,' and I knew. I realized my dad was gone."

I wanted someone other than my mom to know how I felt, what I went through. And I wanted that person to be Jessie.

"The world stopped spinning. It was my greatest fear come true. When I was eight years old my dad's partner was killed on duty. Ever since then I was terrified the same thing would happen to him. I lived in fear for so many years, waiting and expecting that call from my mom, and when it actually happened, it seemed surreal. It still doesn't seem real. It just feels like I haven't seen him in a really long time. It's hard to believe he's actually gone."

"Oh, baby, I'm so sorry." Jessie's eyes sparkled with tears as she pulled me into her arms, rocking me gently. She held me for several minutes before we lay back in the bed, with my head resting on her chest.

I never wanted her to let go. And she never did, as I fell into a deep sleep still in her embrace.

❖

My head was pounding something awful. My eyes felt like they were swollen shut and filled with sand. I rubbed my eyelids, trying to relieve the burning, itching sensation. My stomach churned with every painful throb in my temples. I felt like something was missing. It was the sensation of feeling exposed, unprotected. Then I remembered the night before. What was missing was Jessie's arms around me.

"Good morning," Jessie said. "I thought you might want some coffee." She handed me a cup as I sat up in bed.

"What time is it? It feels late."

"Almost ten. I thought you might need to sleep in a bit."

"Did you rest any?" I looked at Jessie over the rim of my coffee cup as I took a sip. She looked exhausted.

"I slept a little." Jessie sat on my bed and blew into a steaming cup of coffee, attempting to cool it.

"Jessie, about last night…thanks."

Jessie looked at me with tired green eyes, a slight grin on her lips. "You don't have to thank me. You can talk about your dad anytime you need to. I'll always listen and be there for you."

I gave her a weak smile, hoping my eyes conveyed how much last night had meant to me. I stared at Jessie's profile as she turned her attention back to her coffee. An array of emotions passed through me. Surprise, coupled with relief, that I had opened up to Jessie. An unexpected lightness emerged in my solar plexus where sorrow usually resided. But most of all, I felt a warmth radiating from my heart in appreciation for the woman sitting beside me.

Chapter Nineteen

Rumi Reincarnated

What in the world was I doing here? That's what I wondered during a morning meditation class. Lizzie was with her ex, I was stuck at a lesbian resort alone, and my plans were shot to hell. It wouldn't have been so bad if Lizzie hadn't said yes to dating me, if she hadn't kissed me or held my hand. If I hadn't felt like a couple.

The only good thing out of this was that Jessie and I had become friends. More than friends, really. After that kiss and then seeing her naked, I had to admit my thoughts were more of a carnal nature than about friendship. How could Lizzie do this to me? If she hadn't left with Heather then we'd be dating, and I wouldn't have to resort to meditation to try and get the image of Jessie's naked body out of my mind.

I wanted to throw something but resisted the urge to rip the round cushion out from under my numb butt and hurl it across the room. Not very Zen of me, I know. I pictured the cushion flying through the air like a UFO, crashing through the window and shattering glass everywhere, speeding down the highway and conking Heather right in her third eye. Hey, maybe I was good at this visualization stuff after all.

Opening one eye, I scanned peaceful faces. I could probably dance around naked and no one would notice. Everyone was in a deep trance with their eyes closed. I seemed to be the only rebel who ever dared peek. No Jessie in sight. Where was she and what was she doing? Maybe she'd go on a hike with me later. I'd barely seen her since my breakdown about my dad a few nights ago. I missed her.

Three chimes sounded. Thank you, sweet Jesus…or Buddha… or the devil even. Meditation class was over! I wandered back to the cabin, not feeling any more relaxed than I did before.

Clarissa poked her head into the cabin. "Hey, Malley, is Jessie here?"

"No, I haven't seen her all day. I don't know where she disappears to. What's all that?" Clarissa had an armful of books.

"I want to get Jessie to sign these."

"Why would you want Jessie to sign books?"

"I'm giving them as presents to some friends. I thought it would be a nice touch. It's her book," Clarissa said, as though that clarified things.

"*Her* book?" My lips pursed as I scrunched my eyebrows together.

"The one…wait, do you not know about this?" Clarissa handed me a book titled *The Seeker: Poems from the Soul*.

I was still confused until Clarissa turned the book over and I saw a photo of Jessie. Jessie was an author? Of poetry?

"I can't believe she didn't tell you about this." Clarissa shook her head. "How does she expect anyone to ever get to know her?" She said that last part more to herself than to me.

"Jessie writes poetry? And she's published?" It just seemed… so…weird, although it did explain what all that notebook writing was about.

"Ever since I can remember she wanted to be a writer. She's written short stories, essays, but mostly poetry. This is her first published book and I couldn't be prouder."

"I had no idea. Can I borrow a copy? I'd really like to read it."

"I'll do you better than that. You can have a copy. Listen, can I leave these here and she can sign them when she gets in? I don't want to lug them back to my cabin."

"Of course. And thanks for the book."

I walked to the pond still in a daze. Jessie…a poet? It just didn't seem to fit her. Sitting in the shade with my back against a ponderosa pine, I cracked open the book and read the dedication page: *To Rumi. My Inspiration.* Who the heck was Rumi? After I Googled the name on my phone I learned he was a thirteenth-century Persian poet considered to be a great spiritual master. Who knew?

I immersed myself in Jessie's book all afternoon. Not that it was a huge book, but I took my time reading each line, savoring the meaning of every word. I was more than impressed. The book was sensitive, romantic, and deep, the poems about love, beauty, and being one with everyone and everything. Poems about living from your soul, peace, and happiness. I adored each verse and couldn't help but adore the person who'd written every word my eyes feasted on. I was in awe.

Did Jessie have any other secrets?

❖

I couldn't wait to find Jessie to tell her I'd read her book and punch her arm for not telling me she was a published author. My excitement plummeted when I walked into a cozy scene in our cabin. Jessie was sitting at the table signing books with Nicole standing behind her, her arms wrapped around Jessie's neck, looking over her shoulder.

"What's up?" I said, raising an eyebrow. I still couldn't understand what Jessie saw in Nicole and why she let her hang all over her. I mean, weren't Nicole's polyester shirts itchy wrapped around Jessie's neck?

"Oh, Malley," Nicole said, looking terribly disappointed to see me. "We're signing Jessie's book." Okay, first of all Jessie was signing her books, not *they*, and Nicole said it in a way that made it sound like she'd known for years that Jessie was an author. "Did you know our Jessie is an author?"

"Yeah," I said. " I do now." I held up Jessie's book. "Clarissa gave me a copy. Why didn't you tell me?"

"I don't know," she said, looking embarrassed. "I didn't think you'd be interested."

"Why in the world would you think that? I loved reading it. It was beautiful." Jessie and I looked at each other until I turned and walked out of the cabin.

Later that night, when Jessie and I were in our respective beds, I lay awake, unable to sleep.

"Malley, are you awake?"

"Yeah."

"It's not that I didn't want to tell you about my writing. It's just…I don't know. It's just so personal, you know? My heart and soul are in those poems. It makes me feel…exposed, you know?"

I did know.

"I understand. But I'd hope by now you think of us as friends. You can trust me."

"I know. Good night, O'Brien."

"Good night, Jessie."

CHAPTER TWENTY

BED, SHOWER AND BEYOND

I was standing as stiff as a Buckingham Palace guard, not wanting to budge until Lizzie gave me a straight answer. I stood in the middle of the cabin, the phone pressed tightly against my ear.

"Are you getting back together with Heather?" My voice commanding, strong.

"I need to make sure, Malley."

"Is that a yes? I want a simple yes or no."

"I need some more time."

"I can't talk to you anymore. I care about you, but I don't want to hear from you until you know what you want." I heard a sharp intake of breath on the other end of the line. I was being harsh, but I was beyond tired of this. "Good-bye, Lizzie."

I clenched the phone in my hand. Winding up my arm I slung it in a pitch any rookie ballplayer would be proud of. Luckily, it only bounced off the bed and onto the floor rather than crashing into the wall.

I stared at my phone for several seconds before I walked across the room, picked it up, and plopped down on my bed. Deflated. Abandoned. That's how I felt. Like someone had let all the air out of my balloon. I was also thinking logistics. The retreat ended in a week. How would I get home if Lizzie got back together with Heather? She was my ride. No way in hell would I sit in a car with her for eight hours back to LA.

The thought made me incredibly sad. As much as I wanted to date Lizzie, our friendship would suffer. We'd had so much fun together on the road trip to Sedona, laughing and talking until we were hoarse. The thought of not even wanting to be in the same car with her broke my heart. I regretted asking her to date. If I'd just held off a few days I could have continued secretly worshipping her. She wouldn't have had a clue, and I'd still have my best friend.

I sat on my bed in the same position for God knows how long after I hung up with Lizzie. With no lights on in the cabin, it was quickly getting dark. Jessie would probably be back any moment.

"Why are you sitting in the dark?" Jessie flipped on the light as she walked into the cabin. "Malley? Are you okay?" When I didn't answer, she sat beside me on the bed. "Did something happen?"

"I think Lizzie and Heather are back together." I stared straight ahead, fixing my eyes on a knot in the pine wood paneling.

"I'm sorry."

"I think I just lost my best friend." Verbalizing that statement immediately brought tears to my eyes. I licked my lips and tasted salt. I couldn't believe I was crying in front of Jessie again. She'd think I was a blubbering fool.

"Come here," Jessie said, putting her arm around me. "Things have a way of working out. You and Lizzie care about each other. Try not to worry." Jessie moved a strand of hair from my face and looked at me.

"What is it with you?" I said through a forced laugh. "I never cry in front of anyone, but here I've done it twice now."

Jessie lifted my chin so we were eye to eye and gazed at me with such tenderness it warmed my heart. "Your eyes are so beautiful, Malley. I could drown in them."

The compliment was sudden and unexpected. I wanted to tell her my eyes could never compare to her jade ones, but I couldn't form intelligible words. My mind was mush with Jessie so close.

Everything in the room disappeared except for her green eyes. She gazed at me like she actually *was* drowning, just as I was in hers. Normally, I'd feel uncomfortable with someone inches away from my face, staring right at me. But this wasn't just someone. It was Jessie.

"It hurts me to see you cry, but when you do, your eyes look like crystal-clear blue lakes. I could just…drown in them. Did I already say that? I need to…"

I must have been expecting it, or maybe wishing, because I wasn't surprised when Jessie leaned closer and kissed me. The kiss was tentative at first, as though she was making sure she had my permission. Wanting more of her, I pressed my mouth harder against hers, slowly slipping my tongue between her lips. She moaned and laid me back on the bed. I had a sense of déjà vu followed by a sudden fear. This was the position we were in when Jessie halted our first kiss. I'd die if that happened again. I needed to let her know I wanted more, even at the risk of sounding like a cheap romance novel.

"Jessie," I whispered. "Don't stop." A shiver ran through me when she stopped kissing me and looked into my eyes.

"I'll do anything you want. Anything."

Jessie's warm lips were on my neck, kissing their way down to my chest, making me breathe heavily. Was it possible to have a heart attack from kissing alone? How embarrassing would that be? Jessie lifted my shirt and nibbled on my breast through my bra. Easily finding my erect nipple she sucked on it through the material. I desperately wanted to feel her lips on my skin, so I unhooked my bra and tossed it aside. Her tongue played with my nipple, causing a pulsating sensation between my legs. Thinking I could have an orgasm simply from her feasting on my breasts, I pulled her up to me, kissing her hard.

I wanted to feel Jessie's skin against mine, so I lifted her shirt over her head, pleased to see she wasn't wearing a bra. Rolling her over, I covered her body like a blanket, feeling her breasts pressed against mine. As much as I loved being melded together, I wanted to see Jessie, all of her. As I lifted myself from her, I drank in the most beautiful sight. Even though I'd seen her naked coming out of the shower, nothing compared to an up-close view. I gazed from her sultry eyes to her breasts, and lower to her toned stomach. Wanting to see more, I unbuttoned her shorts, lowered the zipper, and slipped them off. I ran my fingertips lightly over her satin panties, which were wet. I felt dizzy just imagining how warm and soft Jessie would feel deep inside. Kissing her breasts, I flicked my tongue against her nipples, which hardened instantly. Slowly, I slipped my fingers underneath her panty line, lightly stroking her soaked, trimmed hair.

"God, Malley, you're driving me crazy. Touch me," Jessie said.

"Like this?" I fondled her slick lips, barely entering her, teasing her with my touch.

"Deeper." She was practically begging.

Two fingers easily entered as I moved them slowly in and out. Jessie was so hot and I was so incredibly turned on. More than I'd ever been with any other woman.

"Take your shorts off," she demanded. "I want to feel you against me."

I did as ordered, removing my panties as well, feeling the wetness on my inner thighs. Jessie's hands slid down my back and around to touch my swollen lips. "You're so wet," she said.

"I want us to come at the same time."

I'd never done this before. It was always an I-do-her, she-does-me sort of thing. Pushing deeper inside of Jessie, I found her engorged clit with my thumb and could actually feel it throbbing against my fingers. Her hips undulated to meet my touch as I traced circles around and around. Jessie reached underneath me and lightly rolled my clit between two fingers, which drove me wild.

"Oh baby, I'm so close," I said. The chills that always preceded an orgasm coursed through my body.

On the edge herself, Jessie grabbed me hard as she became rigid and shuddered. Jessie's excitement, coupled with her caresses completely set me off. Every nerve in my body exploded. We held each other tight as we both climaxed at the same glorious moment. Both panting hard, we collapsed, still in each other's arms.

❖

Something was wrapped around me, like a warm, comforting quilt. Except it wasn't a quilt. I felt an arm draped over my shoulder as I clutched a hand pressed to my breast. Jessie. Memories of the night before flooded back. Kisses. Caresses. Orgasms. Multiple orgasms. Jessie and I had sex. Actually, that sounded crude for what we'd shared. It hadn't felt like sex just for the sake of getting each other off. It was more than that. We'd connected.

The more I woke up and began thinking clearly, the more fearful I became. What if Jessie thought last night was a mistake like our first kiss? What if she regretted sleeping with me? I stiffened as she moved behind me. I'd find out soon enough.

"Malley?"

Oh God, she doesn't remember who she slept with. I didn't respond. More movement. I felt a light kiss on my bare shoulder. Okay, that was a positive sign. Kisses are usually a good thing.

"Are you awake?" she asked.

"Barely." Reaching behind me, I caressed her naked hip. My stomach soured, afraid of what Jessie might say next. If she regretted sleeping with me, I'd have to play it cool no matter what I felt otherwise. Finally mustering the courage, I rolled over and was greeted by gorgeous green eyes.

Jessie kissed me lightly on the lips. "Morning," she said.

"You look absolutely adorable in the morning." I kissed her forehead, her right cheek, her left cheek, and then her lips.

Looking into her eyes, I saw a flash of something, a realization of where she was and what we'd done. I had a good ten minutes of awake time on her to grasp the reality of the situation, whereas it was just hitting her. I backed away a bit to give her some space.

"Are you okay?" I asked.

"Yeah." Jessie ran her fingers through her hair. "Are you?"

"Actually…I'm better than okay." There it was. I put it out there. A slow smile crept onto her face. "Yeah. Me, too."

Jessie pulled me close and kissed me in a way that instantly made me wet. We spent the morning exploring every inch of each other—touching, tasting, moving in rhythm as our bodies paired together perfectly. Slowly and deliberately, Jessie brought me to the brink over and over without allowing release. Teasing me with her touch—her tongue—until I begged for relief. I was completely at her mercy.

After many blissfully torturous caresses, Jessie quickened her touch where I craved it most until I screamed out in pleasure. The delayed gratification made for the most powerful orgasm I'd ever had. It left me in a sweat-drenched ecstatic exhaustion, completely fulfilled, lying in her arms. Jessie rained tender kisses all over my body as I lay helpless, unable to utter a word.

"You are so sexy." Jessie said it in a way that actually made me believe her.

I gave her a sensual kiss, which I hoped conveyed the passion I felt in that moment. Finally breaking apart, we collapsed back on the bed, breathing heavily. As we turned toward each other, we said in unison, "Wow," then giggled. Was this the best night and morning *ever*?

"The only thing that could possibly get me out of this bed is a growling stomach," Jessie said as she cupped one of my breasts with her palm.

"If you keep touching me like that I'll never let you go. But as much as I hate to admit it, I'm starving, too."

"How about we shower? Together?" Jessie wiggled her eyebrows in the cutest flirt I'd ever seen.

"Oooh, another first," I replied.

"Another first?"

"I've never taken a shower with anyone. And well…I never had an orgasm at the same time with a woman before. I've always wanted to experience that with someone."

Jessie flashed a sexy smile and pulled me closer. "And we did. Over and over again." She gently kissed my neck before moving to my lips.

After being thoroughly kissed, I reluctantly suggested we get up. I snatched my T-shirt, which was draped over the lamp, and pulled it over my head as Jessie grabbed my arm.

"What are you doing? I thought we were going to, you know, take a shower."

"We are," I replied.

"Then why are you putting your shirt on?"

Parading around naked wasn't something I'd ever felt comfortable doing, and certainly not in front of anyone. It's not like I was a prude when it came to being nude when having sex, but walking around in broad daylight in my birthday suit? No thank you.

"I'm just putting my shirt on. I'll take it off in there." I pointed to the bathroom. Jessie lifted my shirt up and over my head. I felt suddenly exposed, which I know sounds weird since she'd just seen and touched every part of my body.

"Malley, you're beautiful. Don't you know that?" Jessie looked up at me as I stood by the bed, resisting the urge to cover my breasts.

No, I guess I didn't know that. Jessie looked so sincere, and what she said pierced my heart in a way she'd never understand. I'd battled body-image issues the last several years after gaining weight, but even before that I never would have described myself as beautiful. But here, as I stood completely exposed in front of this gorgeous woman, I felt more beautiful than I ever had.

Jessie sat up on her knees in the bed and gently kissed me. "I believe you promised me a shower," she said.

As we stood under the warm spray, stimulating each other with slippery, soapy hands, I wondered what the Guinness World Record was for the most orgasms in a twelve-hour period. I wasn't sure, but I'd bet a million dollars Jessie and I were well on our way to breaking it.

CHAPTER TWENTY-ONE

BELL ROCK BIRTHDAY WISH

I'd never felt so light on my feet, especially while hiking uphill. I could have practically skipped up Bell Rock. And I was downright giddy. My insides were quivering with excitement. I attributed this to having hot sex all night and well into the morning, although I couldn't remember ever feeling this energized after sex before.

I resisted the urge to analyze sleeping with Jessie, but I had a million questions. Was it a one-night stand, would we do it again, should I feel guilty about Lizzie, does this make me a cheater, and if I held Jessie's hand right now would she pull away? I pushed all those questions out of my mind, trying to milk the hot-sex afterglow for as long as I possibly could.

Bell Rock, 550 feet tall, is a sandstone rock formation aptly named since it's shaped like a bell. Neither Jessie nor I had ever climbed to the top, so we thought we'd put all this excess energy to good use. The first part of the hike was steep, and we had to use our hands to grab ahold of jutting rocks to avoid falling backward. Frequently, small pebbles from above would rain down on us.

This was by far the most treacherous hike I'd ever done. At one point, we considered turning back since it didn't look like we were on a clearly marked path, but we'd gone so far already and were determined to get to the top. Needing to take a breather, we stopped and took swigs of water.

"Why do people do that?" I pointed to a perfectly balanced stack of about ten small sandstone rocks, one on top of the other. I'd noticed impromptu piles of these rocks on hiking trails all around Sedona.

"They're called cairns. Some people erect them to mark the trail. Others build them as a symbol of something, like balance, or sometimes as a memorial to someone or something." Jessie handed me a rock. "Here. Make your own."

I scoured around and gathered a handful of rocks, which I precariously balanced one on top of another. The last rock was a small triangle, which I carefully placed on the tip of another rock. Jessie must have sensed I was in my own little world as I erected my cairn. She didn't disturb me or try to coax me into telling her what it represented. Grabbing my cell phone to snap a picture of the cairn, I saw a text from Lizzie. I snapped the photo and stuck my phone into my backpack without reading it.

Jessie and I did it. Although we were dirty, sweaty, and exhausted, we were standing at the summit of Bell Rock. As with all views in Sedona, this one didn't disappoint. A sea of bright crimson and pink soaring rock formations stretched as far as we could see. Sedona always took my breath away. Weary from the rigorous climb, Jessie and I rested side by side on a flat sandstone rock. I lay back and put my hands behind my head, feeling the warmth of the hard surface beneath me. The cloudless sky was a rich cobalt blue.

"Is this one of those vortex sites?" I asked. We couldn't drive fifty feet in Sedona without seeing a sign about vortexes. Supposedly, there were four power locations, with the Kachina Woman being one of them. "What exactly is a vortex anyway?"

"It's energy. Some people think Sedona has certain vortexes, with Bell Rock being one of them, but I think all of Sedona is one giant vortex. It's a magical place that vibrates with energy." There was that word magical again. The guy in the ghost town had said the same thing.

"What are people supposed to do on a vortex? Since we're sitting on one, after all."

"Different things," Jessie said. "You can meditate, pray, or hold a ceremony. Whatever you want to do to connect with nature or the universe or whatever you believe."

"How do you know about all this stuff?"

"As I said before, my parents were New Age hippies. I guess I picked up more from them than I thought. I'm not religious, but you could say I'm spiritual."

"So what do people do when they have a ceremony?" I sat up so we were face-to-face.

"We could do one, if you'd like."

"Uhh, we aren't going to slit our writs and become blood brothers or anything, are we?" I asked, halfway kidding.

"No." She was smiling. "I thought about this before we left and put some sage in my bag. If you want, we could light it and dedicate a ceremony to something we want to manifest."

Jessie seemed to be treading lightly, not sure how I'd take all this sage-ceremony stuff. Sedona must have been rubbing off on me, because surprisingly I was interested in giving it a try. Jessie took out a match and lit a bundle of sage, the wind swirling the smoke around us.

"What do we do now?" I asked.

"Think of something you want to manifest into your life. It can be anything. Visualize it and then mentally place that image inside the smoke that's surrounding us and allow the sage to carry your wish to the universe. The key is to let it go and not try to control how it'll come about. Trust."

"That's a hard one for me," I said.

"I know."

Normally I would have taken offense to that response, but Jessie hadn't said it in a nasty way.

"I don't have to tell you what I want to manifest, do I? It's like a birthday wish, right? It won't come true if I tell?"

"That's right," Jessie said with a chuckle. "It's like a birthday wish."

It didn't take much pondering for me to know what I wanted to manifest. I wanted to be in love and to be loved. I wanted a partner. That's what I visualized and was surprised to find that I didn't put an image of Lizzie in the smoke.

I'd yearned for her for almost a year, been obsessed with her to the point of completely disregarding the possibility of being with anyone else. I didn't know what the future held for us, but if we weren't meant to be together, I would let her go.

Wow, I sounded freaking healthy. I opened my eyes and looked at Jessie, who was still lost in her own visualization. What did she want to manifest, what was she thinking? I desperately wanted to know her birthday wish.

CHAPTER TWENTY-TWO

TWO TIMES THE CHARM

Any questions I had about whether Jessie and I would sleep together again were answered the moment we stepped into the cabin. Wrapping her arms around my waist, she pulled me close.

"I know we're both filthy and smell like red dirt, but it's been killing me all day not to do this." As Jessie kissed me lightly, my stomach turned upside down and inside out. How could she do that with one kiss? We walked together, still entwined in each other's arms, to the shower, where we had a repeat performance of our time together that morning.

"Do you remember when I walked in on you coming out of the shower?" Jessie and I were lying in bed that night, my head resting on her chest.

"Of course. How could I forget?"

"Well, I never forgot," I said. "That image of you stayed with me. You looked so sexy."

"I couldn't forget the way you looked at me. It was like you were almost pleading for me to walk toward you."

Raising my head, I gazed into Jessie's beautiful eyes before pressing my lips against hers. I didn't think it was possible to feel more wanted and cared for as I did the first time Jessie and I slept together, but I did now. Her touch was gentle when and where I needed it most, mixed with wild abandon when our desires heightened. Several times Jessie told me how beautiful I was. And slowly, I was beginning to believe her.

❖

There was no question about it. Clarissa knew. She'd walked up to the screen door the next morning when Jessie and I were coming out of the bathroom. Luckily we weren't naked. With us, there was no guarantee of that. I had my arm around Jessie's waist, and we were giggling as she nibbled on my ear. Clarissa's jaw dropped.

"Ah, hi," Jessie said.

"Hi," I said too.

"Hello?" Clarissa responded as she opened the screen door. As if the scene was finally registering, she smiled broadly and clasped her hands together. "You two?" Rushing into the cabin, she embraced us in a group hug that nearly knocked Jessie and me over. "I'm so happy for you both! I was hoping, but I had no idea!"

"Wait," Jessie said, trying to break free. "We're not…I mean, I'm not sure…" She looked at me helplessly.

Not having analyzed anything yet, I wasn't sure what to say. Luckily, Clarissa was too excited to let us utter a word.

"Oh my God, I'm horrible for bursting in like this. But you've been MIA for a couple of days, so I wanted to check on you and invite you two to a concert tonight. And oh my gosh, I just had no idea. Listen, I'll get out of your way. I'm not one of those intrusive sisters. So you two continue with what you were doing. Just let me know later if you're interested in the concert." Clarissa kissed my cheek and then Jessie's before practically running out the door.

Several moments passed as we stood stiffly, staring at the screen door after it had slammed shut.

"Sooo," Jessie said.

"Yeah, right, sisters, huh?"

"She, you know, thinks we're a couple," Jessie said, still staring at the door.

"That's what she thinks all right."

Jessie turned to face me. "And what do you think?"

"I don't know. I mean, everything was…wow…just there, you know? And then we…well, you know. And with everything else going on…" Okay, that made absolutely no sense whatsoever.

"Maybe we shouldn't analyze it. Just go with the flow and take things as they come."

Okay, that made sense.

"Yeah, maybe." It wasn't easy for me not to analyze. Typically, I'd have my laptop out, well on my way to listing the pros and cons of sleeping with Jessie in an Excel spreadsheet entitled "What the hell did I just do?"

Speaking of which, what the hell *did* I just do? Jessie was a cop. I could never date a police officer. Not after losing my dad. That was totally out of the question. So I guess this was a fling? I'd never had a one-night stand, or I guess this would be a two-night stand, but I didn't see anything inherently wrong with doing so. But weren't Lizzie and I technically still dating? She didn't actually break up with me. Or did she? So many unanswered questions.

"I don't regret the past two nights, Jessie. It was amazing." I meant it, and it was important to me that she know that.

"It was amazing," she said. I wanted to kiss her but wasn't sure if I should. Things between us felt a little awkward.

"I'll talk to Clarissa, so she doesn't get carried away. Wouldn't want her to start planning our wedding just yet," Jessie said with a nervous chuckle.

"Like I'd let Clarissa plan our wedding. No one likes a vegan wedding cake."

Jessie smiled and gave me a squeeze before walking into the kitchen for a bottled water.

I followed her, leaning against the counter. "What would you like to do today?" I asked.

Jessie peered over her water bottle and wiggled her eyebrows in a suggestive manner.

Just that one gesture caused my face to flush. "I do like the way you think, Officer Barnett."

Chapter Twenty-three

Sex, Lies, and Mandalas

I couldn't take my eyes off it. Staring into the huge mandala mural, I felt like Alice in Wonderland falling down the rabbit hole. It sucked me in, swallowing me whole. Vibrant, swirling reds and greens encircled a yin/yang, which had a flaming red heart with wings in the center. Countless rainbow-colored butterflies flitted within and around the circle. When Jessie looked at me, I had to make a conscious effort to peel my eyes away from the mural. She appeared just as moved as I was.

The mural was painted on the side of The Spirit Soundstage, which was a small purple building at the edge of a cliff overlooking Sedona. Dominic, a guy Clarissa was dating, owned it. She'd invited Jessie and me to attend a New Age concert by an artist named Satori, which I was fairly certain wasn't her real name. Clarissa headed inside to find us three seats while Jessie and I studied the mandala.

"What do you think it means?" Jessie asked. The heart in the center reminded me of the heart-shaped rock the Indian at Boynton Canyon had given me, but I didn't want to get into all that.

Jessie slipped her arm around my waist. "I think it's about freedom. Releasing your heart and letting it fly where it's meant to be. That's the only place where you can find true happiness and balance."

Warmth radiated from my solar plexus to my heart. I wasn't sure if that was because of the mural or Jessie's touch.

"Dominic painted it."

"Seriously? Clarissa's boyfriend? It's amazing. Absolutely beautiful."

"Yes, it is beautiful," Jessie said, looking right at me.

I smiled and kissed her lightly. Just that one action sent my heart soaring—with wings and all.

The venue consisted of a stage facing fifty seats. Connected to the building was a community center where Clarissa said a reception would be held after the concert. Hopefully, I'd get to meet the man who painted the mandala.

I wasn't sure what to expect. New Age music conjured images of a woman in an incense haze, sitting in lotus position while chanting. Not exactly my kind of thing. When Satori walked onstage looking like the Zodiac Goddess of the Universe in a royal-blue flowing gown sprinkled with the twelve astrological signs, I wondered if this was destined to be the longest night of my life. But once she started singing, it wasn't half bad. Granted, one entire song had only four words, and I had no idea what language they were, but I loved her voice. It was simple with a smooth, crisp quality that pulled me in.

"This is the Gayatria Mantra. It's Sanskrit," Jessie whispered in my ear. She stayed close, as though she was going to say something else. I inhaled the scent of lavender, making a mental note to ask Jessie later what perfume she used, if any. Her warm breath tickled my skin, and just the nearness of her made my breathing shallow. Jessie moved closer, expertly nibbling my earlobe, which sent shivers down my spine. She lightly grazed her lips on my neck before pulling away, leaving a scent of lavender hanging in the air.

I don't think she had any idea what she did to me. I put my hand on Jessie's knee and slowly ran my fingers up her thigh. She was wearing low-riding jeans that fit her body perfectly, along with a white shirt that buttoned up the front. The thought of ripping her shirt open later that night, knowing what I would find underneath, made me dizzy.

With my hand resting on her leg, I lazily traced circles with my fingertips inside her thigh. Around and around. Her breathing increased as her chest rose and fell quickly. Feeling completely satisfied that I'd affected her as much as she did me, I grazed her thigh once more before placing my hands back in my lap. When Jessie turned to look at me, she had such longing in her eyes it took all I had not to kneel in front of her right there.

After the concert everyone piled into the reception hall, mingling and socializing. When Jessie went to get us a glass of wine, Clarissa pounced on me like a monkey on a banana.

"So, are you and Jessie dating?"

I squirmed, feeling suddenly hot and itchy. Clarissa had a way of backing you into a corner, her face inches away from yours, and never breaking eye contact. God, I don't think the woman even blinked. Intense stares must run in the family.

"No, I mean, I dunno. I'm not sure. We're going with the flow."

"But you like her, right?"

"Of course. Jessie is…she's amazing."

"That's good." Clarissa looked relieved. "Jessie really cares about you, Malley. She doesn't always show her feelings, but you mean a lot to her. I don't want to see her get hurt."

"I would never hurt Jessie. Not purposefully. Not for anything in the world."

Just the thought of doing so made my stomach sour. Maybe I did need to analyze this situation after all. I'd never gone with the flow with anything in my life before. What made me think I could do it now?

"Here we are," Jessie said. She handed Clarissa and me each a glass of red wine.

"What should we toast to?" Clarissa held her glass in the air. Before we could answer, she said, "Love. Let's toast to love." Clarissa peered at Jessie and me over her glass. Maybe she was planning our wedding after all.

"I'd love to meet Dominic," I said.

"He has to play host at these events, but we should be able to steal him for a minute." Clarissa glanced around the room. "There he is." They made eye contact as Clarissa waved him toward us. "For someone who owns a New Age center and puts on events, he actually dislikes crowds and entertaining. He'd much rather be in the background or locked away painting all day."

A stout, chubby Italian approached us. He was balding, with laugh lines at the corners of his dark, sparkling eyes. If I'd passed him on the street, I would have thought he looked like a nice guy, with no clue as to how talented he really was. But ever since that Circle of Enlightenment, I looked at people differently when first meeting them. I wasn't so quick to judge, knowing they had a lot more under the surface.

"Hello, darling," he said. Dominic planted a light kiss on Clarissa's cheek.

"I'd like you to meet Malley, and of course you know Jessie."

Dominic grabbed me in an embrace. Normally, that would have felt intrusive coming from a stranger, but for some reason it felt natural. He then wrapped his arms around Jessie in a tight hug.

"It's so good of you to come, and so wonderful to meet a new friend. Did you enjoy the concert?"

"Oh yes," we all said in unison.

"Jessie tells me you're the artist who painted the mural on the outside of the building," I said.

"You like?" he asked.

"I love it. It touched me very much."

"Well, I have some—"

"The singer was wonderful tonight, Dominic. She had a beautiful voice." Jessie cut him off, which seemed a little rude.

"We were lucky to get Satori. She's very popular."

Clarissa clinked her ring against her wineglass and cleared her throat, seemingly demanding our attention. Dominic beamed as he slipped his arm around her waist.

"Since my love here can't make it to dinner with us, we would like to make an announcement." They gazed at one another with the sweetest of smiles.

"An announcement?" Jessie said. She raised an eyebrow, with a slight grin.

"How would you, little sister, like to be a bridesmaid?"

It took a couple of seconds before Jessie let out a whoop and flung her arms around both Clarissa and Dominic.

"Are you serious?" Jessie's eyes came alive. God, she was adorable when she was excited.

"She finally roped me in," Dominic said. He kissed Clarissa on the cheek.

"Congratulations! That's so awesome. When's the wedding?" Jessie asked.

"October first, and you better be here."

"October? That's only three and a half months away! I wouldn't miss it for anything." Jessie gave Clarissa another hug.

"Congratulations, you two. I'm very happy for you," I said.

"Malley, we'd love for you to come as well," Clarissa said.

"Well, I'll see what I have going on then. Thank you for the invitation." Three months was a long way away. Would I be with Lizzie? Jessie and I wouldn't be together, since she wasn't someone I could ever date. I should probably sit down and analyze this situation before one of us got hurt. The thing, though, was that I was afraid to analyze. I might decide to end this affair—or whatever it was—with Jessie, and the thought of doing so made me incredibly sad.

We continued talking, celebrating, and making toasts until Dominic had to get back to his other guests. I was beginning to feel a little tipsy from the wine since I never drank, so I was glad when we left for the restaurant.

Clarissa took us to a quaint café with a beautiful view of Cathedral Rock through a wide bay window. I'd never look at Cathedral Rock again and not think of being wrapped in Jessie's arms in the rain. We had the best garlic bread doused in butter and meatless lasagna I'd ever eaten. I seemed to have abandoned counting Weight Watchers points and surprisingly lost a few pounds in the process. Maybe Jessie was right about letting go and trusting. I'd been so obsessed about counting points that it seemed to have a counterproductive effect. I made a mental note to delete the app from my cell phone when we got back to the cabin.

"Malley, there's something I need to come clean about." Clarissa was suddenly serious, which piqued my interest.

"What is it?" I asked.

"Well, this was terrible of me. I've never done anything like it before." I looked at Jessie, who shrugged. "I may have...well, no...I did...sort of rig it so you and Jessie roomed together."

"Clarissa, wait." Jessie held up her hand.

"What do you mean?" I asked.

"The two number-seven keys weren't exactly random when it came to you two. I purposefully put you and Jessie together. I'm sorry. That was wrong of me."

"I don't understand," I said. "Why would you do that?"

Clarissa looked at Jessie, who appeared to be very uncomfortable. "Maybe I shouldn't have said anything," Clarissa said. "I should just keep my big mouth shut is what I should do."

"Wait a second. Did you know about this?" I asked Jessie, who was busy fumbling with her napkin.

"It's not Jessie's fault. It was all my idea," Clarissa said quickly.

I turned and faced Jessie directly. "Did you know?"

"Yes, but not at first."

"When?" My anger was rising.

"Right after we both got the keys. It was too late then."

"It wasn't too late. I asked you that night if you'd switch rooms with Lizzie, and you said no because of Clarissa's rules, but there were no rules. You lied." My last two words hung in the air. We were all silent, unsure of what to say.

"I think we should go," I said. "It's been a long day." I pushed my chair back forcefully and headed to the front door.

The tension in the car was palpable. No one said a word all the way back to the lodge. Clarissa was visibly shaken and probably feeling horrible that she'd mentioned anything. But she wasn't the one I was angry with. It was Jessie. I glared at the back of her head from the backseat, hoping she could feel the heat of my anger.

As we pulled up to the lodge I thanked Clarissa for dinner before bolting out of the car and heading to the cabin. Jessie walked in about ten minutes later.

"Listen," she said.

"No, you listen. You outright lied to me, Jessie. How could you do that? Why would you do that? One thing I can't tolerate is lying. You knew I'd come to Sedona to spend time with Lizzie."

Jessie flinched. I grabbed my toothbrush and PJs and headed for the door. Just as I swung it open, Nicole was standing on the porch about to knock.

"She's all yours," I said.

"Malley, wait. Where are you going?"

"Out!" I dashed past Nicole and bolted off the porch. Where *was* I going? I hadn't thought it through that far. All I knew was that I wasn't sleeping in the same room, or especially the same bed, as Jessie. So I went to the only place I knew that had an empty bed.

"Do you have any idea what time it is?" Rhonda said. She rubbed her eyes and yawned.

"Yes, it's late, and I'm tired and I need a bed to sleep in." As I strong-armed my way through the door, Rhonda stood and stared at me. "Look, I know Lizzie isn't here and I need someplace to sleep for the night, so sorry, but you're stuck with me."

Rhonda's eyebrows shot up and she flashed a grin. "Ahhh, so you want to spend the night with *moi*?"

"Settle down there, Tex. It's not like that. I just want to sleep."

"Lovers' quarrel?"

"Listen, I don't mean to be rude, but it's been a long day and I just want to fall into bed. Alone."

Rhonda shrugged, went back to bed, and was snoring within five minutes. But sleep didn't come easily for me. It's hard to sleep when your mind is raging. As furious as I was at Jessie, I was even angrier at myself. Angry for the empty ache I felt inside as I lay alone in bed, yearning to be wrapped in Jessie's arms.

I felt incredibly guilty being in Lizzie's bed and not even thinking about her. I did miss her. I missed talking to her, laughing, and having fun. How did things get so off track in such a short time? What was I even doing with Jessie? I'd vowed never to date a cop and here I was sleeping with one. I could never live with the constant fear of waiting for that phone call, the one that said my girlfriend was in the hospital...or worse.

Maybe it was good I found out Jessie had lied. It was the perfect excuse to cut her off. And maybe if I stayed angry, the ache in my heart would dissipate. At that moment, I vowed never to sleep with Jessie again.

❖

I felt like the weird kid no one wanted to eat lunch with. Glancing around the dining hall, I searched for a familiar, friendly face. Guess I hadn't exactly made an attempt to make friends. I'd barely spoken to half these women. I plopped down next to two chicks who were obviously a couple because they were deeply enthralled in a conversation. My heart clenched when Jessie walked in. Our eyes locked. As she approached me, I placed my backpack in the empty chair next to me.

"Can I sit here?" she asked.

"I'm saving it for someone." I lied.

"Malley, can we go somewhere and talk?"

"I have a packed schedule today, Jessie." I pushed the scrambled tofu around on my plate. Jessie sighed and walked away. I know I wasn't being very mature. Sophomoric, even, but I needed to get my head on straight, and being around Jessie wasn't the way to do it.

Yoga. That's what I needed. Even though I'd never done it before, I was in relatively good condition, somewhat flexible, and

I looked great in yoga pants. After only one pose, though, I had horrifying flashbacks of playing Twister. I was so uncoordinated I'd fall over after two minutes into the game of trying to put my left foot on yellow and my right hand on blue. And what made yoga class even worse was that Jessie was right in front of me and looked ten times better in her yoga pants than I did. Damn her. I almost quit and walked out of class several times, but I didn't want to give Jessie the satisfaction of thinking that having her near me affected me in the least. Even though it did.

After class, Jessie grabbed my wrist and pulled me outside.

"Hey, where are you taking me?"

She didn't say a word but continued to drag me all the way to the pond.

"Sit," she demanded, pointing to the bench.

"I'll stand, thank you."

"Suit yourself. Malley, I have something to say and you're going to listen."

"I don't—"

"You were right."

Okay, she had my attention. I sat on the bench and listened.

"I lied. I'm sorry. I knew Clarissa had rigged the cabins so we'd be together, and I lied about why I didn't want to switch rooms." Jessie paused. When I didn't respond she asked, "Don't you want to know why?"

"There's never a good reason to lie, Jessie."

"I did it because…because I wanted to be with you." She sat down beside me. "I wanted to get to know you better. I wanted us to get closer. I did it because…I care about you."

"Oh," I said, softening considerably. "That's actually sweet. You care about me?"

"I have for a long time now."

"You still should have told me the truth."

"Would you have been my roommate if I had?"

We both knew the answer to that.

"No, I suppose not. But I didn't know you as well then. If you were to ask me now, I might have a different response."

"Malley, would you like to be my roommate?"

I knew I should say no. Nothing good could possibly come out of sleeping with Jessie again. But the tender, vulnerable look in her eyes caused the words to tumble out of my mouth before I could stop them.

"More than anything." Frightening how much I meant that. "But…what are we doing? We're going home in four days. What happens then? And I don't even know if I'm still dating Lizzie. I feel like I'm cheating on her."

"You're not cheating. She left. She's with her ex-girlfriend."

"I know, but things have gotten so confusing. It scares me." I stared down at my tightly clasped hands.

Jessie turned my face to meet her gaze. "What scares you?"

"I can't date you, Jessie. I can't ever be with a police officer. Not after my dad. I couldn't live with the constant fear of worrying about you. I couldn't. I just couldn't."

"I know, baby," Jessie said, pulling me into her arms. "Malley, I don't know what I'm doing either. I don't have any answers. We can't always plan and predict everything in our lives. All I know is that I want to be with you. I want to be close to you."

"Even if it breaks your heart in the end?" My voice cracked with emotion. The absolute last thing I wanted to do was break Jessie's heart…and mine.

"I'm willing to take that chance. I want to be with you for as long as I can. I'm not ready to give you up. Do you want to end it?" Jessie's voice was shaky and she looked near tears.

Feeling the powerful emotion radiating from this beautiful woman's eyes, I think I would have promised her anything in that moment. How had Jessie snuck under my radar? When did she steal my heart? How was it that I wanted to spend every waking moment with her? Those feelings had crept up on me slowly, without me even realizing it.

Sitting on the bench, being near Jessie, feeling our mutual passion and affection, I didn't doubt my feelings in that moment as my heart swelled a thousandfold.

But I didn't tell her any of that. Verbalizing it would have made it too real. Instead, I leaned in for a sweet kiss that melted me on the spot. So much for my vow to be celibate with Jessie.

Chapter Twenty-four

Making Up Is Fun To Do

It was the most romantic thing anyone had ever done for me. Hundreds of tea-light candles flickered in the dark cabin, with the scent of Nag Champa incense in the air. Dinner sat on the table—veggie burgers from the Red Planet and red wine sparkling in glasses. And best of all, a gorgeous woman stood in the center of the room, who pulled me into her arms and kissed me with those lips of hers I'd come to adore.

"Jessie, it's absolutely beautiful. When did you do all of this?"

"Well, I have to admit I did elicit Clarissa's help a bit."

"Clarissa? Oh, wait. You mean her all-important Excel project was a ruse? I spent over an hour helping her set up that budget worksheet. You're in trouble now."

"And just what are you going to do about it?" Jessie grinned as the candlelight sparkled in her eyes.

"This," I said. Pushing Jessie against the wall I kissed her hard while I let my hands roam up and down her body, finding their way under her shirt and straight to her breasts. Feeling taut nipples as I stroked, I edged my thigh between her legs, pressing hard against her. When I lifted Jessie's shirt over her head, I was greeted with a sheer, lacy bra. I circled her nipple through the material with my thumb as I reveled in the way her body responded to my touch.

I unbuttoned her jeans and slowly let the zipper down while kissing her fervently. Slipping my hand into her pants, I felt her wet silk panties.

"God, Malley," Jessie moaned.

"Oh baby, you're so wet already. Mmmm...you're aching for me to be inside you, aren't you?"

"Yes." Jessie whimpered. I don't know what had gotten into me. I wasn't the type to take control, nor had I ever talked dirty before. All I knew was that I wanted to ravish, delight, and surprise this woman.

"Now. Please." Hearing Jessie beg turned me on so much I thought I'd come from the friction of her thigh pressed against me. But this wasn't about me. I wanted to please Jessie.

Painstakingly slow, I parted her lips, barely entering her. Jessie's breathing quickened as she released an agonizing moan. With her head thrown back, I assaulted her neck with my lips, nibbling, sucking, then tracing my tongue in circles. Jessie was so aroused I easily penetrated her with three fingers, slowly moving in and out.

"Mmmm...you feel so good. I love touching you."

"Deeper," she said breathlessly.

I obeyed her request, stroking tender flesh. Jessie was getting wetter with each caress. With my thumb, I lightly grazed her clit, which was hard and swollen. Feeling Jessie tightening, twitching inside, I removed my thumb, causing a guttural groan.

"God, you're driving me crazy."

"You're so beautiful. Open your eyes. Look at me." I'd never felt as close to Jessie as I did at that moment. Our eyes locked, connected in the most intimate of ways.

I would never describe myself as sexy, but in that moment I was channeling Marilyn Monroe herself. Passion I'd never felt before rose within me as I kissed Jessie's crimson lips and devoured her with a hunger I desperately tried to quench. I had an aching, almost animalistic, desire to be as close to her as possible. Grabbing her hips, I pulled her into me, our bodies becoming one.

After thoroughly kissing Jessie, I let my lips roam down her neck and to her breasts. Unhooking her bra, I kissed the tender skin underneath her breasts. With my tongue I traced down her stomach as I knelt before her.

"I want to taste you." I slipped Jessie's jeans and panties off. The smell of her made me dizzy. I wanted her so much my body ached.

"Malley, I don't think I can stand up much longer."

I ignored her comment as she braced her back more firmly against the wall. Spreading her legs, I kissed her inner thighs, licking my way upward. Jessie gasped as I kissed her wet, protruding lips over and over, allowing my tongue to barely touch her. I sucked on her slick lips as her fingers ran through my hair. After I couldn't wait a moment longer, I penetrated her with my tongue—stroking, licking, tasting.

"That feels so amazing. Please, Malley."

With featherweight caresses, I licked around her swollen clit. Around and around until Jessie grabbed my head, urging me closer. My lips surrounded her as I lightly sucked before increasing the pressure. Jessie moaned as her hips undulated. With fingers pumping in and out of her, I sucked harder until I felt her throbbing and contracting against my fingers. She cried out as her body shook.

Lovingly caressing her soaking lips, I looked up to quite possibly the most beautiful image I'd ever seen. Past the swell of Jessie's breasts, I could see her head thrown back, eyes closed, ecstasy etched on her face. I froze the moment in my memory so it would always be with me, no matter what the future held.

❖

After hours of lovemaking amongst hundreds of twinkling candles, Jessie and I ate dinner and sipped wine. We talked about everything—our dreams, her poetry, our childhoods. Then I braved broaching an uncomfortable subject between us.

"Do you like being a cop?"

"I love it. It's exciting. An adventure. No two days are the same. I could never work in an office, sitting at a desk all day. It's just not for me."

Not the answer I wanted to hear. "Do you worry that it's dangerous?"

Jessie reached across the table and placed her hand over mine. "No, not really. I understand why that would concern you because of your dad. But it's not something I worry about. It is part of the job, but in a way that's what makes it exciting."

We were both silent, contemplating.

"Malley…"

"It's okay, Jessie. I'm glad you love your job. I really am. But it's not something that works for me. I'd hoped you'd say you didn't like it, or that you'd rather be a full-time poet, but the way your face lights up when you talk about it, I know that'll never change."

I didn't want to put a damper on our romantic evening, which had been absolutely perfect until that point, but I couldn't help the heaviness in my heart. Jessie looked sad. Defeated.

Trying to lighten the mood, I forced a smile and blew her a kiss across the table. "You didn't try to catch the kiss," I said.

"You throw like a girl. It went over my head," she responded. We sat in silence, looking into each other's eyes, holding hands across the table.

"Hey, I have a present for you," Jessie said.

"A present? For me? Where? What? When? Give it up, girlie."

"You have to close your eyes and put out your hands."

She was so cute. I did as ordered, patiently waiting. Within minutes, I felt a heaviness in the palms of my hands.

"Can I open my eyes?" I asked eagerly.

"You're adorable when you're excited. Yes, open those beautiful baby blues."

I was staring at a large, square gift haphazardly wrapped with an enormous amount of tape used. I smiled broadly.

"Did you wrap it yourself?" I put my hand on her cheek to let her know I thought that was the sweetest thing ever.

"Yeah. Maybe I could quit my job and go into professional gift-wrapping."

"I think you definitely should," I said.

"So open it already."

I ripped open the package and my heart stood still. With wide eyes I looked at Jessie, then back at the present.

"Oh my God, where did you get this? How?" It was a framed print of the heart-mandala mural that was painted on the side of the Spirit Soundstage.

"You like it?" Jessie beamed.

"Jessie, I love it!"

"Dominic almost blew the surprise when he was about to tell you that he sells prints of the mural. I thought you might like it."

I threw myself into her arms, hugging her tight. "It's the most thoughtful gift anyone has ever given me. And this night, with all the candles, dinner, and being close to you, has been absolutely perfect. I love...loved it all."

CHAPTER TWENTY-FIVE

GRANDMA'S RECIPE

Soft lips on my bare shoulder, kissing their way up my neck and then slowly to my lips. I loved the sensation of Jessie's lips on mine. Mmm…the taste of sugar and cinnamon. That was new. One hand slipped under the covers, down my thigh and then back up again, lightly caressing my skin. Lips pressed harder against mine as her hand roamed upward, stroking my bare breast.

How dare she attempt to break our kiss? I slipped my hand behind her neck, pulling her closer to me. She had woken me after only a few hours' sleep from making love for half the night. I was exhausted and sore, but the thought of going back to sleep wasn't an option. Not when she was kissing me.

"Malley," Jessie whispered in my ear.

"Kiss me again." I groaned with enough vigor to let her know I would possibly die if she didn't. She complied, and I tasted sugar on her lips.

"Mmm…I could kiss you forever," I said.

Jessie lightly kissed my closed eyelids. "Go back to sleep. You need your rest."

"What are you doing up and dressed? You didn't sleep either. Come here and lie with me."

Jessie lay beside me, enveloping me in her arms.

"Why do you smell like cinnamon and vanilla?" I asked.

"I have something to show you."

"Now you're talking. I'm ready to see it all."

"Not that," Jessie said. "And didn't you have enough last night?"

"Never. It could never be enough." I turned to face Jessie and kissed her lightly on the lips.

"Yes," she said. "I could kiss you, and touch you, and be with you all day and all night. And it still wouldn't be enough."

❖

Later that morning, Jessie pulled me through the front door and out of our cabin. "Where are you taking me?"

"You'll see." That's all she said. She led me into the main cabin, through the dining hall, and toward the kitchen. The place was empty. We'd taken our time getting out of bed so it was almost eleven by then. When Jessie swung the doors to the kitchen open, I saw dozens of items stacked on the counter. Sugar, flour, cinnamon, butter—you name it. It was there.

"What's all this?" I asked.

"After hearing you describe how much you love baking, I asked Clarissa if we could borrow the kitchen for a bit." Jessie looked as excited as a kid on Christmas morning. "I thought maybe you could make some of your butterscotch cinnamon buns. I had no idea what ingredients to get, so I Googled cinnamon buns and went out this morning and bought some stuff. I hope I got everything in your grandma's recipe." When I didn't respond, Jessie looked grief stricken. "God, this was a stupid idea, wasn't it?"

I shook my head. "Jessie, this is so thoughtful. You took the time to research the ingredients and then gathered all this together because you know it's something I love to do." Slipping my arms around her waist, I looked up into her eyes. "I would absolutely love to make you something."

Jessie smiled, lightly kissing my forehead. "Good, 'cause I'm starving."

"Okay, let's see what we have here." I picked through the varied ingredients on the counter. Everything I needed was there and then some. "You did a great job. I can totally work with this."

Jessie smiled proudly.

"All right, now you get out." I lightly slapped Jessie on the rear end and tried to push her out the door.

"What? I'm not leaving. I want to watch you cook. I can even help."

"No way. What part of *secret* recipe don't you understand? Plus, I don't like anyone watching me cook. Would you stand behind Picasso and stare at him while he paints?"

Jessie considered the question for a moment with her hands on her hips. "Why yes, I believe I would."

She was so cute. I pursed my lips to try to keep from smiling so she'd know I was serious. "Out." I pointed to the door. "Why don't you go for a walk and come back in about an hour."

"An hour!? I'll be starved by then." I guided Jessie out the door and could hear her muffled protests until her voice slowly faded away.

Memories of my grandmother flooded back the moment I started combining and mixing ingredients. I could hear her voice, instructing me to knead the dough for three minutes and allow it to rest for ten. Then to roll the dough out and spread it with melted butter, brown sugar, and cinnamon. For a moment I could have sworn Grandma was standing right beside me.

I cleaned the kitchen as the cinnamon buns sizzled in the oven. The air was thick with the scent of butter and sugar. After the buns cooled, I swirled whipped cream on top of each one and dotted two eyes and a smiley face on them with caramel. Grandma always did that to make me smile. She called them fun buns.

Jessie was back in forty-five minutes. Clearly, patience wasn't one of her strong points. She inhaled deeply as she poked her head into the kitchen.

"Lucky for you I'm done. Even though you are a little early."

I held out a plate with the butterscotch cinnamon bun smiley face.

Jessie leaned down and breathed in the fragrant pastry. "Oh my God. That smells incredible."

We sat at the table as I cut a bun in half for each of us to taste. Not wanting to miss a moment of Jessie's reaction, I held off on taking a bite. With eyes closed, she sank her teeth into the dessert. I resisted the urge to lick the whipped cream from her lips. She chewed slowly, a look of rapture on her face.

Opening her eyes wide, Jessie groaned. "That's amazing," she said. "It melts in your mouth. Malley, this is so good."

I smiled proudly, glad I could make something she enjoyed so much. I truly wanted to make Jessie happy.

"You should sell these," she said. "I've never tasted anything so scrumptious before."

"Thanks."

"I'm serious. Have you thought anymore about opening a bakery?"

"Not seriously. I don't know a thing about running a business. It sounds so risky. It's not very realistic."

"You shouldn't let that stop you. You could take a class and learn. Your mom said your dad left you money."

"But I have a stable, well-paying job. There's a lot to be said for that."

"Yes, but you should do something you love. That's all I'm saying. Just think about it, okay? I'll say the same thing to you that Clarissa did to me when she told me to send my poetry to publishing companies. She asked, 'If not now, when?'"

That night, I got my laptop out and Googled how to start a bakery. Sometimes when Jessie and I talked, she made the impossible seem very possible.

CHAPTER TWENTY-SIX

BACK TO BOYNTON CANYON

What are we doing here?" I asked. A vise clenched my stomach as I sat on the back of Jessie's motorcycle.

She dismounted the bike and took off her helmet. "This is the hike I wanted to surprise you with. Is something wrong?"

"We're not hiking here," I said.

"I don't understand. Why not? There's a rock formation shaped like a woman at the top, and it has a gorgeous view."

"I know. I've been here before." I studied my clenched hands. "With my dad."

"Oh. But I'm still not really getting it, Malley." Her tone was gentle, probably because, she knew the subject of my father was difficult territory.

"He and I used to hike here. We sort of…had an experience the first time we were here. This became our special hiking spot."

"Oh, honey, I'm sorry. I had no idea." Jessie wrapped an arm around my shoulder.

"I know it sounds crazy. It's just…my dad is the only person I've ever been here with."

"Don't worry about it. We can go someplace else." Jessie mounted her bike, but before she could start the engine I stopped her.

"Jessie, wait. Maybe we could go. I don't know. Maybe I could erect one of the cairns where he and I used to sit."

Jessie rotated in her seat to face me. "Are you sure? I'm fine with whatever you want to do."

After pondering a few moments, I nodded. "I want to go. And I'm glad you're the one here with me. My dad...he would have really liked you." Jessie smiled, kissing me on the cheek.

It was strange being on Vista Trail again after so many years. Every step reminded me of my dad. Things he'd said, a specific tree he'd pointed out, or some dumb joke he'd tell me to try to make me laugh.

Jessie was very thoughtful. She'd ask me every so often if I was okay and if I wanted to turn back. Remarkably, I felt pretty strong emotionally. I missed my dad, but I wasn't near tears, which was what I was expecting.

It wasn't until we reached the top of the summit and saw the Kachina Woman that sadness overtook me. I could picture my dad sitting cross-legged under the juniper tree. Even though it had been a year since his death, it surprised me how raw and close to the surface my emotions were. Walking to the Kachina Woman, I placed my hand on her crimson body. Vibrations flowed into my palm.

"Do you feel that?" I asked. Jessie placed her hand on the rock formation as well. "It's like she's alive. Like we're feeling her heartbeat." I pressed my cheek against the rock and stretched out my arms as far as they would reach around the woman. Normally, I don't hug rocks in front of people, but with Jessie I didn't mind so much.

Jessie sat under the tree, taking in the sights of the canyon below. She was in the same spot the Indian had been so many years ago. Releasing my hold on the Kachina Woman, I studied Jessie's profile. My heart swelled with affection as warmth spread throughout my body. It amazed me how close I felt to her after such a short time. Did she feel the same? Did she think every moment we spent together was bliss? Was she scared out of her mind about what would happen when the retreat ended tomorrow?

Jessie turned, locking eyes with mine. "Are you okay?"

"As long as I'm with you, I am." God, that sounded corny, but it's really how I felt. I walked over to Jessie and sat beside her.

"I want to tell you something I've never shared with anyone," I said. "Something that happened when my dad and I were here."

Jessie listened intently as I described the Indian and his flute, how he'd disappeared without a trace, and the heart rock I'd kept for fifteen years.

"You probably don't remember this, but when we were in the bakery and you and Lizzie were talking about me opening my own shop, you said the exact same thing the Indian told me, and you also tapped on your heart three times like he did."

"I remember. I said you should follow your heart."

"Do you think…I mean, it's crazy to even ask…but do you think that Indian could have been some sort of spirit? It's just that in Jerome this guy was telling me about the legend of an Indian spirit who's the Kachina Woman's helper. God, that sounds insane."

"I don't think it's crazy. There are a lot of unexplainable things in this world, and most of them usually happen in Sedona." Jessie smiled and put her arm around my shoulder.

"I don't know. It's a little hard to believe. The guy in Jerome also said the Kachina Woman delivers gifts to people through the Indian. Like maybe…maybe the heart rock was a gift from a spirit. What do you think?"

"I think you should follow your instincts. What does your heart tell you?"

I contemplated that question for probably longer than I should have. Listening to my heart wasn't really something I was used to doing. But I gave it a go, concentrating on the area of my chest where the Indian had tapped three times.

"I think it's possible. I believe in souls and spirits. Sometimes I can feel my dad with me so strongly that when I turn around I'm half expecting him to be standing there. So…I guess it's not so far-fetched to think an Indian spirit could exist."

Jessie and I sat in silence, feeling the warmth of the rocks beneath us. Satisfying an urge to be closer to Jessie, I scooted over until our shoulders were touching. She laid her hand on my knee. Reaching around, I gathered loose red rocks and carefully began stacking one rock upon another, erecting a cairn. I handed Jessie the last rock and asked if she would balance it on top.

"This is for you, Pop," I mentally told my dad. I could have sworn he was sitting beside Jessie and me, with a megawatt smile bright enough to light up the heavens.

CHAPTER TWENTY-SEVEN

FANTASY ISLAND HURRICANE

I was terribly afraid Jessie would walk in at any moment. She was at the pond spending some quiet time writing, and I was sitting outside reading a book she'd suggested. A book by a psychic who talked to dead people was the last thing I thought I'd ever read, but it was geared to losing a loved one and I found it comforting. That's when Lizzie drove up. A torrent of emotions went through me: shock, confusion, uncertainty, but most of all pleasure in seeing her again. I'd missed her.

"Hi, Malley." Her voice was shaky.

"Lizzie, how are you?"

"Mostly ashamed." She lowered her head and stared at the ground. "Can we go inside and talk?"

I led Lizzie into the cabin and we sat on my bed, since that was the only free space. Suitcases and clothing were strewn around the table and chairs, as it was the last night in the cabin and I wanted to get a head start on packing before the end-of-the-retreat party that night.

"Where's Heather?"

"Heading back to LA, I guess. I don't really care. Oh, Malley, I'm so sorry about everything. I'm such an idiot. I thought maybe she'd actually changed, but she hadn't." I was silent, not knowing what to say or what was happening. Lizzie reached for my hand. "I hope you understand that I had to try once more with her. I had to make sure it was truly over. And it is. Believe me. This time is for good."

"Did you sleep with her?" I was such a hypocrite. I think a part of me was hoping Lizzie would say yes so I'd have an excuse to break up—if we were even still dating, that is.

"No, I didn't. That was one of my conditions to staying with her. I wanted to see if we had anything between us besides sex. We don't."

I felt like such a scoundrel. The minute Lizzie left to work on personal issues, I'd jumped into bed with Jessie.

Jessie. Oh, God. I so hoped she wouldn't walk into the cabin with Lizzie sitting on my bed, holding my hand.

"Do you think you could forgive me? That...maybe...we could pick up where we left off? You're the one I want to be with."

For almost a year I'd dreamed of hearing those words come out of Lizzie's mouth. I should have been ecstatic at the turn of events. But I wasn't. Not by a long shot.

"Lizzie..." My heart sank as I heard the screen door open behind me. Lizzie looked past me and I knew Jessie was standing in the doorway. I didn't want to turn around.

"Hey," Jessie said.

"Um, Lizzie's here." Completely unnecessary to point out, but I didn't know what else to say.

"Yeah," Jessie said. "I guess I should leave you two alone."

My heart melted as I turned around to wounded eyes.

"Hi, Jessie," Lizzie said. "It's good to be back. And to be with Malley." Lizzie squeezed my hand tighter, accompanied by a wide smile.

"Listen, I'll just get out of your way. Take all the time you need." Jessie quietly closed the door behind her.

My heart ached. I couldn't just let her leave like that. I needed to talk to her. I needed to look into her eyes and make sure she was all right.

"Lizzie, look...I just need to talk to Jessie for a minute." I stood up, looking at the door.

"Where are you going?"

"I'll be right back. I promise."

Before Lizzie could protest, I darted through the door.

Jessie hadn't gotten very far. She was leaning against the oak tree outside the cabin. I lightly touched her shoulder from behind.

"What are you doing out here?" Her beautiful jade eyes were filled with an emotion I couldn't quite pin down.

"I wanted to make sure you're all right."

"I'm fine. So, Lizzie came back, huh?"

"Yeah. I had no idea she'd just show up."

"Is she with Heather?"

"No. She said it's over."

"What happens now? Is she...are you...still dating?"

"I don't know. She said she wants to be with me."

"Of course she does. Who wouldn't want to?"

My heart pounded as Jessie gazed into my eyes. "Jessie..." I reached for her hand, but she pulled away.

"This is what you wanted, Malley. This is the whole reason you came to Sedona—to be with Lizzie and tell her you love her." Jessie's voice cracked with emotion.

"I know, but things have changed. I've changed."

"You should get back to Lizzie. She's the one who can make you happy." Jessie took a step back.

Closing the gap, I moved toward her and said, "How do you know what would make me happy?" Jessie looked at me with such affection it broke my heart. I reached for her hand again, but she pulled away once more, putting more distance between us.

"Why are you doing this?" I took a step toward her. "Didn't the past weeks mean anything to you? Are you so ready to be done with me? Why are you pushing me away?"

"Malley, don't—"

"Was this just a fling to you? A quick summer affair?"

"No, of course not." Jessie looked at me tenderly. For a moment I thought she was about to wrap me in her arms, but instead her eyes turned cold. "I don't need to remind you that I'm a cop," she said sternly. "After hearing how painful your father's death has been and that you could never date a police officer, I don't see any choice here."

The realization of our situation flashed across my eyes. Jessie saw it and continued. "We've been living a Sedona fantasy, Malley. This isn't real life. The moment we'd get back to LA everything would come crashing down. I won't be the cause of fear in your eyes every time I walk out the door to go to work."

My entire body was numb. Jessie was right, as much as I wanted her not to be. I felt like someone had punched me hard in the gut. Jessie backed away slowly, still holding my gaze. I wanted to run and throw myself into her arms, but I couldn't. I was rooted into the ground, just like the heavy, immoveable oak tree standing beside me.

❖

Jessie was gone. Or at least her stuff was. The cabin felt empty without her. I lay in my bed and curled into a fetal position. It hurt physically to feel the absence of her arms around me. I didn't know what to do. I knew Jessie cared for me. I could see it every time she looked into my eyes, every time she kissed me. In her mind, she was evidently doing some heroic thing by letting me go without a fight. She cared about me enough to put my happiness first, and I think she genuinely believed I'd be happier with Lizzie. But I wasn't happy without her, and I never would be.

Worse, I knew Jessie was right. Sedona had been a fantasy. This wasn't real life. I couldn't live with the constant fear of getting that dreaded phone call that she was hurt, or worse. I couldn't watch her leave for work every day and not worry that something would happen. It was crazy of me to sleep with Jessie, to get close to her. But I didn't regret it. How could I? She was an amazing, kind, captivating woman. My heart ached, and I hadn't a clue as to what to do about it.

❖

The end-of-the-retreat party looked like a blast. And it would have been if I'd been anywhere near a party mood. I wouldn't have even gone, but Lizzie dragged me there. Technically, I hadn't said yes to dating again. She just assumed we'd pick up where we left off, like nothing had ever happened. I wasn't sure when I'd tell Lizzie about Jessie and me. Call me selfish, but I wanted to keep my best friend around a little longer. I had a distinct feeling our friendship would be over the minute I told her that Jessie and I had slept together, several times, several mind-blowing orgasmic times. Well, I'd probably leave that last part out.

Women were dancing, laughing, drinking, and munching on snacks. I scanned the room, hoping to spot Jessie, but wasn't surprised that she was a no-show. I wasn't sure what I'd have said, anyway, but I wanted to see her, wanted to look into her eyes. Nicole stared at me from across the room with a sneer. As she headed my way, I looked for an escape route, as I wasn't in the mood to deal with her. She reached me before I could slip away, putting her hands on her hips.

"You broke her heart, you know," Nicole said.

"This is none of your business." I tried to walk past her, but she stepped in front of me, blocking my way.

"I can't believe someone like Jessie would even want to be with you. She was devastated when she left."

"She left? You talked to her?"

"Not only talked but consoled her. And gave her my number in case she ever wants a real woman next time." Nicole stormed off.

I felt a stab of jealousy at the thought of Nicole consoling Jessie. That was something I wanted to do. Desperately.

Did everyone at the lodge know Jessie and I had been together? Guess we hadn't kept it very quiet. I hoped no one would fill Lizzie in before I could. Clarissa spotted me across the room, and she looked none too happy. This was so not a fun party.

"Malley, I don't know what happened between you and Jessie." Clarissa had backed me into a corner. "Trying to pry information out of my sister is like trying to milk a bull. But I wanted you to know that I really like you. I hope you two can work things out."

"I don't think that's going to happen," I said.

"You know, Jessie has the tough-girl routine down pat. But she's really a frightened little child inside, afraid of getting hurt."

My heart sank. I never wanted to be the cause of anything but happiness for Jessie. I felt horrible that I'd hurt her and couldn't even put my arms around her and make it better.

"Is…uhh…is Jessie coming tonight?"

"No, she left for LA a few hours ago. I told her not to drive at night, but you know how stubborn she can be."

"If you talk to her, tell her…just…tell her…I'm sorry." There was so much I wanted to say to Jessie. So many jumbled emotions and thoughts that I couldn't put into words.

"I will, Malley." Clarissa squeezed my hand before walking away.

"Sooo, this is a fine mess you got yourself into." I rolled my eyes at Rhonda, who'd snuck up behind me.

"I'm not in the mood, Rhonda."

"Let me get this straight. You were dating Lizzie, then you slept with Jessie, and now you're dating Lizzie again. You're just a regular Sedona slut." Rhonda cackled like a hyena.

"See you around, Rhonda. I'll look you up if I ever go insane and decide to visit Texas." Maybe that was mean, but I was in no mood to be teased.

Not being able to handle much more of the party, I told Lizzie I had a headache and headed to the cabin. Alone.

Chapter Twenty-eight

Reality Sucks

I hadn't planned to break up with Lizzie at a Texaco Station in Yucca, Arizona, but that's where it happened.

"What are you reading?" Lizzie had asked as we drove through Phoenix on our way back to LA.

"It's a book about the afterlife. Written by a psychic."

"Oh my God. A psychic? Seriously? Sedona turned you into a New Age nut."

"I'm not a New Age nut!" Strange how three weeks ago I would have laughed off that comment, but now I found it insulting. "It helps me understand what happened to my dad. And how he's still with me."

"Oh, I'm sorry, Malley. I didn't know. After that picture you were so anal about packing in bubble wrap…what'd you call it? A heart mandala? Well, I was afraid Sedona had changed you."

"No," I said. "It wasn't Sedona that changed me." *It was Jessie.*

"Hey, are you okay? You haven't said much since we left."

"I'm fine. Just tired. Didn't sleep very well last night."

That wasn't a lie. Of course, there was a lot more to it, but I wasn't ready to open up to Lizzie. Closing my eyes, I drifted off to sleep. I dreamed that Jessie and I were standing under the oak tree.

Right when she was pulling away, I grabbed her hand, tugging her into a tight embrace. She kissed me passionately, pushing me against the trunk of the tree. My heart was bursting with joy until our sudden stop jarred me awake.

"Where are we?" I asked.

"Yucca. I have to pee something awful. Can you fill up the tank?"

As I pumped gas into the car, Lizzie came out of the Texaco carrying two Diet Cokes.

"Do people actually live here?" I asked. Yucca was hot, windy, and desolate.

"Beats me. Gas is cheap. Might be worth moving here." We both chuckled as Lizzie totally invaded my personal space, standing so close I could feel her breath on my cheek. She had that look in her eyes, that look women have right before they kiss you. I leaned back into the car, trying to put some space between us.

"I don't think Yucca is a gay-friendly place," I said. "Maybe we shouldn't—"

"Shouldn't what? Do this?" Lizzie moved in for the kill as I turned my head to avoid a smack on the lips. "What's wrong?" she asked.

Her eyes were as big as UFOs. (Okay, maybe Sedona did get to me.) That's when it hit me. I couldn't kiss someone when I was in love with someone else. I was in love with Jessie, not Lizzie.

I so did not want to do this here. At a Texaco station, in Yucca, with the smell of gas fumes in the air. And with a five-hour drive left in a tightly enclosed space. But I couldn't pretend. Lizzie knew me too well and she deserved to know the truth. I blew out a long breath, trying to calm my nerves. She took a step back, her eyes still huge.

"Lizzie, I don't know how to say this. I care about you so much. But I slept with Jessie when you were with Heather. I'm so sorry if that was cheating, but I'm not so sure it was."

"Oh," she said. Her eyes got bigger, if that was even possible.

"You're so important to me. I don't want to lose our friendship over this," I said. Lizzie found an oil stain on the ground and stared at it intensely. "Please say something."

"You slept with Jessie?"

"It's not something I planned. And then things just got so...so confusing after that."

Lizzie continued to glare at the oil stain, until finally her eyes rose to meet mine.

"I...I guess I can't blame you. I *was* with my ex-girlfriend. So you slept with her just once?"

Now it was my turn to stare at the oil stain. "Um, no. It was a lot. I'm in love with her."

Lizzie paused before throwing her car keys at me, which bounced off my stomach and clanged to the ground.

"You drive," she said.

I can honestly say that was the longest five hours of my life. I tried to talk to Lizzie several times, but she sat in the passenger seat with her eyes closed and never said a word. I felt nauseous when we pulled up to my West Hollywood apartment and unloaded my bags onto the sidewalk as Lizzie walked around to the driver's side.

"Lizzie, wait. We said we'd never let anything ruin our friendship. Please talk to me."

She glanced at me briefly before slamming her door shut and speeding away. I stood on the sidewalk, gazing back and forth from the taillights of Lizzie's car to my apartment building. My best friend would possibly never speak to me again, and inside, right next door, was a woman who had my heart but who I couldn't be with. Living next door to Jessie would be a curse and a blessing. I couldn't bear the thought of never seeing her again, yet seeing her and not being able to touch her, kiss her, be with her, would be hell. Life sucked something awful.

❖

Few sounds are more offensive than the buzz of an alarm clock after being on vacation for three weeks. Rock 'em Sock 'em Robots duked it out in my stomach as I got ready for work. I was nervous about seeing Lizzie and the possibility of running into Jessie in the apartment building.

After arriving at work, I saw Lizzie standing by the cappuccino machine. That's where we used to meet every morning before starting the workday. It was as though she knew I'd walked up behind her, as she visibly tensed.

"Good morning, Lizzie." It was anything but good. She briefly turned her head and nodded. "Maybe we could talk later?"

Dave, one of our coworkers, sauntered into the break room. "Hey, you two. How was wacky Sedona?"

"It was…different," I replied.

"Different how?" he asked.

"Surprisingly different," Lizzie said with a scowl. She turned abruptly and stormed out of the room.

"Wow, color me confused, but did Lizzie just give you a go-to-hell look?"

Without a word I turned and bolted out of the break room.

If trying to catch up after being out three weeks wasn't bad enough, having Lizzie not talk to me was even worse. She avoided me all day, and when I did see her she dodged eye contact. As uncomfortable as the workday was, things seemed to get worse after I got home.

My thought was that working out in the apartment complex gym would help me relieve some stress. I was wrong. I'd envisioned running into Jessie in the hall, at the mailboxes, or even by my front door. I knew it would happen sooner or later, and I thought I'd prepared myself. But in my imaginings, I never expected her to be sweating, in skin-tight workout pants and a cut-off shirt, and looking superbly scrumptious.

But there she was right when I opened the door to the gym. She was bending over, picking up a dumbbell, when her head shot up and she looked right at me. Damn if she didn't look sexy.

Sweat cascaded down her chest and into the deep recesses of her cleavage. Her beautiful eyes were even greener than I remembered. Even under the painful circumstances, it was so good to see Jessie I couldn't help but smile.

"Hi," I said. Walking toward her, I stayed out of arm's reach so I wouldn't be tempted to touch her. "How are you?"

"I'm okay. It's good to see you. I was nervous about running into you, but now that we have…it's just great to see you."

My stomach flipped when she flashed that beautiful smile of hers. "You, too. I've missed you."

Unspoken desires, thoughts, and feelings passed between us as we gazed into each other's eyes.

Jessie suddenly tensed, her eyes hardened, and she erected a wall between us that seemed almost tangible. "Well, actually, I should get going," she said abruptly. Jessie gathered her things and was out the door before I could respond.

Since I'd caught her in the middle of doing reps, I figured she was leaving on my account. I was incredibly sad we couldn't comfortably remain in the same room together.

I ran on the treadmill as fast as my legs could move, fixing my eyes on a water stain on the wall. I pushed all thoughts of Jessie out of my mind. It was just me, the treadmill, and that water stain. Sweat poured down my back as I panted, gasping for breath. My legs burned as I pumped my arms. Just when I didn't think I could take another step, I pushed myself to do so. A lump formed in my throat as tears threatened, but I held them back. Instead, I ran, attempting to outrun my feelings.

When I got back to my apartment all I wanted to do was call my best friend and tell her how wonderful and painful it was to see Jessie. But I couldn't, because my best friend wasn't speaking to me. I collapsed on the floor of my living room, exhausted. Closing my eyes, I tried to meditate. I visualized a relaxing garden filled with vibrant green plants, but I saw Jessie sitting on a bench in the garden. Then I visualized being at the ocean, feeling the spray of the salt water in the breeze. And then

I saw Jessie and me walking along the shore, hand in hand. I couldn't get her out of my mind.

Restlessness overtook me that night. It took all I had not to bang on Jessie's door. She was so close—just beyond the wall. Maybe if I listened closely enough I could hear her breathing, hear her heartbeat. Maybe if I pretended hard enough I could actually feel her arms around me. Like when we were in the velvet blackness of the cabin. And maybe if I whispered loud enough, she would actually hear me when I said, "Good night, Barnett. Sweet dreams."

Chapter Twenty-nine

Lovesick in LA

I felt like a sugar-addicted teenager whose parents were away for the weekend. Double Stuff Oreos, a bag of marshmallows, rocky road ice cream, and four giant Snickers. That was the contents of my shopping cart, along with a bottle of Midol just in case my depression wasn't entirely Jessie-related.

"Oh, I see someone needs a sugar boost today." There are few things I dislike more than a chatty checkout girl. Nobody wants a wafer-thin teen named Misty, as indicated by her name tag, scrutinizing their diabetic-inducing goods. The bag boy giggled. Obviously, they were in cahoots. "I'd be as big as a house if I took even one bite of this." Misty surveyed my Snickers. My fingers flew across the debit machine. Couldn't she see I was too busy to respond? "Well, this explains it," she said when she got to the Midol. The bag boy looked down, embarrassed. Served him right for giggling at my marshmallows.

Grabbing the paper sack, I stormed out of the grocery store, running smack dab into a couple smooching. They were wearing T-shirts with the American flag printed on the front and red, white, and blue striped shorts. They looked happy. And why wouldn't they be? They were joined at the lips in sickeningly cute matching outfits, oblivious to the fact that not everyone had the luxury of being with the one they love on Independence Day. Ignoring their apologies for blocking the entrance, I headed down the sidewalk to my apartment, anxious to begin Sugar Fest 2015.

I was stretched out in my La-Z-Boy recliner, ice cream perched on my frostbitten knee as *The Brady Bunch* blared on the TV. I had already ingested two Snickers, half the bag of Oreos, a half-dozen marshmallows, and was kicking myself for forgetting to buy Alka-Seltzer.

I balanced a marshmallow between two fingers, squishing it three times before popping it into my mouth. It was like ingesting a spongy cloud plucked down from the heavens. A sugar rush awakened my senses. I was alert, alive, and poised to pop another shot into my mouth before the high wore off.

I was pathetic, I know. But in my defense, it was the first time Cupid had reached into my chest, yanked out my bloody heart, and tossed it into a blender. Sorry to be so graphic, but that's how I felt. It's not like Jessie was my first breakup. Not by a long shot. But it was the first time I'd been in love.

My only salvation was that the pain wouldn't last forever. I was well aware of the stages of grief as described by my therapist after my dad died: denial, anger, depression, and acceptance. I was clearly in depression, so just one more step to go and I'd be back to normal.

Feeling completely stuffed, I stretched out in my recliner focusing on the TV. It was *The Brady Bunch* Christmas episode. I challenge anyone not to shed a tear at that last scene. Thanks to Cindy's plea to Santa Claus, Mrs. Brady received a miracle by regaining her lost voice in time to sing at the Sunday service. The camera panned to the six kids and Mr. Brady sitting in the pews. They were all misty eyed. A close-up of Cindy's sugarcoated smile at her dad did me in. I grabbed for a tissue. Maybe I needed that Midol after all.

Clicking off the TV, I closed my eyes and drifted to sleep. It was a deep slumber, filled with chaotic dreams. Had it not been for a blast outside, I probably would have stayed in a sugar-induced coma all night. Disoriented, I bolted upright. An earthquake? No, I didn't feel shaking. Another blast. I jumped. A gun shot? Through closed shades I could see flashing lights. Fire trucks? Marshmallows fell to the floor as I heaved myself from the recliner. I pulled the shades aside just as a red burst flashed across the dark sky. Fireworks. I'd forgotten it was the Fourth of July.

My balcony provided a great view of the Hollywood Bowl fireworks display. Lizzie and I used to spend every Fourth sipping wine and watching the light show in the sky. I wondered what she was doing, if she was thinking about me, missing me. Probably not. She greeted my many attempts to talk with silence and icy glares. Grabbing a bottle of red wine and a glass, I slid my balcony door open. I didn't intend to let Lizzie or Jessie ruin my Fourth.

My resolve melted when I saw Jessie on her balcony, which practically adjoined mine. She was leaning against the railing, looking into the sky, wide-eyed with anticipation. The joy in her eyes faded the moment she saw me. I looked at the ground, not wanting to see the pain in her eyes. Jessie turned her attention back to the fireworks as I sat in a lounge chair, pouring myself some wine.

"It's beautiful, isn't it?" Jessie didn't take her eyes off of the exploding gold-and-red starbursts.

"Yes, it is," I said. We watched the rest of the display in silence. I found something comforting about sharing the experience with Jessie, even if we were on separate balconies.

The grand finale was spectacular, with hundreds of blasts setting off colorful sparks in the sky. Gray smoke hung on the clouds as the last gold sparkles of light trickled downward, the scent of gunpowder in the air.

"I think I should move." She spoke in a monotone, emotionless voice, without even looking at me.

"What?" Had I heard her right?

"I think I should move." Jessie looked at me, her expression tense, her eyes blank.

"You don't have to do that." I really wanted to say, Don't do that.

"I think it would be easier if I did." She looked at the smoky sky.

Heat crept up my neck, my breathing shallow. Did she really think not ever seeing each other again would make it easier? Is that what she wanted?

Jessie looked at me when I didn't respond. The muscles in her face softened, her eyes appeared compassionate. She still cared for me. I could feel it. She wouldn't move. She couldn't.

In the span of two minutes I had gone from depressed, to angry at Jessie for wanting to move, to denial that she would do so. I was back at step one on the grief scale, a far cry from acceptance.

You know it's bad when the Prozac commercials are piquing your interest. The days rolled into weeks, my misery not lessening. It was hard to get out of bed in the mornings. I couldn't eat. I couldn't sleep. An empty ache, which nothing quenched, took up permanent residence in my stomach. I even called in sick, faking the flu. My only aspiration was to be a couch potato and find comfort in the fact that soap-opera characters had screwed-up love lives worse than mine. No matter what I did I couldn't stop thinking about Jessie. And to make matters worse, Lizzie still wasn't talking to me.

My first tactic was to keep busy. I immersed myself in spring cleaning even though it wasn't spring, worked out so hard I couldn't even walk the next day, speed-read huge novels in record time—anything I could think of to keep my mind occupied and off how much I missed Jessie. But when none of those things worked, I resorted to the couch-potato plan.

One particular day when I was home "sick" flipping through the channels, I paused at the sight of an African American woman and a young boy making a plea to the camera. My arms and legs went limp and my stomach turned sour. Apparently, the woman's husband, who was a police officer, had been gunned down in the middle of Wilshire Blvd while on duty. The woman was begging the public for any information. The suspects were still at large. It had happened in broad daylight on a busy street in LA. Someone must have seen something.

She pulled her young son, who looked about ten years old, close to her as she spoke. At first, I thought it cruel to subject him to cameras and press, but these people were desperate. They wanted to find the suspects, and I didn't blame them for trying anything they could to get information.

I couldn't take my eyes off the kid. His big brown eyes were filled with shock, with fear and sorrow. It was a look I'd seen in my own eyes dozens of times after my dad was killed. Sometimes when I'd stare in the mirror I wouldn't even recognize my own reflection. This scared, sad girl looked back at me. I wanted to reach through the TV screen, grab this kid, and embrace him. I wanted to whisper in his ear that it's okay to cry, it's okay to yell and scream, and it's okay to be terrified for as long as he needs. He didn't have to be strong for his mom or anyone else. He didn't have to be a brave little boy. I wanted to tell him everything I'd wished someone had whispered in my ear when my dad died.

Without thinking, I grabbed the phone, called information, and got the number for KTLZ TV station. Within minutes I was talking to the station manager, asking him what I could do to help. I told him my father had been killed on duty and I wanted to do anything I could for these people. He took my name and number and said he would pass them off to the woman.

Sometimes all it takes is a little dose of reality to put things in perspective. My love life wasn't such a horrible thing compared to the pain that woman and her son were going through. It was high time I got off my butt, stashed the marshmallows in the cabinet, and ended my pity party.

Chapter Thirty

Possible Dream

A re you sure this isn't crazy?" I was sprawled out on my couch, looking up at the ceiling, talking to my mom on the phone.

"No, honey, this is the best idea you've ever had. You know your dad left you plenty of money. He'd want you to use it for something you want."

"But maybe I should save it for the future, as a security blanket for retirement."

"Malley, you're thirty-two years old. Do you want to be stuck at your job for the next thirty years?"

That hit a chord. Thirty years was a long time. Not that I hated my job, but for some reason it wasn't the same after I got back from Sedona. And it wasn't just because Lizzie was ignoring me at work. Most days I'd catch myself sitting at my desk, staring at my stapler or tape dispenser, daydreaming. I'd visualize owning that cute bakery in Sedona, or maybe even one in West Hollywood. A place I could build from scratch, making it my own.

"You're right. So you think I should go ahead and do it?"

"Definitely," Mom said.

After we hung up, I swung my legs around and opened my laptop on the coffee table. Leaning forward, I stared at the screen:

Learn How To Start and Run a Small Business. I poised the cursor on the submit icon, having already filled in the registration and payment information. All it needed was one click of the mouse. One small action that meant the difference between parasailing hundreds of feet in the air or staying firmly planted on the ground... where it was a hell of a lot safer.

I leaned back into the sofa, still staring at the screen. If I had reservations about spending so much money on a class, how would I feel when it came time to drop the big bucks? Like remodeling, rent, supplies, employees, and on and on. I closed my eyes and took a deep breath. Maybe if I tuned in to my dad he'd tell me what to do. It was his money, after all. I could feel him around me, as I often did when I quietened my mind. Warmth radiated down my arms and chest, settling into my heart. *What would make you the most proud of me, Dad?* The answer came as it always did, with a knowing. He was okay with any decision I made, as long as I was happy.

I wished I could talk this out with Jessie. She'd know what to say. Actually, we'd discussed it in Sedona and she was all for it. Jessie's voice echoed in my ears: "If not now, when?"

I sat up, covered the mouse with my palm, and firmly pressed the button. The screen flashed: Thank you for Registering for the Small Business Course. I did it. I had taken the first step in achieving my life-long dream. Uncertainty vanished as I turned the corners of my mouth upward into a huge grin. I had a sudden urge to high-five someone. Being alone didn't stop me, as I raised both hands in the air and clapped them together.

"Whoo hoo!" I'd never said *whoo hoo* in my life, but it felt right in that moment. I pranced around West Hollywood that day, hovering a foot above the ground. The excitement lasted several days, until the first night of class.

After the two-hour introductory course, my head was spinning. There was so much I didn't know about starting a business: health regulations, business plans, insurance, sales permits, and much more. As excited as I was to scout out a location for my bakery, I had a ton of other items to sort through first. It was a huge undertaking, more so than I'd ever imagined. But I stuck with it. I didn't give up, and by class five, things were starting to jell.

I'm all about organization, so I felt better after I designed a spreadsheet listing everything I needed to accomplish. Only one thing stood in the way: my job. Eight hours, not counting the commute, was a big chunk of time I could have spent pursuing my dream. So I did something crazy. Really crazy. For me, anyway. I turned in my two-week notice to my stunned boss. And that's when it really hit me. No longer having a job as a security blanket, I was actually going to make this happen.

I was so excited and proud of myself it took all I had not to share the news with Jessie. I wanted her to be proud of me as well, and I wanted to thank her. She was the one who'd opened my eyes to the possibility of opening a bakery. I didn't feel right having something this monumental in my life and not sharing it with the woman I loved. Since returning from Sedona, my feelings for Jessie hadn't faltered. If anything, they'd become stronger.

"Malley?" My heart stopped. I hadn't heard that voice say my name in months. I turned around from the cappuccino machine at work to see Lizzie with tears in her eyes. "Are you quitting because of me?"

"God, no, not at all. I'm going to open a bakery. Well, I haven't even found a location yet, but it's really going to happen. Are you okay?"

"No. I'm so sorry, Malley. I've been a complete ass. I've wanted to apologize so many times, but I didn't think you'd ever want to talk to me again."

"Of course I would." I took a step closer to her. "You're the best friend I've ever had. No matter how I feel for Jessie, you'll always be my best friend." And that's all it took for both of us to burst into tears and fall into each other's arms. My heart felt lighter than it had in months.

"I was hurt and felt rejected," Lizzie said through sobs. "It was terrible of me to give you the cold shoulder and not even discuss things. I've missed you so much."

"I've missed you as well. You have no idea." We pulled out two chairs in the break room and sat down, not caring who walked in or overheard our conversation.

"Tell me, how have you been?" Lizzie asked. "How's Jessie?"

"I wouldn't really know."

"What do you mean?"

"Well, we're not together or anything." I realized Lizzie didn't know the whole story since we hadn't spoken in months. "We... or I guess she...broke it off when you came back. I've only seen Jessie around the apartment complex a couple of times since then."

"You aren't dating? Why?" Lizzie's eyes filled with concern. God, I missed her.

"You know why," I said.

"Oh, Malley." Lizzie reached across the table and put her hand over mine. "I understand how you feel. I know what a difficult time you've had with your father's death. But you can't let fear rule your life." I nodded in agreement, but we both knew I wouldn't do anything differently. "You said you were in love with her, right?"

"Yes," I said quietly. "She's the first woman I've ever really been in love with. I cared about my exes, but it wasn't like this." I couldn't believe Lizzie and I were actually discussing this subject comfortably.

"Then you need to give it a chance. I don't care how many books you read by psychics. You're not psychic. Anything could happen."

"Exactly. Anything could happen."

I knew what Lizzie meant. I shouldn't try to predict the future, but when you've had a hard blow straight to the chest, it's difficult to get back in the batter's box. Yet I promised to think about it, and I meant it.

CHAPTER THIRTY-ONE

REACH OUT AND TOUCH SOMEONE

Why was it that the few times I'd run into Jessie she was half naked, sweating, and achingly breathtaking? I was lying by the pool one Saturday on a typical gorgeous, sunny Southern California day. It was pretty crowded, mostly with gay boys lying on top of each other in one lounger, so I didn't think she noticed me. At first anyway. She was wearing that little red bikini she wore at Slide Rock, the one that had my eyes popping out of my head. She was beyond cool in her sunglasses as she scanned the scene searching for a free lounge chair. Spotting one beside me, she paused for a moment, but then walked over since it was the only free chair.

Seeing Jessie caused a mixture of joy and pain. I didn't think it was possible to miss one person so much. I missed her kiss, her voice, her smile, her company, her gentleness, her touch, her kiss. Did I already say that one? I hadn't seen Jessie in almost two months, since July fourth. I was afraid she'd moved without me knowing. It was killing me to think she could disappear from my life forever. Having her next door meant I could at least see her every now and then. It wasn't ideal, but it was better than nothing.

"Is this chair free?" she asked.

"Yeah, help yourself."

Jessie spread a towel across the lounger before sitting. "I hope you put a lot of sunscreen on," she said. "It's hot out here." I had a flashback of Clarissa saying that Jessie had told her about my fair complexion. Seemed odd at the time. Maybe Jessie had a crush on me back then? Either way, it didn't really matter now. I closed my eyes as the scent of coconut oil assaulted my senses.

Seriously? She couldn't have oiled up in her apartment? She was going to torture me out here? I tried to keep my eyes closed but soon found myself squinting them open, catching sideways glances of Jessie rubbing oil up and down her legs. I almost groaned, thinking about how much I wanted to help her with that task. Catching me gawking at her, she smirked. Watching her made me breathless and she knew it.

"How have you been?" she asked.

"Okay. I did something sort of crazy." I couldn't help but smile. "I quit my job and I'm going to open a bakery."

"Malley, that's wonderful!" Jessie looked as though she might hug me before she changed her mind and retreated. "Tell me all about it."

"I took a small-business course, because I have so much to learn, and I'm trying to find an accountant right now. And, I haven't told anyone this yet, but I think I found the perfect location. There's a place for lease on the corner of Santa Monica Blvd and Crescent Heights."

"That's a great area. You'll get lots of traffic. Do you have a name picked out yet?"

"Fun Buns."

"Oh, that'll be a popular place with the gay guys in West Hollywood," Jessie said with a wink. "I'm kidding. I know that's what your grandmother used to call the cinnamon buns."

I couldn't stop the big, goofy grin on my face. Was there anything better than being with Jessie? I couldn't think of a thing in that moment.

"It's amazing how everything has fallen into place. I guess that's what happens when something is meant to be." Those last words stuck in my throat. Jessie and I should've been meant to be, but things hadn't exactly fallen into place for us.

"So, have you written any more poems?" I asked.

"A few. I haven't felt very inspired lately."

"You're so talented. Don't ever stop writing. I look forward to your next poetry book and expect a signed copy."

Jessie smiled in a way that ignited my heart. "Clarissa said she sent you an invitation to her wedding in a couple of weeks. I hope you can make it."

"I don't think I can, with everything going on. And it might be a little uncomfortable, you know?"

"Think about it, okay? It'd be nice to have you there." Jessie took her sunglasses off, looking directly at me. "How are you and Lizzie doing?"

"Great," I replied enthusiastically. Then I realized she probably thought Lizzie and I were dating. "I mean, we're not together as in dating. I broke it off with her on the way back from Sedona. We had a rough patch for a while, but we're friends again and I couldn't be happier."

"Why aren't you dating?"

I didn't even bother to respond but instead looked at Jessie with a raised eyebrow. She already knew why. "So," I said, pulling a thread on my beach towel. "Are you moving?" I didn't dare look at Jessie. Instead, I wrapped the loose thread around my finger.

"I am." My heart toppled out of my chest, slamming into the hot cement below. "I found a place in Westwood."

"Perfect. You can find a cute UCLA coed to date. When are you moving?"

"In about a month, after Clarissa's wedding. I think it's best if I leave." She looked dejected. "Having you next door is torture."

It's like she was reading my mind. I sat up to face Jessie, a hard lump in my throat. "And you think never seeing each other again wouldn't be torture?"

Jessie sighed, shaking her heard. "Malley, I don't know what else to do. I miss you so much. You're all I think about."

I laid my palm over her hand, needing to make contact. "Me too. I've tried to put you out of my mind, but I can't."

"Do you think maybe we could talk sometime? I don't know. Just…maybe try to work things out?" Jessie leaned closer, intertwining her fingers with mine.

I studied our clasped hands. They fit perfectly together. "Maybe," I said, seriously considering the idea. Perhaps Lizzie was right. I needed to stop imagining the worst, live in the moment for once in my life. It was clear Jessie and I cared about each other. My fears were making us both miserable. "Are you free for dinner tonight?"

Jessie's posture straightened, her face lighting up in a smile. "I have to be on duty in a couple of hours. How about tomorrow night?"

My heart dropped. On duty. Those two words held so much weight for me. "Sure," I replied, feeling more reluctant than I had a few seconds ago. "That would be nice." No matter the outcome, at least I'd get to spend some time with Jessie again. Maybe I could convince her not to move.

We soaked up the warmth of the sun in silence. Jessie touched my arm when she got up to leave, which sent electricity coursing through my body. How did she do that with just one touch?

"I better get ready for work. I'll see you tomorrow night?"

"Yeah. And Jessie, please be careful."

She nodded as a film of sadness settled over her eyes.

After Jessie left, I lay in the lounger reliving our time together in Sedona. I was still in awe at the turn of events. I'd been so sure Lizzie was what I wanted. But I was playing it safe. I loved Lizzie, but I'd never felt passion for her. Not like with Jessie.

After getting way too much sun, I packed it in and headed to my apartment. Jessie was coming out of her door just as I was unlocking mine.

"We meet again," she said with a smile.

A vise gripped my heart at the sight of Jessie in her blue uniform with a gun strapped around her waist. Staring me in the face was the not-so-gentle reminder of how dangerous her job could be. I knew how, in one moment, everything can be taken away. My eyes settled on her gun.

"Malley, are you okay?" Jessie put a hand on my arm.

"Jessie…" I didn't need to explain. I could see it in her eyes. She understood.

She squeezed my arm, nodding a few times. "I guess we won't be getting together tomorrow night after all."

Tears immediately formed in my eyes. "I'm so sorry. I can't." I stepped into my apartment, quickly closing the door behind me, staring straight at the heart mandala hanging on my wall.

❖

I was deep in thought, trying to perfect my business plan, when my phone rang and scared the crap out of me.

"Hello?" I said a little too harshly.

"May I speak to Malley O'Conner?"

"This is she." I didn't recognize the voice.

"Malley, my name is Juanita. My husband was killed on duty and a police officer just gave me your name and number, saying you called to help my son."

"Of course, yes. I remember. I saw it on the news. I'm so, so sorry for your loss. Have they caught the perpetrator yet?"

"No. In fact my son and I are here at the station right now. I didn't want to bring him, but no one was home to watch him. Ordinarily, I wouldn't bother you, but…well, I don't know what else to do. Sammy refuses to speak to the counselor they assigned us. He just…he won't speak to anyone. Not even me. I thought maybe because your father was a police officer, as well, that he might feel more connected to you. I know it's a long shot, and I hate to bother you."

My heart sank as I remembered the frightened look in that little boy's eyes. "Oh my gosh. It's no bother at all, Juanita. I'm not a therapist or psychologist, but I could meet with him if you'd like. I'd do anything I could to help. What police station are you at right now?"

"Beverly Hills, and they said you live in West Hollywood, but I don't want to trouble you."

"It's no trouble. I'll be there in twenty minutes."

Without even thinking about what I was about to do, or most of all what I'd even say to the little boy, I slipped on my shoes and headed out the door.

It wasn't until I saw the Beverly Hills P.D. sign that I thought about Jessie. I hoped I wouldn't run into her. We hadn't seen each other since the day at the pool.

A queasiness overcame me as I walked into the police station. This wasn't exactly my scene. In fact, after my dad was killed I avoided even looking at a policeman or police station for months. If I'd put any thought into the situation beforehand, I would have suggested we meet someplace else.

Juanita and Sammy were easy to spot. They were sitting on a bench with the same look of desperation I'd seen on their faces in the TV screen.

"Juanita? Hello, I'm Malley." The woman stood and shook my hand, thanking me before I'd even done anything.

"Sammy, I'd like you to meet Malley."

I crouched down to be at eye level but saw no eyes, since Sammy had his head bowed, staring intently at something clutched in his hands.

"Hi, Sammy," I said. "Is that a rocket?"

"One of the officers gave it to him." My eyes followed where Juanita pointed and landed smack dab on Jessie, who was staring directly at me. As much as I wanted to get lost in her eyes, I had a more important task at hand and not a clue as to how to handle it.

"You know what," I said, "let's get out of here. There's a park across the street. Why don't we see if this rocket will fly?"

No response from Sammy, who kept his gaze cast downward.

"Come on, Sammy. Let's take a walk with this nice lady." Juanita coaxed her son off the bench. I searched for Jessie as we walked through the station, disappointed I didn't catch a glimpse of her before leaving.

It was a beautiful, sunny day, almost too nice considering the heartbreaking circumstances that brought the three of us to the park. Juanita lagged behind, sitting on a bench, while Sammy and I walked a bit farther down the path to a sycamore tree.

"I love trees," I said, sticking my nose into the bark and taking a big whiff. "This one doesn't have much of a scent. Now pine trees are a different story. My favorite are the yellow-bark pines. They smell like butterscotch."

Sammy stood stiffly, looking down at the ground. I was in big trouble here. I had no idea what to say to this kid, no idea how to reach him.

"How about we sit?" I plopped down in the grass, resting my back against the tree, and tried to appear relaxed. Sammy continued to stand. "I know the last thing you probably want to do is talk to some stranger. But I do know a little about what you're going through, Sammy. See...my dad was a police officer. And like your dad, he was killed on duty."

Sammy gave me a quick glance, then stared back at the ground with his rocket clutched in his hand.

"I was a lot older than you are. In fact, it just happened a little over a year ago. But it was still really hard. One minute he was there, and then the next he was gone."

"Did...he get shot? Like my dad?" At least I thought that was what he'd asked. His voice was so quiet, barely a whisper.

"Yeah. He made a traffic stop and the driver shot him. Were you close to your dad?"

Sammy nodded a few times.

"I was close to my dad, too. We were buddies."

"Why would someone do that? Shoot my dad?"

Ugh. When the kid finally decided to speak he asked the most difficult question possible.

"I don't know, Sammy. I really don't. But it's okay to be angry, and cry, and yell, and scream, if that's what you want to do. After my dad died I didn't talk to anyone about it, and I never wanted to cry in front of anyone. I guess I thought it would make me look weak. But talking about it helps. Maybe when you're ready you could talk to the counselor."

Sammy was quiet and motionless.

"So have you tried to fly that rocket yet?"

Sammy opened his clutched hand, tossing the plastic toy toward me. "It's just a cheap toy. It doesn't even run on batteries."

"So how does it work?" I purposefully fumbled with the thing, trying to engage the kid.

"Not like that," Sammy said, kneeling beside me. "You have to pull this rubber band back and place the rocket here. And then let go and it's supposed to fly into the sky."

"Let's try it." I pulled the rubber band back as far as it would go before releasing the little yellow rocket, which soared through the air.

Sammy's eyes widened, and for the first time I saw a flicker of joy. "Wow, it really worked. I didn't think it'd fly without batteries." Sammy ran to retrieve the rocket, bringing it back to me for another go.

"One of the favorite things my dad and I used to do together was make paper airplanes," I said. "His always flew ten times farther than mine did, and one day I made him show me his secret. It's all in the way you fold the paper."

"Maybe you could show me sometime?" Sammy asked.

"You can count on it."

"One of the favorite things me and my dad did was ride bikes together," Sammy said. "We'd pedal really hard up this big hill by our house, and then we'd fly down as fast as we could. We never told my mom because she'd have made us stop. You won't tell her, will you?" His big brown eyes filled with apprehension.

"No," I said, laughing. "My dad and I did a lot of things together we'd never tell my mom, so I understand completely."

He looked relieved.

"Sammy," Juanita yelled from the bench. "We need to get going."

Sammy ran to his mom and I could hear him tell her how we had made the rocket fly. Tears came to my eyes, thinking about this sweet little boy who would have to grow up without a father. Life seemed terribly unfair sometimes.

"I don't know how to thank you," Juanita said when we got back to the police station and Sammy sat waiting in the car. "I haven't seen him smile in weeks."

"I don't know if I helped him. I hope he decides to talk to the counselor. That'll make all the difference in the long run."

Juanita and I hugged like we were long-time friends. Funny how I felt like I knew these people after only meeting them an hour ago.

"Feel free to call me anytime," I said.

"Thank you, Malley. Sammy told me you two have a date to make paper airplanes."

"And that's a date I won't miss."

I waved at Sammy and his mom as they drove away. I didn't need to hear Jessie's voice to know she was standing behind me. I could always sense when she was near.

"Do you think he'll be okay?" I asked without turning around.

"I don't know. I hope so. How are you?"

"Fine. I really wanted to help him, but I don't know if I did."

"You did a selfless, thoughtful thing, Malley. I know it's not easy for you to talk about your dad."

"You know," I said, still staring straight ahead, "I'm not sure if meeting Sammy didn't help me more than it did him." I heard Jessie take a step toward me.

"Good-bye, Jessie."

I walked to my car without ever turning around. If I had, I couldn't have resisted melting into her embrace.

Chapter Thirty-two

Blackout

That was weird. An incoming call on my cell phone had a Sedona area code, but it wasn't my mom. Jessie was in Sedona for Clarissa's wedding, but why would she be calling me? I knew something was wrong the minute I heard the voice on the other line.

"Clarissa? Is that you?"

"Malley, I wasn't sure if I should call." She sounded like she was crying.

"What's wrong? Is it Jessie?" I held my breath, waiting for her response, even though I already knew the answer. It was like when I got the call from my mom about my dad. I just knew.

"She had an accident. She's at Verde Valley Medical Center."

I closed my eyes. My heart stopped beating. "Oh my God. Is she…" I couldn't bring myself to ask the question.

"She's alive. It was a motorcycle accident. Malley, she's in a coma." Saying the word coma released a torrent of sobs from Clarissa.

"Listen," I said, "I'm on my way. I'll be there late tonight and will stay with my mom. I'll be at the hospital first thing in the morning."

"I was hoping you'd say that." Knowing that Clarissa was too upset to give me any details, I asked her to call me later when I was on the road.

One great thing about me is that I'm awesome in emergency situations. I stay calm and cool, focusing on what needs to be done in an orderly manner and as quickly as possible. I would have made an excellent EMT. Emotion doesn't enter the scene until after the emergency's over or I've reached my destination, which in this case was Jessie.

Within an hour, I was packed and heading out the door. Something stopped me, though, when I was halfway into the hall. I went back into my apartment, opened my top drawer, and grabbed my heart rock.

From the car, I called my mom and Lizzie, filling them in. They both said Jessie would be okay, and I was trying my best to believe them. My mantra for the next seven hours was, "Please let Jessie be healthy, safe, and well." I said it over and over again, sometimes out loud. It wasn't directed at God or Buddha or anyone in particular. It was meant for any spiritual being who could possibly help, even my dad.

Halfway into the drive, Clarissa called and filled me in on the details. Jessie had never made it to the wedding, which in turn didn't take place. She crashed with a big rig on the freeway, just outside of Sedona. She had a broken arm, cuts, and bruises, and was unconscious. She was in a medically induced coma in the ICU because of a head trauma, which was by far the worst of her injuries. The CT scan showed no fractures or hemorrhage, so that was about the only good news.

Sweet Jessie. My wounded heart reached out to her across the 200 miles I still had left to drive. Tears threatened to flow, but I held them back. Now wasn't the time to fall apart.

Please let Jessie be healthy, safe, and well. Please.

❖

The last time I was in a hospital was when my dad died. Memories of that horrible day flooded back. Unbelievable, gut-wrenching pain. Shock. Disbelief. Enormous heaviness weighing me down. I tried to push the memories out of my mind. Jessie was all that mattered.

Clarissa and Dominic were in the waiting room when I arrived. Both looked as though they hadn't slept in days.

"Malley, I'm so glad you're here." Clarissa hugged me fiercely.

"How is she?" I asked.

"The same as yesterday."

"So what are they doing? Is she still in a coma? Is this the best place for her to be?" I had a lot of questions.

"Jessie's brain swelled from the accident, so they want to keep her in a coma and make sure her body temperature is cold. That allows her brain to rest and controls the swelling."

"So, do they know…if she has brain damage?" Just the thought of that possibility made me want to puke.

"They won't know until she's awake and breathing on her own. After she's stabilized they'll run another MRI. At least she doesn't have any fractures or blood clots."

Fearing my weak legs wouldn't hold me any longer, I slumped into a chair. Clarissa whispered something to Dominic about getting us coffee, and away he went. Clarissa sat beside me and held my hand.

"Clarissa…is Jessie going to be okay? She needs to be okay."

Clarissa pursed her lips to hold back tears. "You know my sister. She's a strong, stubborn woman. She'll make it through this. She will." Clarissa sounded as though she was trying to convince herself just as much as me. "Do you want to see her? Visiting hours are about to start."

"Of course. Yes. That's why I came. I want to be with her."

"Malley, I just…I want to prepare you. She doesn't look good."

No, of course not. She was in a horrible accident. I was prepared, or so I thought.

My calm, cool, awesome-in-emergencies stance crumbled with one look at Jessie. Tubes were everywhere, connecting her to a loud, hissing machine, which I assumed was helping her breathe. Another machine, probably a heart monitor, was beeping. Her right arm had an IV in it, and her left was in a cast. The right side of her face—her beautiful, perfect face—was scratched, red, and swollen. She had cuts on her forehead and around her lips, with bruising under her eyes.

Clarissa slipped her arm around my waist and grabbed my hand. I couldn't stop the tears from flowing. Jessie looked so small, so helpless. My heart broke. We inched toward her. Despite all her injuries, she looked so peaceful, like she was completely content where she was.

Don't get too comfortable there, Barnett, I mentally said. We...I...want you back. And soon.

"Can she hear us?" I asked one of the nurses who'd walked into the room.

"We encourage everyone to speak to patients in this state," she said with a sympathetic smile. "A great majority come out of the coma saying they remember everything that was said to them. Others don't. It depends on how deep the coma is."

After the nurse left, Clarissa said she would give Jessie and me some time alone. Afraid to touch her, and not sure of what to say, I stood by her bed letting the tears flow. Remembering the last time I saw Jessie at the police station, I felt guilty for not embracing her. Christ, I hadn't even turned around to look at her. What if that was the last chance I'd ever have to hold her? To look into her beautiful green eyes? I couldn't think like that. Jessie would be okay. Gently, I placed my hand over hers. My stomach clenched with the coldness of her skin, but then I remembered Clarissa saying what she did about her body temperature.

"Jessie...God, Jessie. You have to be okay. Do you hear me? You better not leave me. That's an order, Barnett. I need you here. With me. Please be okay."

Chapter Thirty-three

Ladies in Waiting

I wanted to spend every moment with Jessie but didn't want to be greedy. ICU had sporadic visiting hours and allowed only two people in at once, so I shared the time with Clarissa and Dominic. Sitting in the waiting room, I couldn't get the image of Jessie out of my mind. I tried to visualize her healthy and happy, but all I could see was the array of tubes keeping her alive, her beautiful face cut and bruised, and her green eyes closed to me and everything around her. I wondered if her soul was even in her body. It felt like she were someplace else, somewhere far away where even I couldn't reach her.

The avocado-colored chairs in the ICU waiting room made me want to puke. The backs weren't high enough to rest my head, and the hard seat made my butt numb. They were impossible to sleep in. If that wasn't bad enough, I was sick of staring at the disgusting greenish color that reminded me of slime. I grabbed a two-year-old *People Magazine* and aimlessly flipped through the pages.

Clarissa and I had been camped out at the hospital for three days, either in the ICU waiting room or sitting with Jessie. Three days of fear, worry, and a helpless, empty sensation in the pit of my stomach that grew like an out-of-control tumor. I couldn't do anything to help Jessie except wait.

"Hi, Lizzie." I answered my cell phone, thankful for the diversion.

"How's Jessie?"

"The same. They're doing an MRI right now to see if the swelling has gone down. They don't want to bring her out of the coma until they get the results."

"Do they know if she'll have any brain damage?"

"We're not sure until they wake her up. We'll know a lot more after that."

"How are you doing?" The sincerity in Lizzie's voice touched my heart.

"I'm hanging in there."

"Don't lie to me, Malley."

"What do you want me to say? It's…hard. I just…I hate seeing her like this. And then not knowing if she'll even come out of the coma or if she'll be okay if she does." I was surprised I could say that out loud without crying, but then again I'd cried so much the past few days I probably didn't have a tear left in me.

"Just take one day at a time. Try not to worry about something that hasn't even happened yet."

"Easier said than done. Especially with me."

"Take care of yourself. I love you, Malley."

"I love you, too. I'll let you know when I hear something." I hung up the phone and sighed, leaning my head back and almost breaking my neck in the process since I forgot these damn chairs didn't have a headrest.

"That so does not look comfortable," Clarissa said.

Attempting to find some level of comfort, I'd scrunched down in the chair with my legs hanging over one armrest and my head halfway resting on the side table.

"Can you help me up? I think I might be permanently stuck in this position." Clarissa grabbed my hand and pulled me upright. I rubbed my aching neck. "Any word from the doctor?"

"Yes," she said brightly. "The swelling has gone down, and they're going to wean Jessie off the sedatives tomorrow morning."

"And what does that mean?"

"They'll remove the ventilator to see if she can breathe on her own and wait for her to come out of the coma. That could take up to six hours or so."

"So, tomorrow, huh?" My stomach clenched.

"I have a good feeling about this. We could be talking to Jessie as soon as tomorrow afternoon." Clarissa smiled and sat in the chair next to me, reaching for my hand.

"I hope you're right." I wanted to think positively. I really did. But something inside said there was a distinct possibility Jessie might never wake up. A possibility I would never hear her voice again, talk to her, hold her. I tried to shake the gut-wrenching thoughts from my mind.

"Malley, I'm so glad you're here. I don't know what happened between you two, but I know how much Jessie cares about you."

"I care for her, too. Very much."

"Before the Sedona retreat she made me swear, on a Bible no less, that I would never breathe a word of this to you."

"What are you talking about?" I looked at Clarissa, who was pursing her lips. She glanced around the waiting room, obviously nervous about something. "Clarissa?" I asked when she didn't respond.

"God, my mouth is bigger than the Grand Canyon. But considering the circumstances I think you should know this."

Long pause.

"Know what?" I bent my head in an attempt to meet Clarissa's downcast eyes.

After several seconds she finally looked at me, taking a deep breath. "Jessie is in love with you."

My heart skipped a beat. Had I heard Clarissa right? Could Jessie really be in love with me? I couldn't deny the emotion I had felt from her, but...love? I'm not sure why I was so surprised, considering I had no doubt of my own feelings for Jessie.

"Are you sure? How do you know?" I asked.

"Sugar, are you blind? My sister's been in love with you from the first moment she met you. She called me the day she moved in and said she'd just met the woman she was going to marry. Oh my, she'd kill me for telling you that."

I froze in my chair. I couldn't believe what I was hearing. Jessie had known since the first day we met?

"Wait. Are you sure she was talking about *me*?"

Clarissa laughed and gave me a light punch on the arm. "You are blind. She was so hung up on you, but she said all you'd ever do was talk about some woman. Somebody you worked with. So she never did anything about it. And as much as Jessie puts on a tough act, she's just a scared kitten."

"I had no idea. I didn't even think she liked me. Well, not until Sedona anyway."

"That's why I was sneaky about switching the rooms so you two would end up together. She went to the lodge just to spend time with you."

How ironic. I'd gone to Sedona to be with Lizzie, and Jessie had gone to be with me.

"Please don't tell her I told you. She'd skin me alive."

"No, of course not. I won't say a word."

"Do you think you two might get back together?" Clarissa stared at me with wide-eyed hopefulness.

"I don't know. It's complicated. All that matters now is that Jessie gets better and back on her feet."

"You're right. That's the important thing. You should go to your mom's and get some rest. You look exhausted."

"I don't know. I wanted to see Jessie during the last visiting hours."

"Go get some rest. Tomorrow's a big day. Jessie will need us more tomorrow after she wakes up."

I wanted to share Clarissa's excitement, but I didn't feel as confident as she did about the outcome.

I loved being wrapped in my mother's arms, enveloped in a fuzzy, warm housecoat and inhaling her scent of sugar and vanilla. My eyes focused on my dad's police academy photo as we embraced. In a way, it was like having them both with me at once.

"How's Jessie?" My mom released me, her hands on either side of my shoulders as though holding me upright.

"They're going to try and bring her out of the coma tomorrow." I slipped off my backpack and slung it onto the sofa.

"That's wonderful." My mom clapped her hands together. "But you don't look very excited."

"I have a bad feeling about it, Mom. I don't know."

"Come with me. I'm making some tea." Following my mom into the kitchen, I didn't realize how exhausted I was until I slumped into a chair. I could have easily rested my head on the table and been asleep within minutes.

My mom poured boiling water into two cups, followed by tea bags. "Do you remember what your father used to say?"

"No, what?"

"Reality isn't reality until it happens."

"Yeah, I know. Same thing Lizzie's been telling me. I shouldn't expect the worse. Just wait and see what happens." My mom placed a steaming cup of chamomile tea in front of me.

"Honey, I want to ask you something." She sat at the table across from me. Looking right at me she asked, "Are you in love with Jessie?"

I paused. Not because I didn't know the answer, but because I was too emotionally exhausted to get into a conversation about my love life. However, the sincerity in my mom's eyes told me she deserved an honest answer.

"Yes. Yes, Mom. I love her very much."

My mom bolted out of her chair and embraced me in a warm hug. "Oh, I'm so happy for you. I knew there was something between you two." My mom pulled away and looked me squarely in the eyes. "I like her, honey. I like Jessie a lot."

Her infectious smile was contagious, but my grin faded when I remembered we weren't even dating. "Mom, it's not that simple. Jessie and I aren't together."

"Why not?" My mom rarely raised her voice, so it surprised me when her words were loud and stern.

"We don't fit in some ways. That's all."

"Malley, is it because she's a police officer?" It was useless to try and get anything past my mom.

"Yes. And you of all people should understand that."

"Honey, I wouldn't have done one thing different. I treasured every minute I had with your father."

"I know you did, but didn't you worry about him all the time? It's such a dangerous job. And then…look what happened."

"I did worry about him. But that doesn't mean I'd have changed anything. Your father loved being a police officer. It was his life."

"I don't think I could live with that constant fear." I shook my head, staring into my teacup.

"Malley, look at me, honey." My mom grabbed my hands, holding them between her palms. "If someone had told me before I married your father what was going to happen, I still would have married him. I would rather have had even one week with him than nothing at all. Life is unpredictable. Someone could get hurt on the job, or someone could have an accident on the way to their sister's wedding. There are no guarantees in life…for anyone, not just police officers. "

That hit home. Anything could happen at any time and not necessarily because Jessie was a cop. More than anything, I knew that if something ever did happen I'd want to be by her side. I'd want to be the one to get the call and not hear about it secondhand. I'd want to be there for her, hold her hand, and help her in any way I could.

I kissed my mom on the cheek. "I love you, Mom. I'll be up early tomorrow. I need to do something before I go to the hospital."

❖

I slipped my hand into my pocket to feel the smooth heart rock with my fingertips before ascending the Vista Trail in Boynton

Canyon, not completely sure what I intended to do when I reached the top. With every step, I could feel my dad walking beside me, supporting and comforting me. Books I read about the afterlife had given me some resolution concerning his death. My dad wasn't gone. In fact, he was with me now even more than when he was alive.

As I rounded a bend in the trail, the Kachina Woman greeted me, standing strong and sure of herself. The early morning sun illuminated her bright-red face. She almost looked like she were lifting her chin to meet the sun's rays. After climbing to the summit, I placed my palm on the warm rock, looking up into her eyes. Pulsations traveled up my arms and into my chest. I wasn't sure if the warmth that overcame me was from the sun or the Kachina Woman.

Slipping off my shoes and sitting cross-legged under the juniper tree, I looked at puffy, white clouds. It was going to be a beautiful day, one I hoped would bring good news about Jessie. She had to be okay. She just had to. Holding the heart rock in my palm, I remembered the Indian's words: *Fear is of the mind. Love is of the heart.*

At first, I regretted wasting fifteen years not fully receiving the gift the Kachina Woman had given me through the Indian. Yes, I'd kept the heart rock all those years, but I'd never understood or lived the message. I let the regret go, though, as quickly as it had come. I wasn't ready. That's why she'd given me the rock. As a reminder to follow my heart. And like any loving mother, she'd patiently waited for me to reach this moment in my life when I was finally ready to let go of fear.

From my own heart to the one in my palm, I silently placed all my fears into the rock's center.

Fear of loss.

Fear of the future.

Fear of love.

Even though a large part of me wanted to keep the rock, I knew I had to return it to the Kachina Woman. I no longer needed it, and it was rightfully hers. Scouting around, I gathered a handful of sandstone rocks. Carefully, I balanced one rock upon another to erect a cairn at the base of the Kachina Woman. Looking upward, I gave her a nod and silent thank you before placing the heart rock at the top of the stack.

As I hiked down the trail, I caught sight of a doe running wildly through the forest in the canyon below. She looked so free, so lighthearted as she bounced over rocks and bushes. It's how I felt, like I could practically fly down the mountain. I smiled to myself, thinking Jessie would be proud of me. Jessie. I needed to see her, to touch her.

Please let her be all right.

Chapter Thirty-four

Wake Up, Wake Up, Wherever You Are

It had been eight hours since they stopped the sedatives that kept Jessie in a coma. The doctor had said it could take up to six hours for her to regain consciousness, and it had been eight. No movement. No signs of life. No nothing. The good news, though, was that the oxygen had been removed and Jessie was breathing on her own. Now I just desperately needed her to wake up.

Relishing the few moments alone with her in ICU, I stroked her cheek and placed my hand over hers. "Jessie, you need to wake up. Please, baby. Wake up. You can't leave now," I pleaded. "Not when I finally have things figured out. There's so much I want to tell you." A nurse walked into the room and gave me a weak smile. "Is this normal?" I asked. "For her to not have woken up by now?"

"Try not to worry. Everyone's different." She changed Jessie's IV bag and ran into Clarissa on her way out.

I met Clarissa's eyes and shook my head no. She knew what I meant.

"Why don't you take a break, Malley? Dominic's in the waiting room with coffee."

I studied Jessie, not wanting to leave her. She looked so peaceful, so beautiful. Like she could sleep forever. My heart bled at the possibility.

"Maybe for a minute," I said.

I sat slumped into an avocado chair with my eyes closed, and Dominic held my hand tight. He had such a kind, gentle soul. I'd gotten to know him and Clarissa better since spending endless hours at the hospital with them. If not for me, then Jessie needed to wake up for her sister.

Seeing how close they were made me sad I never had a sister. Jessie had so much to live for. So many people who loved her and needed her. I didn't want to try to fathom the idea of Jessie not making it. Not after I finally got the message of the Kachina Woman. Follow my heart. And I knew exactly where that led. Right into Jessie's arms.

I opened my eyes when I heard rustling down the hallway. Several nurses were rushing into one of the rooms. Jessie's room. I jumped up and darted down the hall. A doctor was hovering over Jessie with two nurses on either side of her. Clarissa was standing to the side with a hand over her heart.

"What happened?" I asked. My heart beating wildly, I was frantic to know what was going on.

"She opened her eyes. Jessie opened her eyes," Clarissa said. I moved by the window so I could get a better view of Jessie and still be out of the doctor's way. Her head was moving back and forth, her eyes fluttering. A quiet moan escaped her lips.

"Can you hear me?" the doctor asked. At the sound of the doctor's voice, her eyes popped open and she looked right at him. Her beautiful green eyes were filled with fear.

"I'm a doctor. You're in the hospital. We'll take good care of you," he said. "Can you speak?" No response. "Do you know what day this is?"

Seriously? I didn't even know what day it was. *Jesus, ask her something she might actually know.*

"Do you know your name?"

No response.

Please, Jessie. Please be all right.

I wanted to push the nurses and doctor out of the way and rush to her side. I wanted to ease the scared, confused look on her face.

Look over here, Jessie. I'm with you. I haven't left your side. And I won't ever leave you again. As I silently pleaded with her, Jessie turned her head and looked right at me. All eyes turned to me.

"Do you know her?" the doctor asked.

I held my breath. *Malley. Please say my name.*

Jessie continued to look at me as the doctor repeated the question.

Slowly she nodded. "Malley," she said. It was barely a whisper, but she said it. She knew me.

I closed my eyes and released my breath. I heard Clarissa gasp.

"Do you know your name?" the doctor asked.

"Jessie," she said without taking her eyes off me.

I gave her a sweet smile and freely allowed tears to flow. *Thank you, God. Thank you.*

❖

Within a few days Jessie was moved out of the ICU into a private room. She didn't appear to have brain damage from her injuries and was getting stronger every day. We were all ecstatic, with Clarissa and me practically bouncing off the hospital walls. I even didn't mind the avocado chairs anymore. In fact, I thought it would be a nice retro color to get for my apartment.

I wasn't able to spend much time alone with Jessie since she'd woken up. It had been nonstop tests, physical therapy, and nurses in and out of her room every half hour. We didn't have any alone time until the afternoon of the day before she was to be released. Jessie was sitting in bed with me standing beside her.

"I'm so ready to get out of here," she said. "I'll be doing desk duty for a while, though, until this heals." She held up her arm, which was in a cast.

"You'll be back on the streets before you know it," I said.

"So, you were here the entire time? When I was out of it?"

"Of course."

"It must have been hard. I'm sorry I put you guys through that."

"Shhh, it wasn't your fault. We're just so thankful you're all right. I was so worried about you."

"You were?"

"Of course. Nothing could have kept me from being with you." I reached out and moved a strand of hair from her forehead, wanting to tell her how I felt about her. But part of me wasn't completely sure Clarissa was right about Jessie being in love with me. After the emotional rollercoaster of the past week, I didn't know if I could handle the rejection right then. It was quite possible Jessie wanted nothing to do with me at all.

"You know, you're the only one who hasn't signed my cast yet."

"Hmmm...you're right." I grabbed the black marker the nurses used to sign Jessie's cast. She'd managed to charm them all. Even the straight ones wanted to go home with her.

I turned her arm over and wrote the only thing I could think to say. Jessie stared at what I'd written, blinking several times, completely silent. She was taking far longer than necessary to read five simple words. My heart pounded as I stuck my hands in my pockets to keep them from shaking. Finally, her eyes met mine.

"You love me?" she asked.

"No," I said. "You read it wrong. It says I'm *in* love with you." Jessie looked at me as a slow smile crept on her face. A moment later, her smile faded as a shadow washed over her eyes.

"But...what about Lizzie?"

"Lizzie is my best friend. I love her, but I was never in love with her. I've never felt this way about anyone before, Jessie. I'm in love for the first time in my life." My voice was shaky, which I hoped didn't minimize the conviction I felt. This was my chance to tell Jessie how much she meant to me. I didn't want to screw it up. Needing the physical connection, I took my hands out of my pockets, placing my palm lightly on her shoulder.

Jessie's eyes were still filled with concern. "What about...me being a cop?"

"A lot has happened the past few days. I'll tell you about it later, but for now just know that I'm ready to let go of the fear. Life is unpredictable. I don't want to live my life by forecasting future events that may or may not happen. Your accident taught me I'd never want to be anywhere but by your side if anything ever did happen."

"But you were so sure you couldn't handle it," she said, still appearing concerned.

"Jessie, look at me." Her eyes rose to meet mine as I leaned closer. "I love you. So much. I want to be with you for as long as we're meant to be together."

Doubt slowly disappeared from her eyes as they turned a striking shade of light green.

"Could this really be happening?" she asked.

"Yes, if I have any say in it."

Jessie's luscious lips turned upward in a smile as she grabbed my hand. "Malley, I'm totally, completely in love with you. I have been for so long."

"God, I missed you so much." I leaned over and brushed my lips against hers. The slight contact alone melted me. Resting our foreheads together, I stroked her arm.

"Me too, baby," she said. "You're all I ever think about. You're all I ever want."

"Oh yeah? What about all these signatures from the sexy nurses?" I'd missed teasing Jessie. We were a perfect combination of fun and passion.

"This is the only thing I see." Jessie pointed to what I'd written.

"Keep it that way, Barnett." I gave her another searing kiss.

Epilogue

Lucky Number Seven

There's nothing more romantic than a winter-wonderland wedding. The early December snowfall was an unexpected surprise. Snow drifted downward, blanketing the red rocks of Sedona. It provided a beautiful backdrop in the glass cathedral that was filled with flickering candles. Clarissa looked beautiful in a flowing white dress, and Dominic so handsome as he proudly stood at the altar, holding his soon-to-be bride's hand. As breathtaking as the surroundings were, I couldn't take my eyes off Jessie. She was standing by Clarissa at the altar wearing a white tux, looking gorgeous. I was so in love with her that sometimes my feelings literally took my breath away.

The past two months after Jessie's accident had been the happiest of my life. We practically lived together, even though we still had separate apartments. We had such a connection, such a pull between us, that it was nearly impossible to be next door and not be together. Fears crept in every now and then, but I didn't allow them to rule my thoughts and emotions. Nothing could have kept me from being with this amazing, sensitive, giving woman.

Dominic planted an overzealous, passionate kiss on Clarissa's lips while dipping her backward, causing the guests to laugh. My heart was filled with such love as they walked down the aisle as man and wife. Jessie followed them, giving me a wink as she passed.

The reception was held at Dominic's spiritual center. Plenty of wine, vegan cake, dancing, and, most of all, joy and love filled the room.

When "It Had To Be You," sung by Frank Sinatra, blared over the loudspeaker, I looked around for Jessie. I knew how much she liked Sinatra. Dominic had been twirling me around the dancefloor, but he became a little awkward when the slow song interrupted his rhythm. Jessie tapped his shoulder from behind.

"I believe this next dance is mine, brother-in-law." Jessie swept me into her arms, guiding me across the dancefloor. "Have I told you how beautiful you look tonight?

"As a matter of fact you haven't," I said with a smirk.

Jessie leaned closer, whispering in my ear. "You take my breath away. I could look at you for the rest of my life and be perfectly happy."

Pulling Jessie close to me, I reveled in the sensation of her body melding with mine. I rested my cheek on her shoulder, not stopping the contented sigh that escaped my lips. I never thought it was possible to feel so loved and happy.

As the celebration was winding down, Clarissa cornered Jessie and me.

"I have something for you two," she said. Clarissa held out a number-seven rainbow keychain. "Tonight is all about love. Not just for Dominic and me, but for you as well. I thought you might want to return to the place where you first fell in love." We gushed over the idea, embracing Clarissa in a three-way hug.

"I love it," I said. "That was so thoughtful."

"Well, I know Jessie is a romantic, so I thought this would be right up her alley."

"It's absolutely perfect," Jessie said.

With the newlyweds off to their honeymoon, Jessie and I headed to the lodge. The cabin was just as we'd left it. Being in the space again triggered memories of our first kiss, making love, and our late-night talks in the dark. Jessie pulled me into her arms, giving me a warm kiss.

"So, do you think Clarissa wants us to re-create our time here?"

"I think she does," I said. "Well, at least some of it."

"And what part do you think we should re-create?" Jessie nibbled my earlobe, which always drove me wild.

"Do you remember our first kiss?" I asked.

"Considering I replayed it in my mind a million times, yes, I do believe I recall." Jessie slipped my earlobe between her lips while lightly blowing into my ear, which sent shivers down my spine.

"I think that's what we should re-create." Taking Jessie's hand, I led her to the bed. Lying on my back, I guided her with me. Jessie hovered above me as I slipped my hands around her back, pressing her closer against me.

"I love you, Malley." No matter how many times I heard those words from Jessie, it always made my heart clench. "Do you remember when we were on Bell Rock and did that manifestation ceremony? Well, this is what I wished for. My wish was for you and me to be together. For as long as we're meant to be."

"I wondered what you were wishing for. In my heart, I believe that's what I wished for as well. Do you know the first time I think I fell in love with you?"

"When we first met?" Jessie asked.

"Actually, that was more lust for me than love. No, it was our first kiss."

"Do you mean like this?" Jessie pressed her lips against mine.

I loved the taste of her, the touch of her, the sensuality with which she kissed me. Her kiss, teeming with love and passion, was filled with the promise of a future together. Her kiss melted all my remaining fears away.

The End

About the Author

Lisa has been writing stories ever since she could hold a crayon and Big Chief tablet. She's an ultimate romantic and loves creating genuine characters who seem so real that she finds it sad they don't actually exist.

When Lisa isn't writing on her laptop, in her mind, or with a crayon (old habits die hard), her absolute favorite pastime is perusing bookstores—so much so that they should really start charging her rent. A self-professed new age nut, Lisa meditates daily in a haze of incense to stay centered and is a student of metaphysics.

Lisa has a bachelor's degree in communications and journalism from Midwestern State University, TX, and has completed creative writing courses at Santa Monica College, CA. Lisa lives in Los Angeles, CA, for the ocean, mountains, totally awesome weather, and only occasionally thinks about moving when she feels an earthquake tremble.

Lisa can be contacted at www.lisamoreauwriter.com.

Books Available from Bold Strokes Books

Love on Tap by Karis Walsh. Beer and romance are brewing for Tace Lomond when archaeologist Berit Katsaros comes into her life. (987-1-162639-564-0)

Love on the Red Rocks by Lisa Moreau. An unexpected romance at a lesbian resort forces Malley to face her greatest fears where she must choose between playing it safe or taking a chance at true happiness. (987-1-162639-660-9)

Tracker and the Spy by D. Jackson Leigh. There are lessons for all when Captain Tanisha is assigned untried pyro Kyle and a lovesick dragon horse for a mission to track the leader of a dangerous cult. (987-1-162639-448-3)

Whirlwind Romance by Kris Bryant. Will chasing the girl break Tristan's heart or give her something she's never had before? (987-1-162639-581-7)

Whiskey Sunrise by Missouri Vaun. Culture and religion collide when Lovey Porter, daughter of a local Baptist minister, falls for the handsome thrill-seeking moonshine runner, Royal Duval. (987-1-162639-519-0)

Dyre: By Moon's Light by Rachel E. Bailey. A young werewolf, Des, guards the aging leader of all the Packs: the Dyre. Stable employment—nice work, if you can get it...at least until silver bullets start to fly. (978-1-62639-6-623)

Fragile Wings by Rebecca S. Buck. In Roaring Twenties London, can Evelyn Hopkins find love with Jos Singleton or will the scars of the Great War crush her dreams? (978-1-62639-5-466)

Live and Love Again by Jan Gayle. Jessica Whitney could be Sarah Jarret's second chance at love, but their differences and Sarah's grief continue to come between their budding relationship. (978-1-62639-5-176)

Starstruck by Lesley Davis. Actress Cassidy Hayes and writer Aiden Darrow find out the hard way not all life-threatening drama is confined to the TV screen or the pages of a manuscript. (978-1-62639-5-237)

Stealing Sunshine by Tina Michele. Under the Central Florida sun, two women struggle between fear and love as a dangerous plot of deception and revenge threatens to steal priceless art and lives. (978-1-62639-4-452)

The Fifth Gospel by Michelle Grubb. Hiding a Vatican secret is dangerous—sharing the secret suicidal—can Felicity survive a perilous book tour, and will her PR specialist, Anna, be there when it's all over? (978-1-62639-4-476)

Cold to the Touch by Cari Hunter. A drug addict's murder is the start of a dangerous investigation for Detective Sanne Jensen and Dr. Meg Fielding, as they try to stop a killer with no conscience. (978-1-62639-526-8)

Forsaken by Laydin Michaels. The hunt for a killer teaches one woman that she must overcome her fear in order to love, and another that success is meaningless without happiness. (978-1-62639-481-0)

Infiltration by Jackie D. When a CIA breach is imminent, a Marine instructor must stop the attack while protecting her heart from being disarmed by a recruit. (978-1-62639-521-3)

Midnight at the Orpheus by Alyssa Linn Palmer. Two women desperate to make their way in the world, a man hell-bent on revenge, and a cop risking his career: all in a day's work in Capone's Chicago. (978-1-62639-607-4)

Spirit of the Dance by Mardi Alexander. Major Sorla Reardon's return to her family farm to heal threatens Riley Johnson's safe life when small-town secrets are revealed, and love may not conquer all. (978-1-62639-583-1)

Sweet Hearts by Melissa Brayden, Rachel Spangler, and Karis Walsh. Do you ever wonder *Whatever happened to...*? Find out when you reconnect with your favorite characters from Melissa Brayden's *Heart Block*, Rachel Spangler's *LoveLife*, and Karis Walsh's *Worth the Risk*. (978-1-62639-475-9)

Totally Worth It by Maggie Cummings. Who knew there's an all-lesbian condo community in the NYC suburbs? Join twentysomething BFFs Meg and Lexi at Bay West as they navigate friendships, love, and everything in between. (978-1-62639-512-1)

Illicit Artifacts by Stevie Mikayne. Her foster mother's death cracked open a secret world Jil never wanted to see…and now she has to pick up the stolen pieces. (978-1-62639-472-8)

Pathfinder by Gun Brooke. Heading for their new homeworld, Exodus's chief engineer Adina Vantressa and nurse Briar Lindemay carry game-changing secrets that may well cause them to lose everything when disaster strikes. (978-1-62639-444-5)

Prescription for Love by Radclyffe. Dr. Flannery Rivers finds herself attracted to the new ER chief, city girl Abigail Remy, and the incendiary mix of city and country, fire and ice, tradition and change is combustible. (978-1-62639-570-1)

Ready or Not by Melissa Brayden. Uptight Mallory Spencer finds relinquishing control to bartender Hope Sanders too tall an order in fast-paced New York City. (978-1-62639-443-8)

Summer Passion by MJ Williamz. Women loving women is forbidden in 1946 Hollywood, yet Jean and Maggie strive to keep their love alive and away from prying eyes. (978-1-62639-540-4)

The Princess and the Prix by Nell Stark. "Ugly duckling" Princess Alix of Monaco was resigned to loneliness until she met racecar driver Thalia d'Angelis. (978-1-62639-474-2)

Winter's Harbor by Aurora Rey. Lia Brooks isn't looking for love in Provincetown, but when she discovers chocolate croissants and pastry chef Alex McKinnon, her winter retreat quickly starts heating up. (978-1-62639-498-8)

The Time Before Now by Missouri Vaun. Vivian flees a disastrous affair, embarking on an epic, transformative journey to escape her past, until destiny introduces her to Ida, who helps her rediscover trust, love, and hope. (978-1-62639-446-9)

Twisted Whispers by Sheri Lewis Wohl. Betrayal, lies, and secrets—whispers of a friend lost to darkness. Can a reluctant psychic set things right or will an evil soul destroy those she loves? (978-1-62639-439-1)

The Courage to Try by C.A. Popovich. Finding love is worth getting past the fear of trying. (978-1-62639-528-2)

Break Point by Yolanda Wallace. In a world readying for war, can love find a way? (978-1-62639-568-8)

Countdown by Julie Cannon. Can two strong-willed, powerful women overcome their differences to save the lives of seven others and begin a life they never imagined together? (978-1-62639-471-1)

Keep Hold by Michelle Grubb. Claire knew some things should be left alone and some rules should never be broken, but the most forbidden, well, they are the most tempting. (978-1-62639-502-2)

Deadly Medicine by Jaime Maddox. Dr. Ward Thrasher's life is in turmoil. Her partner Jess left her, and her job puts her in the path of a murderous physician who has Jess in his sights. (978-1-62639-424-7)

New Beginnings by KC Richardson. Can the connection and attraction between Jordan Roberts and Kirsten Murphy be enough for Jordan to trust Kirsten with her heart? (978-1-62639-450-6)

Officer Down by Erin Dutton. Can two women who've made careers out of being there for others in crisis find the strength to need each other? (978-1-62639-423-0)

Reasonable Doubt by Carsen Taite. Just when Sarah and Ellery think they've left dangerous careers behind, a new case sets them—and their hearts—on a collision course. (978-1-62639-442-1)

Tarnished Gold by Ann Aptaker. Cantor Gold must outsmart the Law, outrun New York's dockside gangsters, outplay a shady art dealer, his lover, and a beautiful curator, and stay out of a killer's gun sights. (978-1-62639-426-1)

White Horse in Winter by Franci McMahon. Love between two women collides with the inner poison of a closeted horse trainer in the green hills of Vermont. (978-1-62639-429-2)

Autumn Spring by Shelley Thrasher. Can Bree and Linda, two women in the autumn of their lives, put their hearts first and find the love they've never dared seize? (978-1-62639-365-3)

The Renegade by Amy Dunne. Post-apocalyptic survivors Alex and Evelyn secretly find love while held captive by a deranged cult, but when their relationship is discovered, they must fight for their freedom—or die trying. (978-1-62639-427-8)

Thrall by Barbara Ann Wright. Four women in a warrior society must work together to lift an insidious curse while caught between their own desires, the will of their peoples, and an ancient evil. (978-1-62639-437-7)

The Chameleon's Tale by Andrea Bramhall. Two old friends must work through a web of lies and deceit to find themselves again, but in the search they discover far more than they ever went looking for. (978-1-62639-363-9)